THE KERRIGANS
A TEXAS DYNASTY
THE DEVIL TO PAY

Look for these exciting Western series from bestselling authors

WILLIAM W. JOHNSTONE
and **J. A. JOHNSTONE**

The Mountain Man

Preacher: The First Mountain Man

Luke Jensen, Bounty Hunter

Those Jensen Boys!

The Jensen Brand

MacCallister

Flintlock

Perley Gates

The Kerrigans: A Texas Dynasty

Sixkiller, U.S. Marshal

Texas John Slaughter

Will Tanner, U.S. Deputy Marshal

The Frontiersman

Savage Texas

The Trail West

The Chuckwagon Trail

Rattlesnake Wells, Wyoming

AVAILABLE FROM PINNACLE BOOKS

THE KERRIGANS
A TEXAS DYNASTY
THE DEVIL TO PAY

WILLIAM W. JOHNSTONE

with J. A. Johnstone

PINNACLE BOOKS
Kensington Publishing Corp.
www.kensingtonbooks.com

PINNACLE BOOKS are published by

Kensington Publishing Corp.
119 West 40th Street
New York, NY 10018

PUBLISHER'S NOTE
Following the death of William W. Johnstone, the Johnstone family is working with a carefully selected writer to organize and complete Mr. Johnstone's outlines and many unfinished manuscripts to create additional novels in all of his series like The Last Gunfighter, Mountain Man, and Eagles, among others. This novel was inspired by Mr. Johnstone's superb storytelling.

ISBN-13: 978-0-7860-4048-3
ISBN-10: 0-7860-4048-3

First printing: June 2018

10 9 8 7 6 5 4 3 2 1

Printed in the United States of America

First electronic edition: June 2018

ISBN-13: 978-0-7860-4049-0
ISBN-10: 0-7860-4049-1

BOOK ONE

The Wolves Gather

Chapter One

Don't you hate it when a bullet splits the air an inch from your head and spoils an interesting conversation? Well, Kerrigan ranch hand Chas Minor sure did.

He'd had been out for four days checking on the state of the early fall range, and in that time, he hadn't seen another traveler, not even a drifting cowhand looking for a winter berth. As lonely riders often do, Minor spoke to his horse, not that the little dun paid any attention to his chatter apart from the occasional flick of his ears and ill-tempered snort. Behind them, the pack mule took no interest in anything, least of all the ramblings of the puncher breed, for whom it harbored an undying hatred.

"We'll camp in the timber tonight, hoss," the young puncher said. "Stake you and the mule out on some good grass while I belly up to some salt pork and pan bread." Minor leaned from the saddle and stared into the dun's mean right eye. Its left was twice as mean but out of sight. "How does that set with you, little feller, huh?"

Tired and irritated by the constant tug of the rising wind, the horse tossed his head, jangling the bit.

Minor took that as a sign of approval. "Good, then it's a plan." He looked ahead of him at the tree line. "I reckon we're right close to the New Mexico Territory border." The puncher nodded. "Yup, seems like fer sure."

It's possible that man and mount would have kept up this one-sided conversation for quite some time had not the bullet cracked close to Minor's head followed by another that kicked up a startled exclamation point of dirt a few feet in front of him.

Chas Minor was a gun hand, fast on the draw and shoot, as game as they come, and nobody ever considered him a bargain. But the dun was green, already jumpy from the wind, and he wanted no part of the earsplitting bangs that had shattered the afternoon quiet.

As a result two events happened very fast. The mule, full of deviltry and spitefulness, took the opportunity to turn and bolt, tearing the lead rope from Minor's hand. At the same time the dun bucked and all four hooves left the ground at the same time in a move worthy of the most homicidal rodeo bronc. Minor, in the act of shucking iron, was thrown and landed hard on his back, his Colt spinning several feet away. As a bullet thudded into the high heel of his left boot, the puncher rolled to his right and grabbed his fallen revolver. He caught a fleeting glimpse of smoke drifting from the tree line, thumbed off a fast shot, and then dusted a couple more into the timber. Minor was rewarded by a shout of pain.

A man's voice yelled, "We're done! Don't shoot no more!"

Tree branches shook and running feet rustled through brush.

A moment later a woman cried out, "Pa! Over here! Jed's been shot again."

Chas Minor, his eyes never leaving the trees, took the opportunity to eject the empties from his Colt and load three fresh shells. Uncomfortably aware that he was out in the open without cover, he hardened his voice and said, "You in there. Git the hell out here where I can see you. I got faith in this here six-gun and right about now I'm good and mad."

Minor was tense. Any number of gunmen could be hidden in the trees. This far out on the Kerrigan range was a lawless place where bad men continually came and went, some headed south, fleeing the law in the New Mexico Territory, others riding north, away from the Texas Rangers who weren't too fussy about bringing wanted outlaws back alive. In dangerous country, the man who shot first was the one who'd live to drink coffee the following morning.

Only a few months before and not far from where Minor stood, the Rangers had tracked down and gunned Indian Bob Henman, a rapist and murderer who had a pistol reputation going back to his time as a cow-town lawman in Kansas. "Killed while trying to escape," was the official line, but everybody knew that taking a hard-to-handle prisoner like Indian Bob back to El Paso for trial was never on the cards. It was rumored later that the outlaw had his mitts in the air when he took a baker's dozen bullets to the chest and most folks figured it was a natural fact.

So, Chas Minor had every right to be wary. A hundred different kinds of hell could walk out of the trees and land in his lap. The young puncher adjusted his thinking for a gunfight and then adjusted it again for no gunfight.

"We're coming out," a man yelled from the trees. "Give us time. My son is shot through and through."

Minor decided to take a tough stand. "You either show yourselves in five minutes or I'm coming in after you. Mister, seems like you got a decision to make."

"You're a hard and demanding man."

"Yup, I sure am," Minor said.

"Be patient. Give us time."

"Well, right now I'm running out of patience and I didn't have much to begin with."

Then, something unexpected came from the man in the trees. "You hunting us? Did Blade Koenig send you?"

After his initial surprise, the young puncher said, "Never heard of the man. Name's Chas Minor. I ride for the KK ranch, and, Pilgrim, right now you're trespassing on it. You're down to four minutes to git the hell out of there and be sociable."

A couple minutes of silence followed, the only sound the rustle of the gusting south wind through the pines and wild oak. To the north the sky had turned a gloomy purple black over the Caprock, and Minor figured by dark he'd need his slicker. His patience wearing thin, he studied the tree line and decided he had to bring this . . . whatever it was . . . standoff, to a close that was agreeable to all parties.

Colt in hand, his chin set and bunched, Minor stepped toward the timber then stopped in his tracks as a team of skinny Morgans hauling a wagon appeared from a clearing to his left. A pair of women were up on the seat, the reins held by the older of the two. Thin and shabby, her face was hidden by a blue poke bonnet. Her companion was bareheaded and the front of her dress was partially unbuttoned as she held a baby to a swollen breast. In the back of the wagon an undersized young boy stared at Minor with round, brown eyes that were curious but unafraid. After the wagon pulled out of the trees, the older woman drew rein and then turned her head, revealing a pleasant but weatherworn face. She ignored Minor and looked behind her. Two men emerged from the timber, one with his arm around the other's waist, helping him stagger forward on dragging, unsteady legs.

Chas Minor thumbed back the hammer of his Colt, its triple click loud in the quiet. "I don't want to see any fancy moves. I'm almighty sudden with this here iron."

The older man said, "Damn you, mister, look at the blood on my son's shirt, front and back. He's sore wounded and like to die. We're not gunmen. Hell, boy, you taught us that lesson."

"Sometimes the best lessons are learned the hard way," Minor said. "Set him down on the grass and I'll have a look at him."

"You a doctor?" the older man said. One of Minor's bullets had grazed his left cheek, leaving an angry red welt. He was tall and gaunt, his black beard threaded with gray, and his shoulders were narrow, stooped; he was a tired man with no fight left in him.

"I'm not a doctor," Minor said, "but I've seen a passel of bullet wounds in my time."

His voice bitter, the man said, "And I've no doubt that half of them you caused your ownself."

Minor nodded. "Seems about right. Now lay that feller down before he bleeds to death."

The wagon creaked as the woman in the poke bonnet climbed down and stepped quickly to her menfolk. She helped lay the wounded man on his back as the younger woman buttoned her dress and, with her baby in her arms, hurried to the man's side.

Still wary, his eyes everywhere at once, Minor lowered the hammer of his Colt and slid the revolver back into the leather. He took a knee beside the wounded man. He was young, somewhere in his late twenties, and as tall and gaunt as his father, with a shock of black hair and an untrimmed chin beard. He was still conscious, his brown eyes wide, frightened, betraying obvious pain. He didn't have a fighter's face—a farmer's face maybe, and one raised on scripture and prune juice.

No one ever mistook Chas Minor for a nurse, and he made that clear as he tore open the man's shirt and examined his wound. After a while he said, "It's a high chest wound and it's bad. My bullet drilled him all the way through and probably broke his shoulder on the way out." He looked up at the older man. "He'll live if we can get him to a doctor before an infection sets in." He frowned. "Who the hell are you people? Bushwhacking folks sure don't fit your pistol."

"I told you, we pegged you as one of Blade Koenig's hired guns, and we was mistaken," the older man said. "My name is Poter Tillett, and this here a-bleedin' on the ground is my son Jed." He nodded to the slack-breasted woman in the blue poke bonnet. "My wife, Phoebe, and over there holding the young'un is Jed's wife, Edna. The youngster over yonder looking at you like you just grew horns is Miles, my other son."

"Name's Chas Minor. Where are you from and what the hell are you rubes doing in Texas?"

Phoebe Tillett, her anger rising, answered. "We're from the New Mexico Territory, up Luna County way, and what we're doing in Texas is running—running from Blade Koenig and his killers."

The Tillett clan had a story to tell, but as the day shaded into dusk, Chas Minor decided it wasn't the time to hear it. The Tilletts had tried to kill him, so he had reason enough to dislike them, but there was something about them that he could not figure. Maybe the fact that they were . . . pathetic. It was not a good-looking family. The men were not handsome, the women plain without any trace of prettiness, and all of them seemed dull and unintelligent. Even Miles, the youngest, stared vacantly out on the world with eyes that showed no spark of life or interest, as though he watched whitewash drying on a fence. Withal, the Tilletts were an unattractive bunch, mired in the mud of mediocrity as though they couldn't help it.

But then Poter showed some spark. "We don't blame you none for what happened. We brought it on ourselves. Me and Jed, we was pretty much firing blind. I guess we should have done some asking before shooting."

"Maybe you should have at that," Minor said. "Look before you shoot is generally how it's done in this part of Texas. You got horses back in the trees, Tillett?"

"Yes, a couple."

"Then bring one of them out here. I need to round up my dun and pack mule. After he's done that, you women help him carry Jed into shelter."

"Will my husband live, Mr. Minor?" Edna Tillett

said. She was a homely young woman with unkempt hair and leathery skin scarred by smallpox, then a frontier scourge.

Chas Minor made up his mind. "He needs a doctor. I'll take all of you back to the Kerrigan ranch, where he can be treated."

"But will he live?" the woman said, pleading for the kind of reassurance that a young, gun-handy puncher could not give her.

"I don't know if he'll live or not."

"When he's well, Jed is a strong man. He can lift an anvil."

"Guess all that depends on the size of the anvil."

"He's my man. I don't want him to die."

"If the wound doesn't become infected he'll probably be all right," Minor said. "We can make the ranch in a couple days, so he'll have a chance."

"Why are you doing this for us, Mr. Minor, after . . . after . . . what happened?" Phoebe said.

Minor shook his head. "Lady, the hell if I know."

Chapter Two

Kate Kerrigan woke with a start. Her heart pounded in her chest and remembered fear spiked at her. Oh, dear God, she'd been dreaming of Queen Victoria and foggy London town again.

The faint gray light of the clean Texas dawn filtered through the lace curtains of her bedroom window and from outside she heard a cussing puncher turn the air blue as he tried to throw his saddle on a paint mare the hands had named Rat's Ass because of her somewhat less than friendly disposition. Marco Salas, the ranch blacksmith, was already at work, and the steady clang of hammer on anvil dropped into the new-aborning morning like the pealing of a church bell.

Kate turned her head, her red hair spreading across the pillow like scarlet silk, and her eyes moved to the far wall, where the frowning portrait of the old queen hung beside the equally scowling visage of Hiram I. Clay, the mustachioed president of the West Texas Cattleman's Association and Kate's most ardent suitor.

For long moments she stared into the cold, intolerant eyes of Queen Vic, by God's Grace Queen of the United Kingdom of Great Britain and Ireland, Defender of the Faith, Empress of India. Good heavens, had it really been a three-month since those same eyes stared at her across a table set for afternoon tea in the monarch's parlor in Buckingham Palace?

"We are most pleased that you accepted our invitation to tea, Mrs. Kerrigan," Queen Victoria said, still wearing black mourning weeds for her late husband, Prince Albert, dead these twenty years and more. "Our most loyal subject His Grace the Duke of Argyll speaks very highly of you." The queen allowed herself a rare smile, pouring Kate's tea with her own hand. "How fares that stalwart Mr. William Cody, who recently entertained us with his tales of your adventurous derring-do among the wild natives who assail Christians with their dreaded tom-a-hawks? Milk and sugar?"

"Please, milk and no sugar, Your Majesty," Kate said. "As for the Indians, I was never in any danger. The ones I encountered were just a part of Bill's Wild West Show."

"Well when we visited the show and beheld the bloodthirsty savages so close we were much affrighted," the queen said. "Thank goodness a troop of our Inniskilling Dragoons was close at hand to protect our royal person."

Victorian women in mourning were expected to be miserly with their smiles, and Victoria frugally spent one of hers. "We're so happy that you were not in any danger, Mrs. Kerrigan." She lightly touched the back of Kate's hand. "But we fear that we must take you to task." The queen frowned. "No sugar, Mrs. Kerrigan? We hope that does not mean that you won't make a trial of our sponge cake, of which we are exceedingly proud. Justifiably, we think."

"Oh, I'm most anxious to try it, Your Majesty," Kate said. "I bake a very fine sponge cake myself, using your own recipe."

The queen arched a plucked eyebrow. "Indeed? Then we trust you use the finest quality flour and jam for the filling. Raspberry jam of course, Mrs. Kerrigan. Accept no substitute."

"Indeed, raspberry is what I use. I wouldn't dream of using anything else."

Victoria leaned across the table and tapped the side of her nose with a forefinger. "And we add a secret ingredient. Would you like to know what it is?"

"Very much so, Your Majesty," Kate said, smiling.

"Can you keep a secret, Mrs. Kerrigan?"

"Oh yes, Your Majesty. Back home in Texas I'm quite famous for keeping secrets."

The queen again raised a snobbish eyebrow. "Oh, really? One would think that the wild Texans don't have any secrets."

"They have some, mostly concerning affairs of the heart," Kate said.

"Ah, then you must tell us some of those one day."

"But then they wouldn't be secrets."

"Just so. Then we will tell you ours, Mrs. Kerrigan, and this is just between you and me, understand?"

"Oh, of course. I wouldn't dream of giving away your secret," Kate said.

The queen sat back in her chair and declared with an air of triumph, "Rosewater! There, we've said it. At long last the secret is out."

"Rosewater, Your Majesty?"

"Rosewater! Just a few drops added to the cake batter to taste." Victoria smiled. "It adds . . . what do the French say? . . . a piquancy to the flavor. There, we've given away a state secret at last."

"And I can't wait to try it," Kate said.

"And we, dear lady, can't wait to serve it."

Victoria gave Kate a large wedge of cake and cut a similar portion for herself. As the monarch chewed, Kate was surprised that the ruler of the greatest empire the world had ever seen had crumbs in both corners of her mouth. Now and again that happened to her, but she didn't think it ever happened to queens.

"The cake is excellent, Your Majesty," Kate said. Then, a small fib. "Much better than mine, I do declare."

"We are so glad you like it," Victoria said. "Rosewater! That's the key." She sipped her tea then laid the cup carefully back in the saucer. "We are assured that it takes a remarkable and courageous woman to run the biggest ranch in the American West."

Kate nodded, accepting the compliment. "And an even more remarkable and courageous woman to run an empire."

Victoria spent another smile, depleting her supply. "You are quick, Mrs. Kerrigan, very quick. We like that in a woman, but while we enjoy our tea and cake we will talk only of trivial things. How was your crossing?"

"Most enjoyable, Your Majesty. We made the trip in just seven days since summer is the best time for a transatlantic voyage and the Oceanic *is a new ship, very fast and extremely comfortable."*

"She has first-class accommodations, we trust."

"Yes indeed. The ship's staterooms are wonderfully appointed."

"We would hope so. One doesn't wish to travel like a common sailor." The queen brushed away one of the crumbs from the corner of her mouth with the tip of her pinkie. "And the rail journey from Liverpool was uneventful? It takes four and a half hours, as the Duke of Argyle reminded us. That

is a long time to sit in"—then using the current slang—"a rattler."

"I very much enjoyed the train. Despite the rain, the passing scenery was very green and lovely."

"Ah, you arrived in England on Sunday last, did you not?"

"Yes, I did."

The queen smiled. "An inauspicious day, we are afraid. In England, it always rains on Sundays."

A *tap-tap* on the bedroom door brought Kate back to the present. A moment later Nora, her lady's maid, entered bearing a coffeepot, cup and saucer, and a hot buttered biscuit with strawberry jam on the side. She was followed by the parlor maid, who opened the curtains and then left.

As Kate sat up, Nora placed the tray on her lap. "It's the Sabbath and a gray, rainy morning, ma'am. I don't think we'll see the sun before noon."

"It always rains on Sunday," Kate said. "But it's good for the range. Talking about the range, has Chas Minor returned yet?"

"Not yet, ma'am." Concern in her eyes, Nora poured Kate's coffee and then said, "You look a little tired, Mrs. Kerrigan. Did you dream again?"

"Yes, I did."

"Of London?"

Kate nodded. "Yes, I did, of London and Buckingham Palace. I dreamed about old Queen Vic's sponge cake and the Inniskilling Dragoons . . . but not of that other, dreadful business."

"No indeed, ma'am. That is a business best forgotten," Nora said.

"I'm afraid it will live with me, Nora."

"Time is a great healer, ma'am. You'll soon forget."

"No, not soon, but I hope the worst of the memory will eventually fade."

Even on the frontier among genteel society the length of a lady's skirt was cause for much consideration, and Nora managed Kate's wardrobe with an iron hand. Fashion dictated that the hem of her plain cotton morning dress could be no more than instep length, two inches above the ground. Later in the day, when she might expect visitors, Kate would change into an appropriately tailored afternoon dress with a skirt one-inch longer, called the clearing length. Only after dark would she don evening wear, a more elaborate long sweep dress, so called because it trailed the ground and was worn only indoors.

Thus, it was that later that morning when Chas Minor returned, under the stern dictate of Nora, Kate wore a plain white morning dress with long sleeves, a high neckline, and a minimum of decoration. Before long that white dress would be stained scarlet with the blood of a wounded man.

"Carry him into the guest room in the east wing," Kate said, then turned to Moses Rice, her butler, a gray-haired black man who had been with her since the early days. "Mose, show them the way."

Moses was horrified. "Miz Kate, your dress is covered in blood."

"I know. I had to examine him."

"How is he, ma'am?" Chas Minor said. "He was wounded already, and I plugged him a second time."

"I don't know. The second wound is bad, but there's no sign of gangrene, so he might pull through. I've sent Shorty Hawkins to Hiram Clay's ranch for his doctor." Kate watched the wounded man's father and a couple of her punchers lift Jed Tillett and follow Moses Rice upstairs, the two anxious women on their heels. "Chas, Poter Tillett told you they were on the run from a man named Blade Koenig. Nothing else?"

"Only that Poter claims he and his son had a ranch up in the New Mexico Territory." Minor managed a half smile. "Hard to believe, isn't it? I wouldn't give a month's wages for their wagon and three nags."

Kate nodded. "It seems that the Tilletts have lived a hardscrabble life. Jed is so thin it looks like he hasn't had a decent meal in months, and that's why he might not survive the second wound. He has no reserves of strength to call on."

"He could lift an anvil, and now I'm starting to feel sorry I plugged him," Minor said, a crestfallen look on his freckled, pugnacious face.

"You did what you had to do, Chas. Don't blame yourself." Kate laid a hand on the young man's shoulder. "I'll say a rosary for Jed tonight and ask Our Lady for her help. You might want to say a prayer or two yourself."

"Mrs. Kerrigan, I ain't that sorry," Minor said.

Chapter Three

Frank Cobb, Kate Kerrigan's segundo, was less than sympathetic. He cornered Chas Minor in the bunkhouse. "Hell, a right shoulder wound to go with the one he already had on his left. I thought you shot a sight better than that."

"Frank, I was aiming at gun smoke," Minor said. "I dusted a few shots into the trees. As Mrs. Kerrigan said, Jed Tillett is so skinny it's a wonder I hit him anywhere."

"Yeah, well now we got a problem," Frank said. "You know who Blade Koenig is? Ever hear his name mentioned when men get to cussin' and discussin' around the stove?"

Minor shook his head. "Can't say as I have."

"You've led a sheltered life, seems like."

"Could be, or maybe I don't get around stoves much."

"Well, anyhow, back a dozen years or so Blade made his reputation as a hired shootist out of Trinity County," Frank said. "He was top gun in the Horrell-Higgins feud in Lampasas, did his share of killing in the Hoodoo War in Mason County and then he rode with John Larn and John Selman and that hard crowd in the Shackelford County mob war. You catching my drift, cowboy?"

"Blade Koenig is pretty good with a gun, huh?" Minor said. "Is that what you're saying?"

"Pretty good? Hell, they don't come any better," Frank said. "In the summer of '70 Blade drifted into the Arizona Territory and got lucky. He gunned a hardcase by the name of Ned Titles in the town of Chloride. Shot him clean out of his seat in a Butterfield stage. Then Blade discovered that there was a bounty of five thousand dollars on the feller's head, put there by the Union Pacific Railroad. After that, he bought land in the New Mexico Territory and started a ranch. He's prospered ever since, him and a son he sired by a Trinity County whore when he was just a younker. The kid's name is Seth, and he's supposed to be a bad seed, but I don't know about that. Last I heard Seth had killed three men, but I don't know about that either."

"Frank, sum it up for me," Minor said. "I can't see where this is headed."

"I'll tell you where it's headed. If Blade Koenig has a beef with the Tilletts and comes all the way here after them, well, I know Kate Kerrigan, and she's not going to hand them over to be slaughtered. That means a fight. Blade is a dangerous man, used to getting his own way. He has a history of stomping lesser men into the ground, and nobody has dared challenge him. That's how he grew his ranch and his herds. He won't let Kate stand in his way . . . at least that will be his manner of thinking."

"This ranch can handle gun trouble, Frank," Minor

said, a stubborn set to his chin. His hand instinctively dropped to the butt of his Colt. "This here iron ain't on my hip for decoration."

"If Blade Koenig hired punchers that are the same stamp as himself, he'll bring all the gun trouble we can handle and then some," Frank said. "We have to avoid that. This is a working ranch, and I don't want it turned into a battleground."

"How come you know so much about Koenig?"

"Back in the day when I used my gun on the wrong side of the law, our paths crossed a few times. We were both professional shootists, and Blade didn't push me none and I stepped wide around him. We never had it out about anything, and we were both happy to keep it that way. Since then I've been told a time or two how he's prospered, but I didn't think much about him until now." Frank Cobb shook his head. "Hell, Chas, maybe I'm worrying about nothing. Why would a rich and influential man like Blade Koenig leave the New Mexico Territory to get even with the raggedy-assed Tilletts? Don't make much sense to me."

"Me neither," Minor said. "As far as I can tell they're a worthless bunch, fit for nothing but picking cotton."

"They claim to have had a ranch. That's something."

"Not if they call a couple horses, some hogs, and a milk cow a ranch."

"Sure don't look like they've been eating good."

"And that makes having the biggest rancher in the New Mexico Territory as an enemy all the stranger," Minor said.

"Yeah, that sure don't add up."

"Sure don't."

"Well, we'll wait and see what happens, but in the meantime, I don't want anyone out on the range alone," Frank said. "Make sure all the hands know that."

Minor grinned. "Does that include you, Frank?"

"Especially me. I saw Blade Koenig use a gun, and the man can shade me any day of the week, any hour of the day. He's good, mighty fast and sure on the draw and shoot, and I don't think there's anybody around that's better." Frank smiled. "But maybe I could take my hits and outlast him, huh?"

Kate Kerrigan said a rosary for Jed Tillett, not because she had any real feelings for the man, but because she thought it her Christian duty to pray for him. Her bedroom was cool, so quiet she heard the solemn *tick-tock* of the grandfather clock in the hallway downstairs. Doctors were forever warning that night air was bad for the health, but Kate always slept with a window open. The restless West Texas wind billowed the lace curtains as she stirred restlessly, willing sleep to come.

At times her Irish gift of second sight was a curse, and this business with the Tilletts disturbed her deeply. If Frank was right, Blade Koenig was a looming threat, like thunderclouds on the horizon. By all accounts he was a violent, dangerous man and one not easily dismissed.

Kate Kerrigan finally slept, lulled by the sighing wind. Her rosary was still in her hand and her lips moved as she tossed and turned in troubled slumber.

CHAPTER FOUR

Big Blade Koenig looked through the glow of the campfire at the young man sitting opposite. He considered the youngster a piece of human garbage, walking filth without a trace of humanity or a single redeeming feature, and he asked himself again how the hell he could've spawned such a vile creature, the misbegotten son of a whore. But, for better or worse, Seth was his only child and, God help him, he loved him.

For Blade Koenig, there was much to forgive.

The young man had revealed his true nature as a boy when he beat to death a pointer puppy for tearing his shirt. When Seth was thirteen he'd stabbed and seriously wounded a black youth for looking at a white woman, and it had cost Blade a small fortune to square that with the law. Seth was seventeen when he killed his first man, a teamster he quarreled with over the affections of a saloon dancer. A year later, he shot and killed the vengeful brother of a girl he'd raped, and he celebrated his twenty-first birthday when, in a drunken rage, he gunned a hard-rock miner in a Lincoln saloon. Seth Koenig, a bully and a braggart, was proud of the fact that he'd killed three men, and he often compared himself to John Wesley Hardin, boasting that he was the most dangerous gunman in the West. His father, who'd once been friendly with Hardin, knew Wes would consider Seth a tinhorn and braggart without any real bottom to him.

But over the years as he'd watched his son turn into a bad seed, Blade had said nothing and kept his own counsel.

Things came to a head that evening among the pines at the northern limit of the Kerrigan range.

Lonesome Len Banning, a named shootist out of the Sabine River country, a man with a secretive personality and fierce loyalties, started the trouble. He'd listened to Seth's usual boasting to the rest of the hands about the women he'd bedded, his speed with the Colt, and the bad men he'd killed. Finally, a slight smile on his lips under his sweeping mustache, Banning laid his coffee cup on the ground beside him and said, "Boy, here's some advice—never boast and never brag in the company of men. You know what you're worth and they know it too."

That last brought a few laughs from the punchers.

Blade, sensing trouble, said, "Len, let it go."

Banning shrugged. "Anything you say, boss. Advice is free."

"We're all friends around this fire tonight," Blade said. "We've got gun work to do tomorrow."

Seth Koenig was not a man to overlook what he took as a slight on his honor. Wound up as tight as a watch spring and on the prod, he was ready to kill, but Banning's gun rep gave him pause. This was the man who'd outdrawn and killed Billy Bob Henderson up in El Paso that time, and nobody ever considered Henderson a bargain. Seth was aware that he was being watched, the eyes of a dozen tough punchers on him, waiting to see what he'd do next . . . waiting to see if his rumored yellow streak showed.

Seth Koenig rose to his feet, his hand close to his gun. "You tell me. What am I worth, Banning?"

The puncher's eyes slid to Blade's shadowed eyes and caught the glint of a warning. He returned his attention to Seth. "Forget it, kid. Like I said, a man knows his own worth."

"No, you tell me." Seth stood hipshot, as though he was relaxed and confident. In fact, he was neither. But he pushed it. "I want to hear you say it."

"I don't feel so inclined, kid. Not tonight."

"You're inclined to be yellow. That's what I think."

A man like Len Banning could only be goaded so far. He'd been in a dozen gunfights, taken hits in a few, but had always killed his man. Coming of age in the merciless gunfire of a vicious range war when dark men did darker deeds, he'd learned some hard lessons. He knew how good he was but was also aware of his limitations. He'd ridden with men, sudden dangerous men, who were faster on the draw and shoot than himself. He bore them no ill-will. In Banning's world, such was the natural order of things and he accepted its realities.

As he stood to face Seth Koenig, he'd been pushed to his limit. He would not back down from a spoiled, cowardly ingrate like this one, and his next words spelled his feelings out plain. "All right, Seth, you asked and I'll tell you. I don't reckon you're worth much. Now if you plan on pulling that six-gun, go to it and get your work in." Those words, quietly spoken, smashed into the taut silence like rocks through a plate-glass window.

From his place on the ground, Blade Koenig read the signs and made his move. With a litheness unusual in such a big man, he rose to his feet and stepped next to his son. Emboldened, aware of his father's speed on the draw, Seth stared at Banning and through clenched teeth said, "You're a damned liar."

Seth's hand dropped to his gun, but Blade was faster, much faster. Even as Len Banning drew, Blade's gun slammed into the side of his son's head, and the younger man let out a shriek of surprise and dropped like a felled ox.

Banning hesitated as he took in the unexpected turn of events. A man who rode for the brand, he then slowly returned his Colt to the leather.

Blade looked at the puncher for long moments and then said, "You would've killed him, Len. You were faster, much faster on the draw."

"He wasn't even close, boss," Banning said. "Seen that right off."

"I know you did." Blade reached into his coat pocket, withdrew his wallet, and thumbed off some bills. "Here's your time and then some. Now saddle up and ride, Len. You're done at the Hellfire."

Banning nodded, showing no surprise. Without a word to anybody, he took the money and picked up his saddle.

A few minutes later, as the groaning Seth held his head in his hands, the punchers heard departing hoofbeats fade into the distance. The hands sat in silence. Banning had not been particularly well liked, but he'd been one of them, and his treatment rankled. Railroaded by a fool into drawing, Len had not pulled the trigger, and he left with the respect of every man present.

A towheaded young puncher summed up the feelings of the rest when he said, "Next time I run into ol' Len in a saloon I'll buy him a drink."

"Me too." Blade Koenig raised his son to his feet, but Seth violently jerked his arm away from his father's helping hand.

"Get your damned paws off me." Seth staggered back a couple steps and then twisted his mouth into a snarl of hate. "One day I'll kill you for this."

"Seth, I'm sorry I hit you so hard," Blade said. "But Banning was too fast. He would have killed you."

"You could have shot him," Seth said. "Your gun was in your hand."

"It wasn't my quarrel. A man has to fight his own battles." Blade stepped closer to his son and whispered low enough so that only Seth could hear. "Len Banning didn't deserve to be shot. It's enough that we'll soon kill another man who doesn't deserve to die."

"Would you rather see me hang?" Seth said. "Is that what you want?"

"No, I don't want to see you hang, and that's why I'll kill Jed Tillett. But it doesn't set right with me."

"Then maybe it's time it did. Blood is thicker than water, or had you forgotten that?"

"No, as far as you're concerned, Seth, I've never lost sight of that."

"You're agin' me, Pa. you've always been agin' me."

"No, I'm not agin' you, boy. I just don't think the

killing of Tillett is justified. I'll do it, but it goes against the grain."

"Compared to me, Tillett is nothing, a nobody, a penniless tramp," Seth said. "Who gives a damn whether hayseed trash like him lives or dies?"

Blade let that go and said, "Sit down, Seth. Let me look at your head. You're bleeding pretty bad, son."

Seth touched his fingers to his scalp, and they came away red. "Damn you. I'll take care of myself." His face twisted and ugly, his eyes on fire, he said, "Think about this . . . think real good . . . every day that passes you get older and weaker, but I'm young enough to stay strong and outlast you. A year from now, two years . . . hell, I don't know how many years . . . but one day I'll see the feebleness in you, and that will be the day I kill you and claim the Hellfire as my own."

Blade Koenig looked as though he'd just been gut-punched. "Seth, I'm your father. Do you really hate me that much?"

"More than I can ever tell you . . . Pa."

"Why?"

"Why? You want me to count the reasons?"

"Just give me one. Give me one reason I can understand."

"All right. Here's one you can understand. I hate you because you murdered my mother. Sure, I know she was only a two-dollar whore, but she was the only mother I had and you killed her."

"Seth, your ma died in childbirth. You know that."

"She was frail, sick, her heart was weak, yet you forced another baby on her."

"Force her? I didn't force her. She was delicate and I knew it, and I would never have done anything to harm her."

The punchers huddled around the campfire looked like their shirtfronts had been splashed with orange paint. Every eye was on the Koenigs, father and son. None of them could comprehend a hatred that ran that deep, even those who'd fought a bitter enemy in the War Between the States.

"That's not true, Seth. Your ma wanted another child. She spoke about it all the time. She wanted a girl she could dress up in silk and ribbons who'd grow to womanhood without ever seeing the inside of a brothel."

"And what did you want? I'll tell you what you wanted. You wanted a son, a son to take my place, and you wanted him badly enough that you were willing to kill my mother to get him." Seth spat and then yelled, "Well, it happened to be another boy all right, but he died with Ma, and I'm glad he died because you didn't get what you wanted."

Blade reached out to his son. "Seth—"

"Get away from me!"

Seth's hand reached for his gun, but he stopped when a voice from the darkness said, "No!"

Shield, Blade Koenig's Pima scout and sometimes range detective, stepped into the circle of firelight. Dressed in a red headband, breechcloth, deerskin leggings and a white, Mexican peasant shirt, he held a Winchester across his chest. "This is bad talk between a son and his father. It is no good." His eyes glittering, he turned to Seth. "You stop now. The words from your mouth are as bitter as gall."

If Len Banning was no bargain, Shield was hell on wheels. Bones from the trigger fingers of eighteen enemies, both white and red, hung on a rawhide cord around his neck.

Seth Koenig wanted no part of him, at least not that night. He forced himself to relax, but glared at his father. "Remember what I told you, old man."

"It's something I'm not likely to forget," Blade Koenig said. His face was gray and stiff, as though he wore a mask of iron.

CHAPTER FIVE

"How is Jed Tillett, Kate?" Frank Cobb shrugged, as though the answer meant little to him.

"He seems stronger this morning," Kate said. "I think he'll pull through."

"You're an excellent nurse, Kate."

"I can't take the credit. I think his recovery is due to Jazmine's beef broth and the fussing of the kitchen maids."

"I hope he's worth saving."

"Every person is worth saving, Frank." Kate sounded less than sincere.

For a moment, Frank lost himself in the emerald green depths of Kate's eyes and then said, "All right. Tell me. What's troubling you? You look worried."

"I'm not worried."

"But there's something. Tell me."

Kate shook her head. "Frank, it's nothing really. It's not important."

"Tell me," Frank Cobb said, his voice full of gentle insistence.

"My parlor maid . . ."

"Winifred?"

"Yes, Winifred."

"A fine-looking girl."

"Yes, she is. Well, she told me this morning that the Tilletts have already trashed their rooms. Winifred takes pride in her housekeeping and she's very upset."

"How were they trashed?"

"I don't know. But it seems to be a terrible mess. Winifred wouldn't tell me what they'd done."

"White trash making more trash," Frank said.

"Frank, don't say that. Maybe they just don't know any better."

"Did you look at the rooms?"

"No. Winifred and Nora wouldn't let me see them before they'd had a chance to clean up. I won't go into details, but Nora said the smell was pretty bad." Kate was in the barn with Frank and her son Trace during her usual morning visits to Pretty Boy, a recently purchased paint stud.

Her younger son Quinn was at Cornell studying engineering but had promised to return to the KK for Christmas. Quinn was on the university's boxing team and that gave Kate no end of worry.

Trace had been silent, listening to the exchange before he said, "Ma, how long before Jed Tillett can get out of bed?"

"Not soon enough," Kate said.

Trace frowned. "I don't like them Tilletts—"

"*Those* Tilletts, Trace," Kate said. "Your grammar is getting worse. That's what comes of spending too much time around Frank."

"I didn't like those people from the moment I first set eyes on them," Trace said. "They're a rough bunch and probably thieves."

"Well, I can't throw them out," Kate said. "God knows, they seem to have suffered enough."

"I can throw them out," Frank said. "Just give the word."

"No, I don't want that. Once Jed can get out of bed they'll leave."

"Unless they decide to be squatters," Trace said.

"That won't happen," Kate said.

Frank said, "I hope you're right."

Kate let the subject of the Tilletts end there, though secretly she wished them gone. Not only were they dirty, they were exceedingly loud.

As the hands gathered outside, she watched Trace and Frank saddle their horses. It was time to check on the windmills and to cut winter hay, a task the cowboys hated. The KK had been the first ranch in Texas to install windmills on the range for irrigation, though Hiram Clay told Kate that the Matador and XIT ranches and the Francklyn Land and Cattle Company had quickly followed suit. So far the massive King Ranch in South Texas did not use windmills and none would be drilled until 1890.

Trace swung into the saddle and then looked down at his mother. "Ma, are you sure you'll be all right left alone with them—those—Tilletts? They look like bad news to me."

"As I said before—white trash," Frank Cobb said with great finality, as though he'd summed up the family and would brook no argument.

"I'll be just fine," Kate said. "The Tilletts mean me no harm. Now go cut some hay."

"Ma . . ." Trace began, his face concerned.

"I said I'll be fine." Kate patted the pocket of her suede skirt. "And I've got my derringer."

Then, talking about his sisters, Trace said, "I'm glad Ivy and Shannon are visiting farmer John Wren and his wife. I wouldn't want them to be around the Tilletts either."

"If they were here, they'd probably enjoy the baby," Kate said. "Or you and Frank would have them out helping to cut hay."

Kate watched a deeply troubled Trace and Frank leave with the hands and then went directly to her bedroom, where she picked up a book by Mr. Dickens and tried not to listen to the noise the Tillett clan were making in the kitchen. She shook her head. *Poor Jazmine.*

An hour later Kate was still reading when hell came to the Kerrigan ranch.

What was destined be the most horrific day in Kate Kerrigan's life began innocuously enough with a knock on the front door of her mansion. A few moments later old Moses Rice, the butler, told Kate that some gentlemen were outside and wished to speak with her on a matter of some urgency.

"Do you know them, Mose?" Kate said.

Moses shook his gray head and seemed worried. "No, I don't, Miz Kate, but they're a tough-looking lot. Cattlemen, I'd say. Maybe I should tell them to come back after Mr. Trace and Mr. Cobb and the hands ride in from the range."

"I'm sure they're just visiting," Kate said. "After all, they did have the manners enough to knock."

"It was a loud knock, Miz Kate. Made with a fist, I'd say."

Kate laid aside her book and stood. She noticed a

bulge at the waist under Moses' white jacket. He'd taken time to pack his Colt, a thing he hadn't done in years.

She forced a smile, suddenly her instinct for trouble telling her that danger had come to her door. "It's all right, Mose. I'll talk with them."

"I can send them away," Moses said. "You got no need to talk with their kind, Miz Kate. Some of them boys look like gunmen to me."

Kate stepped to the old man, loosed one of the gold buttons of his coat, and removed the blue Colt. "You won't need this, Mose. Now go tell our visitors I'll be down directly. There is no need to invite them inside until I've had words with them."

"But Miz Kate—"

"I'll be down directly, Mose. Now tell them that." Her voice was firm and a fine line appeared between her eyebrows as she frowned.

Mose had seen that line maybe a hundred times since they'd left Tennessee and he knew what it meant. Kate had made up her mind, and no power on earth would change it. "Yes, Miz Kate." He glanced wistfully at his revolver and then stepped out of the room.

After Moses left, Kate took a few deep breaths to steady herself and then made her way downstairs to the front door.

Two armed men were already standing in the foyer, both so big that they made the large space seem small. The younger of the two, a towhead with a cruel mouth and reptilian eyes, held the Tilletts at gunpoint. Poter had a bruised swelling on his left cheekbone, and his wife, who looked terrified, clung to her young son.

Edna Tillett held her child to her breast, her brown eyes wide and frightened.

The Tilletts' obvious distress annoyed Kate, and her anger flared. "What are you doing in my home? Get out of here. Get out now!"

Seth Koenig's hot stare lingered on Kate for a moment and then he said, "Where is he?"

"Where is who?" Kate said.

"Jed Tillett. Where is he?"

"I have no idea what you're talking about," Kate said. "Now leave before I call my hands."

"Your hands are on the range cutting grass, lady," Seth said. "Now, for the last time, where is Jed Tillett? If need be I'll take this house apart to find him."

Kate looked beyond the towhead to the older man. He could only be the rancher Frank Cobb had spoken about. "Are you Blade Koenig?"

"I am," the big man said. He looked well-fed and prosperous, and his face was strong-boned with a heavy chin, the domineering, bold features of a man who would ride roughshod over any obstacle.

"Then call off your barking dog and get out of here," Kate said.

"Give us Tillett and we'll leave peacefully," Blade Koenig said. "We've come all the way from the New Mexico Territory to find him, and we will not be denied."

"The man is severely wounded and he's under my roof and my protection," Kate said. "Now be off with you. Whatever business you have with Jed Tillett can wait until he's fully recovered."

Seth Koenig turned to several gunmen and an unsmiling Indian who had crowded into the foyer. "Search the house. Find Tillett and bring him here."

A couple of the men headed for the stairs, but Kate stepped in their way. "You will do nothing of the kind."

From behind her, Moses Rice said, "You heard Miz Kerrigan. Get out of this house, all of you." He advanced on the men, his fists balled, and ran into a sledgehammer.

The Colt of a gunman slammed into the side of Moses' head. Moses had been old when he and Kate first met, and his hair had changed from gray to white. He could not withstand such a blow and fell in a heap onto the floor.

A red-hot anger spiked through Kate. She flung herself at the grinning gunman who'd buffaloed Moses, but Seth Koenig stepped between them and viciously backhanded her across the face. Stunned, she staggered and fell heavily. Her head hit the marble floor. Kate saw the horrifying events of the next few minutes through a semiconscious haze . . . a state she would later attribute to one of God's tender mercies.

Two of the Koenig gunmen dragged a naked, screaming Jed Tillett down the stairs by his ankles, the back of his head rapping on every step. Dazed, Kate watched the men haul Tillett into the foyer. She heard Seth Koenig yell, "You spying son-of-a-bitch! It's all up for you!" and then heard the cascading crashes of his Colt as he pumped shot after shot into Tillett's thin body.

Horror piled on horror. Violence on violence.

"No!" Kate yelled. She tried to struggle to her feet as the screaming Tilletts, except for Edna's baby, were dragged out the door. The Indian tore it from the woman's arms and laid the crying child on the floor beside Kate. Her eyes met his, and in a moment of clarity, she understood that the man was saving the infant's life. She also realized that no other lives would be spared that day.

The Indian passed Seth Koenig and a couple other men in the doorway.

Seth grinned and stood spread-legged over Kate, unbuttoning his pants. "Boys, I'll have a taste of the redhead before we leave. Find the maids for yourselves. This one is mine."

He kneeled, straddled Kate, tore off her blouse, and as she struggled, he tried to push up her skirt. As the roars of the other men and the shrieks of the maids rang through the house, Kate tried to reach the derringer in her pocket, but pinned down as she was, she couldn't get to it. She was weakening.

Seth knew it, and his grin widened. "I like 'em sassy," he said as his demanding mouth sought Kate's. She tried to punch her would-be rapist, but he knocked her fist aside and slapped her again, a heavy blow that made her head spin. Claw, bite, knee . . . Kate tried every weapon she could muster, but Seth, laughing as he dragged down her underwear, defeated her every effort.

Kate refused to surrender . . . but she was being overpowered, slapped into submission.

Suddenly the massive bulk of Blade Koenig loomed above Kate.

The square toe of the rancher's boot thudded like a battering ram into his son's ribs, and Seth screeched in pain and rolled off Kate. He kept on rolling, and Blade followed, kicking his son mercilessly until Seth begged for mercy.

Blade hauled him to his feet and slapped him hard across the face, a smashing blow that sounded like a pistol shot. "We have enough villainy to do today without that. Damn you, Seth. Taking a woman who did not want you is how all this started."

Seth's eyes rolled in his head, and drool trickled down his chin as his father pushed him to the door.

Kate, angrier than she'd ever been in her life, finally reached her derringer. She snapped off a shot as Seth staggered through the doorway. Groggy as she was, her aim was off and she splintered the jamb inches above his head. Kate swung the derringer on Blade, but the man ignored her.

The two gunmen who'd accompanied Seth ran into the foyer.

The one with a badly scratched face said, "What the hell happened?" then read Blade's eyes. "We didn't do nothing, boss. Them damned serving women fight like tigers."

"Get the hell out of my sight," Blade said. "Both of you."

The men, their eyes wary, gave him a wide berth as they stepped around him and scrambled out the door.

Kate's derringer had not moved from Blade, but he continued to ignore it. He offered his hand to Kate, but she pushed it away and struggled to her feet.

The big man picked up the baby and said, "Lady, if you want this Tillett brat to live, put the stinger away."

Kate shot him a look of pure hatred, dropped the derringer into her skirt pocket with one hand, and tried to hold her torn blouse together with the other. At that moment the kitchen maid, an Irish girl of seventeen named Biddy Kelly, Winifred the parlor maid, and Nora rushed into the foyer.

Winifred, face bruised, ran to Kate. "Oh, Mrs. Kerrigan, are you all right?"

"I'm fine," Kate said. "I hope I can say the same about you and Biddy."

Biddy Kelly answered that. "We fought them off, Mrs. Kerrigan. They beat us, but we battled them." Tears sprang into the girl's eyes. "But one of them stole me silver claddagh ring. It was me father's ring, Mrs. Kerrigan. After the British hanged him as a rebel, the British took it off his finger and gave it to me mum. Three months later she died of a broken heart and on her deathbed she left the ring to me."

Kate glared at Blade Koenig. "And now the ring of an Irish martyr adorns the finger of a man who's not fit to wear it."

Koenig shrugged as though the matter was of little account. He sniffed and then shoved the crying baby into Biddy's arms. "Take this, girl. It smells." The man turned his attention to Kate. "Don't try to follow us, woman. My son's life is at stake, and if I need to, I'll kill you or anyone else who gets in my way."

Kate would not be intimidated. "When it came to women, children, and an old man you and your toughs acted very brave, Mr. Koenig. How will they do against grown and belted men?"

"They'll stand, be sure of that. And if you don't want this fine house burned down around your ears, you'll hold your impudent tongue." He touched his hat. "Now, good day to you, and pay heed to my warning."

Kate would have challenged Koenig more, but Nora, who cradled Moses' head in her lap, looked up at her and said, "Mr. Rice's head is bleeding, ma'am."

"See to him, Nora," Kate said, breathing hard. "I'll be right back." She hurried across the foyer to the parlor and ran to the adjoining gun room, an oak-paneled space with glass-fronted racks, dozens of gleaming shotguns and rifles standing like bluecoat soldiers on parade. Under the long guns were stacked drawers where the pistols were stored. She grabbed an old .44-40 Henry rifle that was kept loaded in case of emergencies . . . she figured it was an emergency all right.

Kate retraced her steps to the front of the house, levered a round into the Henry's chamber as she ran out the door, and stepped onto the porch. Behind her the maids yelled at her to come back inside, but she ignored them. She wanted just one clear shot at Seth Koenig, the man who'd tried to rape her. Her eyes scanned into the distance, but disappointed, she lowered the rifle. He was already far enough away that he lay beyond the range of her shooting ability and worse, he and his gunmen had roped their prisoners and were dragging them behind their horses. If Kate attempted a shot, she could hit a Tillett.

Moses Rice, blood staining his white hair, stepped beside Kate and gently took the Henry from her hands. "Miz Kate, there are ten of them."

The ranch cook, a plump, red-faced man named Tom Ogilvy who looked jovial but was not, and Marco Salas, the blacksmith, arrived in a wagon a few minutes later and then stood outside the mansion like a pair of lost souls. Ogilvy carried a Winchester, but Salas was armed only with a hammer.

"We was up on the tree line with the Studebaker gathering firewood, Mrs. Kerrigan, and thought we heard shooting, but that old Morgan team will only go so fast." Ogilvy looked crestfallen. "I'm sorry we didn't [illegible]ere in time."

Kate said, "Perhaps it's just as well, Mr. Ogilvy. There were too many of them. They would have killed you for sure."

Ogilvy looked at Kate's torn shirt and frowned. "What happened, Mrs. Kerrigan?"

On any ranch the range cook was a highly respected figure who earned twice as much as a top hand.

Kate would normally have taken time to answer Ogilvy's question, but concerned about Moses Rice, she said, "Talk to Nora. She'll tell you all about it." She took Moses' arm. "Inside, Mose. Let me take care of that cut on your head."

"Those were mighty bad men, Miz Kate," Moses said.

Kate nodded. "Yes, they were, Mose. And I plan to hang every man jack of them from the highest tree I can find."

CHAPTER SIX

Only when Trace and the hands returned from the range as the day shaded into a lilac dusk and lamplight glowed in the windows of the Kerrigan mansion did Kate become aware of the full horror of the day.

Frank Cobb, speaking for Trace, who seemed to be in shock, spared her none of the details as he told her what they'd found out on the range.

"The boy too?" Kate said, unwilling to believe what Frank had just told her. "Are you telling me they murdered the child?"

"All of them," Frank said. "Pa Tillett, the two women, and the boy, lined up and shot to pieces. It seems like someone among the Koenig bunch has a sense of humor." Frank reached into his pocket and produced a page torn from a tally book. "This was placed on the boy's forehead and weighed down by a rock. Here, Kate, read it for yourself."

NITS MAKE LICE
HAHAHA

Kate lowered the paper. She looked dazed. "Frank . . . how . . . how could civilized men do such a terrible thing?"

"Blade Koenig and his good-for-nothing son are far from civilized. They're wild animals who kill to survive."

Trace finally spoke. Under his sun-browned skin, his face was pale. "After what Seth Koenig did to you, I'm hunting him down, Ma. I'll find him and then I'll kill him."

"And I'm riding with you, Trace," Frank said. "Kate, we can't let this attack on the KK stand. There has to be a reckoning."

"And there will be," Kate said. "We saddle up at first light."

"Hell, Ma, you're not going with us," Trace said. "The men we seek are dangerous killers. It's no job for a woman."

A warning crease appeared between Kate's eyebrows. "Since when does the kitlin' tell the cat what she can and cannot do? And if I hear any more profanity from you, Trace, I'll wash your mouth with soap." She glared at Frank. "Perhaps, Mr. Cobb, you should teach my son respect for his elders instead of how to curse, ride like a Cossack, and shoot revolvers." Frank opened his mouth to speak, but Kate closed it quickly when she said, "And some reading from holy scripture now and again about the perils of strong drink and loose women would not go amiss."

Frank, a cautious man, waited until Kate vigorously poked the logs in the parlor fireplace and the line disappeared between her eyebrows before he said, "Kate, Trace is right. A revenge ride is no place for a woman."

Then he saw the frown line appear again and steeled himself for the worst.

It was not long in coming.

"Then perhaps this ranch is no place for a woman, huh?" Kate said. "And perhaps Texas is no place for a woman. What is it men say? Is it that Texas is hell on women and horses?"

Frank swallowed hard. "Something like that."

"Well, let me tell you, mister, let me tell both of you that my place is here on land I fought and bled for. It was my home that was invaded, it was my body and the bodies of my servants that were manhandled and abused, and if there is to be a reckoning, and there will be, then I'll be the leader of it. Do you both understand?"

Frank and Trace nodded, but wisely said nothing.

Kate waited a few moments for effect, then said, "We ride at dawn. Do I hear objections? Good, I'm so glad there are none. Frank, Trace, I'll expect you both for supper and perhaps between now and then you can brush up on your how-to-talk-to-a-lady skills." She gathered up the rustling skirts of her blue taffeta dress and swept out of the room, holding her head high like an Irish warrior princess.

After waiting a few moments to make sure Kate was gone, Frank said, "Do you want to try again, Trace?"

"Try what again?" Trace said.

"Telling Kate that she can't ride with us."

"Hell, no. Do you?"

"Hell, no. She says I taught you to ride like a Cossack. What's a Cossack?"

Trace shook his head. "I don't know. Some kind of Indian or Irishmen, I guess."

* * *

As the bathwater grew tepid, Kate told herself that it had been a terrible day. Nora had burned the clothes Kate had worn when Seth Koenig attacked her. Jazmine Salas, Kate's household cook, upset and fearful, had scorched the roast. Trace had been silent and withdrawn at supper, and it seemed all Frank wanted to talk about was Cossacks, obviously avoiding talk of the attack and further upsetting Kate.

Even steeping in a hot bath for an hour or more hadn't helped much.

"Ma'am, are you feeling a little better now?" Nora asked as Kate stepped into the towel the maid held for her.

"Cleaner," Kate said. "But I still don't feel clean enough."

"It was a terrible thing that happened to the Tilletts."

"I think they were doomed from the start. Born under a dark star."

"Well they're at peace now."

"Yes. I suppose they are."

"The baby is drinking milk, but it's not breast milk."

"Nora, will she live?"

"I have no idea, ma'am. I don't know very much about babies."

"Well, I do, and she seems strong enough."

"Let's hope that's the case."

"Yes. Let's hope so."

* * *

By the time for bed Kate was exhausted and relieved to slip between the cool sheets and close her eyes. But the long, dreadful day was far from over . . . and the sleep she sought vanished amid a racketing volley of gunfire.

Chapter Seven

Kate Kerrigan sat bolt upright in bed as the startled maids in the attic rooms upstairs called out to one another in alarm. From outside, seemingly right in front of the house, a man shrieked in his death agony.

Frank Cobb's voice rang loud in the echoing silence after the shooting ceased. "Git your damned hands up or I'll blow you right off'n that hoss."

A man's voice answered, speaking so low and soft that Kate couldn't make out the words.

"I don't give a damn who you are," Frank said. "Keep them mitts in the air."

Running feet thumped in the darkness and the ranch hands threw questions at Frank.

Chas Minor yelled, "Three of them, Frank."

"They all dead?"

"As they're ever gonna be."

"Get over here, Chas," Frank said. "Take this ranny's pistol and the rifle from under his knee."

As Kate hurriedly threw on a dressing gown, through her open window she heard Minor say, "Frank, feller says he's a deputy U.S. marshal. Says his name is Dunk Jefferson and that you know him from way back."

Frank did not answer at once. Kate ran downstairs, moving through the gloom like a candle flame, and stepped into the front yard.

Lit by the amber glow of the oil lamps on each side of the door, three dead men lay sprawled on the porch, blood staining their hair and beards. Nearby a short, stocky man stood by his horse, the reins in his hands, a silver star within a ring pinned to the left breast of his vest. His holster was empty and Frank Cobb held a gun on him.

When the man saw Kate, he removed his hat and made a sweeping bow worthy of a cavalier. "Forgive my intrusion, dear lady, and for disturbing the tranquility of your evening."

Kate pulled her robe closer around her neck. "Who are you, and did you kill these men?"

Frank Cobb, his face stiff and hard, answered the first part of that question. "His name is Dunk Jefferson and he's a United States deputy marshal, or he was."

"And still am, ma'am," Jefferson said. "As to the dead men, the towheads are Julius and Octavius Duffy and the one nearest you"—he smiled as Kate instinctively stepped away from the body—"is Platte River Burdett Mohan." Jefferson's smile slipped. "I call them men, but they were not. They were mad dogs." He toed Burdett's body with his boot. "Especially this one. He was a pip."

"What did they do that you would kill them so?" Kate said.

"Rape, murder, robbery, leaving a trail of vicious

crimes across three states. Need I go on, dear lady?" Jefferson said.

"No, you don't. My name is Kate Kerrigan, and I own this ranch."

"I have heard of the KK," Jefferson said. "The beautiful widow Kerrigan owns the biggest ranch in Texas, or so I was told. I didn't believe it at the time, but now I do. You are indeed beautiful."

Kate accepted the compliment without comment. "We've already had trouble at my ranch today, Marshal. Mr. Cobb will tell you about it later."

"If you need me, I'll do everything in my power to help." Jefferson gave another little bow. "Consider me your obedient servant, ma'am."

Then the man did something strange. For long moments he stared at his open hands and then said, "Eighteen . . . nineteen . . . twenty . . ." His eyes flicked to Kate. "Counting those three, in the line of duty I've now killed twenty white men, an even score. Think of that." He held up his hands, palm forward. "Do you see blood, Mrs. Kerrigan?"

"No." Kate shivered in the night chill.

"Are you sure?"

"Yes, I'm very sure. I see no blood on your hands."

"But it's there," Jefferson said. "I can see it, red, scarlet, crimson . . . and oh, how it glistens in the lamplight."

Kate stared through the gloom at Frank Cobb. Her voice almost accusing, she said, "You know this man?"

Frank nodded. "Yeah, I do, Kate. Me and him swapped shots a few years back when I was running with Wes Hardin and them over to Uvalde County way."

Jefferson, small, thin but not insignificant, smiled.

"Yes, I seem to recollect that scrape. But I thought it was down at Eagle Pass, huh?"

"No, it was in a dry wash ten miles south of Uvalde," Frank said. "You killed Dave Streeter that day, Jefferson, and winged me."

"Streeter wasn't much, a tinhorn gambler always down on his luck," Jefferson said. "But he was one for the ladies."

"Yeah, that about sums Dave up. His luck sure ran out that day, but I set store by him. He always done all right by me."

"I saw you drop, figured you were done for. You were fortunate that day, Frank. My urgent business was with Hardin, not you, and I didn't wait to see if you were alive or dead."

"I was still kicking and took a pot at you."

"You missed."

"Yeah, I always regretted that."

Jefferson ignored that and turned to Kate. "Can I come inside and wash my hands, Mrs. Kerrigan?"

"There's a water basin and a roller towel at the bunkhouse, Jefferson," Frank said. "You can wash there and then ride on."

"It's been a long day. A fifteen-mile rifle chase, and I'm all used up. I was hoping for some grub and a bed," Jefferson said. "Or do I impose, Mrs. Kerrigan?"

Before Kate could answer, Frank said, "You can bed down in the bunkhouse, and the cook always keeps a pot of beans and bacon on the stove. But I want you out of here at first light, understood?"

"Perfectly," Jefferson said, his face stiff.

Frank said, "Jefferson, I never did like you, and when I get to disliking a man bad things tend to happen."

"Frank, to me, you were just a common outlaw and

you still talk like one. Like or dislike? I never thought about you one way or t'other."

"Good, keep it that way."

"One thing I know is that Hardin was trash. He should've been hung years ago and maybe you with him, Frank."

"That's your opinion about Wes. I have another."

Jefferson nodded. "Yes, you would. Birds of a feather and all that."

"If I had to sum it all up in my mind, I'd say Wes was worth ten of you.

"Only ten? Selling him short, aren't you?" Jefferson patted his belly and smiled. "Well, lead me to the grub. I'm hungry enough to eat a longhorn steer, hide, horn, hooves, and beller."

"First tend to your horse. He's done in. Put him up in the barn," Frank said. "There's hay and oats."

"My guns?" Jefferson said. "I am a lawman after all."

"You can have them back in the morning."

"Relieving a United States deputy marshal of his guns could be a crime, Frank. I'll need to think it over."

"Now I recollect something about you, Jefferson."

"And that is?"

"That you're no longer a lawman" Frank's voice became hard-edged. "Sure, I remember it now. The government took your badge when they sent you to the insane asylum in Kentucky. Or don't you recollect that your ownself?"

"Once a deputy United States marshal, always a deputy United States marshal. That's how it works," Jefferson said. "Like being a priest. When I was released, my badge was restored to me. Why? Because I'm a good lawman."

Jefferson gathered up the reins of his horse and moved toward the bunkhouse. The man stopped after a few yards, turned, and raised his hands. "What do you see, Frank Cobb? Look closely, man. The carbolic soap at the Meadowbrook Asylum took the skin clean off but still couldn't wash them clean of blood." Jefferson shook his head. "Ain't that a pisser? Ain't that a thigh-slapper?" He grinned and continued walking his mount, passing Trace, who stepped quickly to his mother's side.

Jefferson halted again. "I see a family resemblance in that young man, Mrs. Kerrigan. He's a good-looking boy."

"He's my eldest son, Trace."

The marshal nodded. "Trace. May I call you Trace?"

"You can call me anything you want," Trace said. "So long as you smile when you say it."

"Then Trace it is. Now a lesson for you. Do you see those three dead men? I killed them because they broke the law and then attempted to flee the consequences. The Duffy brothers and Burdett Mohan deserved no compassion from me and none from you." His eyes sought Trace's in the gloom. "Do you understand?"

Frank Cobb answered for him. "Yeah, he understands. He's met killers before, Jefferson. The three men were trying to surrender when you gunned them. Mohan had his hands in the air."

"You saw it, Frank?" Trace said.

"Yeah, I saw it."

"They were trying to enter Mrs. Kerrigan's home," Jefferson said.

"There was no fight left in them, Jefferson. They were all used up, done, and you knew it."

"No matter. The law must take its legal course and I am its instrument."

"Damn it, you murdered them."

"No, I executed them." Jefferson looked tough and mean and hard to kill, with all the emotion of a pillar of granite.

Frank stifled his anger and his voice was steady as he said, "That time over to Uvalde way, Jefferson, you were lucky. If you'd caught up to Wes, he would've killed you."

The lawman shook his head, smiling. "No, he wouldn't. I could shade Hardin any day of the week, any hour of the day, same way as I can shade you, Frank."

Frank's anger flared. "Dream on about it, Jefferson. The day you can shade me will never come."

Jefferson did not answer. He looked around him, alarmed, his open mouth yelling silent words as a sudden, roaring wind cartwheeled across the open yard and violently tugged at Kate Kerrigan's robe, as though trying to strip her naked. A spinning maelstrom of stinging sand enveloped Frank and Trace, and Dunk Jefferson bellowed something into the reeling, roaring tempest as he battled to control his rearing horse. The blast smelled of things long dead, and fear spiked through Kate as she saw Frank Cobb and Trace go down on all fours, forced to their knees by a shrieking, elemental power that even they, tough and range-hardened though they were, could not withstand. Her hair streaming across her face like ribbons of red silk, Kate backed toward the shelter of the house. As though trying to foil her escape, the wind caught her and slammed her into the door. Her left shoulder hit the unyielding oak hard and she cried out in agony, her arm falling numb and useless to her side. Through a haze of pain and whirling sand Kate saw Jefferson throw back his head and above the clamor of the storm she heard him scream one word, a feral yelp of hate.

"Bitch!"

Then silence.

As suddenly as it had begun the wind dropped, the stinging sand ceased its onslaught, and the air cleared. The Texas stars again filled the night sky. Slowly, Trace and Frank got to their feet, a pair of spectral figures who looked as though they'd been doused in bread flour, red-rimmed eyes staring from stark white faces.

Frank used his hat to beat sand from his pants and shirt. "What the hell was that?"

Dunk Jefferson, himself looking like Noah's wife, calmed his scared horse. "Damn her, we had a visitation from the Angel of Death. Mexicans worship her as Santa Muerte, but she's no saint. She's a blasphemy who flaunts her evil body in the robes of a Blessed Madonna. Merciless, without pity, she's an evil spirit who carries a reaper's scythe and has the face of a skull and smells like a rotten corpse. I know the bitch well. She stalks my every step. Even in the insane asylum she tormented me."

Kate's beautiful eyes were luminous green in her sand-whitened face. She crossed herself and whispered, "Jesus, Mary and Joseph, and all the saints in Heaven preserve us."

Frank stepped to her. "Kate, it was only a small haboob." He glared at Jefferson. "You make a habit of scaring womenfolks?"

"Yes, yes, of course, that's all it was, Mrs. Kerrigan. Just a pissant sandstorm," Jefferson said.

As the gunman led his horse toward the stable, Frank called after him, "Jefferson! Before you ride out of here tomorrow, bury your dead."

Without turning, the marshal threw over his shoulder, "Hell, the sand buried 'em."

Frank Cobb shook his head. "I should've killed that man years ago." It was only then he noticed how pale was Kate's face and the pain that showed in her eyes. "Kate, you're hurt."

Kate's only answer was a slight nod. Then the door opened behind her and half a dozen maids tumbled outside, led by Nora, her hair covered by a white crown of paper curlers. "Mrs. Kerrigan, after we heard the shooting we thought you were in your room." Nora glanced at the mounds of the sand-covered bodies and then studied her mistress from head to toe. "Oh dear. Look at the state you're in. Let's get you inside."

"I've hurt my shoulder," Kate said.

"You poor thing." Nora helped Kate through the doorway, but before she stepped into the house, she popped her head outside and said, "Frank Cobb, what did you do to my mistress?"

Before the startled segundo could answer, the door slammed in his face.

Frank saw humor in the woman's accusation and smiled. His eyes drifted to the stable where the hands stood around the door silently staring inside. It seemed that a deputy U.S. marshal who'd just gunned three outlaws was a sight to see. Frank's smile grew thinner. What was the old saying? Oh, yeah. *Curiosity killed the cat.* Well, the punchers' curiosity had just earned them an extra chore . . . dragging the bodies away from the front of the house to the rise where Kate had established a cemetery.

Walking toward the barn, Frank said, "I've got a job for you boys."

Eight young men wearing only hats, boots, and long johns turned and stared at him, a questioning frown on every face. Hell, it was too late and too dark for any kind of job.

Frank smiled. "And you're gonna love it."

As the ranch segundo, Frank Cobb merited his own quarters, a two-room residence tacked on to one end of the bunkhouse. Giving the cramped space more dignity than it deserved, Kate called it "The Tara Wing." The cookhouse took up space at the other end, but Kate had never given it a name.

As he lay in bed that night, Frank was a troubled man. Before he turned in, he'd scouted the area and had made an uneasy discovery—the sandstorm had hit only a patch of ground in front of the Kerrigan mansion, entirely missing the nearby barn, corrals, and bunkhouse. Why? Why had it been so selective? Unbidden, the answer came to him. *Because Santa Muerte, the Angel of Death, had passed that way.*

Angry at himself for having such a thought, he sat up in bed and stared through the bedroom window into opalescent, moonlit darkness. No, it had been a rogue haboob, just that and nothing more. Sure, a twister could've make a straight track across the front of the house and touched nothing else. Yeah, that was the answer. Must be.

Frank lay back on the pillow and closed his eyes, courting sleep.

The night held its silence, and the moon rose higher in the night sky and out on the range the hungry coyotes yipped.

He fell into the deep slumber of the young . . . but a grotesque Madonna with a skull for a face haunted the misty canyons of his dreams.

CHAPTER EIGHT

The fall chill had already frosted Gabe Dancer's ancient bones, and his joints painfully reminded him that the rheumatisms had now cozily settled in until the spring thaw. He'd been out in the wild for four years, killed a man in Lincoln in the New Mexico Territory where that Bill Bonney kid was raising a hundred different kinds of hell, and then rode down the spine of the Guadalupe Mountains and swung east through Gunsight Canyon toward a settlement he knew in the Yeso Hills. Years ago, more years than he cared to remember, Dancer had consorted with a fallen woman there, but he guessed she'd moved on, gotten old, or died.

As the settlement buildings came into sight across the flat scrub and grassland, he drew rein and took a ship's telescope from his saddlebags. He scanned into the distance and realized nothing had changed. The false-fronted saloon with its upstairs rooms to rent by the day or the hour, depending on the guest's intentions, still stood. Next to that was the blacksmith's shop with a pole corral out back and the charred remains of a church. Hammered together by a Reverend Shoveler, it had burned down with him in it and had never been rebuilt.

Satisfied, Dancer lowered his glass. Today was his seventy-sixth birthday, as near as he could figure, and a little celebration was in order. He felt tip-top. He had gold dust in his poke, enough for a good-going drunk and perhaps a lady, if one was available and he could rise to the occasion. If there was a Lincoln hanging posse behind him, they'd surely lost interest long ago. He kneed his yellow mustang into motion and charted a course for the saloon door . . . and destiny.

Gabe Dancer was midway to the saloon when a rider heading away from the settlement abruptly changed direction and cantered toward him. In the West few trusting men lived long enough to grow old, but Dancer had gotten to be seventy-six because he didn't like people all that much and trusted nobody. He drew rein, slid a .44-40 Henry from the boot under his knee, rested the butt on his right thigh, and waited.

When the rider was within talking distance, the man raised a hand. "Howdy, stranger."

Dancer nodded. "And howdy stranger right back at ya."

"You headed for the Golden Nugget?" He was a respectable-looking feller who sat his saddle well and rode a two-hundred-dollar horse.

Since there were a few thereabouts, Dancer pegged him for a rancher of middling prosperity. "That is my intention." With a measure of pride, he added, "It's my birthday today and I plan to make merry."

"Best wishes, but aim to do your celebrating

somewhere else, old-timer," the rider said. "Keep on going and don't stop until you're east of the Brazos. Name's Jasper Eaton. I have a ranch north of here, and that's my advice, if you're willing to take it."

Dancer, a man who'd outgrown life's surprises, was nonetheless puzzled. "Why would you give me such counsel? And on the day of my birth when I plan to carouse?"

Eaton affected that deliberate, slow-talking tone that people reserve for explaining things to the very young and the very old. "You ever hear of the Hellfire ranch? It's owned by a feller by the name of Blade Koenig and it's the biggest spread in the New Mexico Territory, or so he says. And maybe it is. I've heard of none bigger." Eaton waited for that information to sink in.

Dancer said, "Go ahead. I'm listening."

"Well, two Hellfire hands are drinking in the Golden Nugget, and they're on the prod. They got a loose woman with them, and she's a sweet distraction to be sure, but they're spoiling for a fight. That's why I got the hell out of there. I don't see much future in gun fighting a couple of bellering punchers with fast hands and hell in their eyes and neither should you. From what I heard one of them tell the woman, they took a hand in a recent killing that didn't set well with them. My guess is that they're drinking to forget and badly want a chance to prove that they're still men."

"What kind of killing would make them boys think that way?" Dancer said.

"I have no idea," Eaton said. "Maybe a woman got gunned or a child or maybe a preacher. Who knows? It's been my experience that all kinds of things happen in the New Mexico Territory."

"Well now, there are some killings that trouble a man."

"I wouldn't know. I've never killed anybody."

Dancer gave a nod. "And that's a feather in your cap, sir. No good ever comes of a killing, whether the dead man deserved it or not."

He was a thin, wiry old man, dressed in the rough, patched clothes of a hardscrabble tinpan. His bleak, blue eyes were faded as though they'd seen too much and he'd plumb worn them out. He was aware of his advancing years, fully conscious of the fact that he was running out of room on the dance floor, but he wasn't quite ready to turn up his toes just yet. He'd done a lot of things in his life, both good and bad, and wanted to do more. By nature, he was a private, close, tight man, who'd never spread his blankets within the sound of church bells, except during a couple visits to Paris, France, and had never bedded a woman without paying her first. He had neither kith nor kin, and in his entire life no one had ever been glad at his coming or sad at his leaving. Dancer had sand and was skilled with the Winchester rifle. He'd killed two men, a Regulator in Lincoln who'd demanded his fine rifle, and a Deadwood pimp who tried to roll him in an alley. Before taking five .44 bullets to his belly, the pimp had cut Dancer, and he still bore a six-inch knife scar across his scrawny chest.

Withal, apart from the seasonal rheumatisms and bouts of the croup, Gabe Dancer was a tough old coot, straitlaced in his way, and by times, if prodded, he could be as dangerous as a teased rattler.

"Mr. Eaton, you've given me a fair warning, and I thank you kindly for your thoughtfulness, but today is my birthday and I will not forgo my merrymaking."

The old man showed his rare smile. "Since you put out your name, let me extend you the same courtesy. My name's been Gabe Dancer, man and boy, and I'm in your debt."

Eaton, a man with iron gray hair, shook his head. "You owe me nothing, Mr. Dancer. Are you sure I can't dissuade you from your planned course of action?"

"No, you can't," Dancer said. "I've met men with hell in their eyes before."

"But maybe you were younger then, huh?"

"Age makes no difference. I'm ready for anything, and that includes my birthday party. Say, you don't suppose that loose woman at the saloon can bake a cake?"

"I don't think she ever baked a cake in her life."

"Pity. I have a notion that I'd be right partial to birthday cake, although I've never partook of one. Now, if you'll give me the road . . ."

"Your funeral, old-timer. Now all I can say is good luck." As he swung his horse away, Eaton's smile was grim. "You're surely going to need it."

The Golden Nugget was a long and narrow building with a bar to the left, a single wood-burning stove along with a barber's chair, a couple poker tables, and a few chairs. Sawdust covered the floor, and the only lighting came from candles and a few oil lamps suspended from the ceiling. The place had the characteristic saloon aroma of unwashed customers, stale beer, fumes from the oil lamps, and the acrid stink of strong tobacco. On the wall behind the bar, hanging at a forty-five-degree angle, was a printed sign that read, HAVE YOU WRITTEN TO MOTHER? The saloon was cold and dingy and depressing, and when Gabe Dancer stepped through the door the atmosphere was none too friendly.

Suddenly he was the elephant in the room, the object of everyone's attention, meaning the two Hellfire punchers at the bar, a blowsy woman in a red dress and fishnet stockings, and the bartender. But this mixologist was not one of the magnificent pomaded, perfumed, and brocaded creatures of the boomtown saloons, but rather a muscular, bald ranny who looked more blacksmith than bartender. Further offending Dancer's Victorian sensibilities, the man had his sleeves rolled up, revealing his wrists, a vulgar display unheard of in polite society.

But it was Gabe Dancer's birthday and he was willing to overlook the man's breach of etiquette. "Good afternoon to all"—he gave a slight bow—"and especially to you, dear lady."

That brought a guffaw from the bigger and meaner of the two punchers. "Lady? There ain't no ladies in here, old man."

"I was a lady . . . once," the blowsy woman said.

That brought another roar of derisive laughter from both men. The big man, showing his teeth in a grin, grabbed one of the woman's breasts and twisted, causing a yelp of pain from the lady in question and occasioning more ribald laughter.

"What can I do you for, Pops?" the bartender said. He was smiling at the woman's obvious distress, revealing bad teeth and a suspect attitude.

Despite what had happened, Dancer laid his Henry on the bar, prepared to be sociable. "It's my birthday today, so give me a bottle of whatever you have that passes for whiskey and a beer to cut the dust in my throat."

"You don't seem too well set up," the bartender said. "You have money to pay for whiskey and beer?"

"Rest assured, I have enough for my birthday party."

"Then show me some coin," the bartender said. A fat blue fly landed on the side of his nose and he irritably brushed it way. "I'm not a trusting man."

Dancer took a leather bag tied with a rawhide string from around his neck and tossed it onto the bar. "Gold dust. Take a look-see."

The bartender seemed skeptical. "Fool's gold, maybe."

"I ain't no fool. Look fer yourself, young feller."

The bartender opened the sack, stared at the contents for a spell, and then rubbed a pinch between forefinger and thumb. He let the dust trickle back into the bag. "It's gold all right."

At the mention of gold the two punchers gave Dancer their undivided attention.

"How much in there?" the bigger man said, touching his tongue to his top lip.

"I'm about to weigh it," the bartender said. "But it's a fair amount." He reached under the bar and blew cobwebs off a small pair of scales. After adding a few tiny brass weights the pans balanced Dancer's poke. "Seven ounces, old-timer. Call it a hundred and forty dollars American."

"I figure that's about right." Dancer took his poke from the scale. "Today being my birthday, I plan to do some celebrating. We'll settle up when the drinking and the festivities are done."

"No, we'll be the ones to settle up," the big puncher

said. "An old coot like you don't need a hundred and forty dollars. Hell, at your age you can get drunk on five."

"Damn right," the other cowboy said. "We'll do the drinking for you."

The blowsy woman, a peroxide blonde with a wide, scarlet mouth, puckered up and blew Dancer a kiss over her open palm. "Listen to the man, Pops. You got no need to be spending all that money when there's so many poor folks like us about."

"Yeah, just like us," the big puncher said, grinning. He had a bad, humorless grin, feral and predatory. "We need money real bad—your money, somebody else's money, anybody's money—if you catch my drift."

Dancer rubbed his cheek, figuring that's where the woman's kiss had stuck like a slug on a wrinkled leaf. It had been the old man's experience that when a man needed a gun in the West he needed it almighty sudden, and to his disappointment that's how things were rapidly shaping up.

But he still tried to defuse what he knew was already a bad situation.

"Hell, the drinks are on me, boys. I reckon between us and the woman we'll burn through a hundred and forty dollars quick enough." He smiled. "And you too, bartender. Join the party. Anybody here know how to bake a birthday cake?"

The big puncher, half-drunk and red-eyed with whiskey meanness, was having none of it and made the second-to-last mistake he'd ever make in his life. "You ain't catching my drift, Methuselah. We ain't sharing. Now give me that damned poke afore I put a bullet in your hide." He took a step toward Dancer.

That step was the cowboy's first mistake, but the only person present who knew it was Dancer. As the old man would tell it later to them who had the time and inclination to listen, the second, and ultimately fatal faux pas, came when the big waddie dropped a hand to his holstered Colt, as threatening a gesture as ever was.

Dancer was a slight old man and stiff from the rheumatisms, but that day when the chips were down he moved as quick as the snap of a bullwhip. In one smooth motion, he lifted his Henry from the bar, took a step to his right as he levered a round into the chamber, and fired.

The .44-40 slug punched a half-inch hole in the puncher's belly even as the big man's Colt cleared leather. Shock, amazement, confusion, and regret, each of those emotions took a fraction of a second to cross the man's face before the pain hit him like a blow to the gut by a mailed fist. The man screamed, dropped his gun, and went down.

Dancer didn't watch him fall. His attention focused on the second cowboy. Slowed by whiskey and appalled by what had just happened, the puncher telegraphed his draw and Dancer gunned him where he stood, a killing shot to the chest that dropped him, all flopping arms and legs, like a puppet that just had its strings cut.

Wreathed in gray gun smoke, his ears ringing, Gabe Dancer thought the shooting was over. The screams of the gut-shot man rang loud in the close confines of the saloon, and the whore had backed away, her face ashen, showing no sign of making any kind of play. Then Dancer saw her attention flick to the bar, and her eyes got as big and round as dollar coins.

Damn that bartender!

Dancer twisted around to his left just as the man raised a sawn-off scattergun, his face ugly with rage. Dancer wiped that expression off the bartender's face with a bullet that smacked right where his eyebrows met above the bridge of his nose like a greeting pair of hairy caterpillars. The man shrieked, fell backward, and crashed into a shelf of empty bottles lined up for display. The sign on the wall and the bartender hit the floor at the same time.

Dancer looked over the bar and saw that the man was as dead as hell in a preacher's backyard, the HAVE YOU WRITTEN TO MOTHER? sign laying on his chest.

Dancer said, "She must be mighty proud o' you."

"Don't kill me, mister," the woman said. "Hugh Flannigan owned the place, and I only worked for him. I'm an entertainer."

Gabe Dancer looked at her. "I make it a rule not to kill women, children, or friendly dogs. Of course, rules are made to be broken, and when it comes to whores who might have a sneaky gun, I'm willing to make an exception."

"You have nothing to fear from me." The woman looked at the two men. The big puncher had stopped squealing but was groaning in pain, his bloodstained hands clutching his belly. "That one chawing up the sawdust is Chester Bird. He hurt me, hurt me awful bad, and laughed while he was doing it. He called the dead one Pete, and he was from Missouri, and that's all I know about him. But they were trash, both lowlife trash."

Dancer had seen a lot in his long life, but what the woman did next surprised even him. A large pot of coffee simmered on the stove and she picked it up, using the hem of her dress to grip the hot handle, and then crossed the floor again and stood over the man named Bird. Without a word, she emptied the boiling coffee over the puncher's crotch. As he renewed his shattering screams, she said, "You won't hurt another woman."

Dancer shook his head. "You ain't one to hold a grudge, are you, honey?" He took a knee beside the tormented cowboy. "Make your peace with God, old fellow. Your time is short, because I'm about to put you out of your misery, on account of how you're shaping up to spoil my birthday party."

Bird had reached the plateau of pain that a man can rightfully be expected to endure and then gone beyond that stratum into a realm of diabolical torment, the hellish kind of agony that makes even a brave man beg for death. But somewhere deep within him the big puncher had sand, and through waves of pain he mustered the strength to whisper, "You . . . go . . . to . . . hell . . ."

"So be it." Dancer raised his eyes heavenward. "For what I'm about to do, Lord forgive me." A single shot from the old man's Henry ended Chester Bird's suffering forever.

His stiff knees cracking, Dancer rose to his feet. "Woman, what's your name?"

"Lily. What's your'n?"

"Gabe Dancer, and I'm right pleased to meet you." He laid his rifle back on the bar and clapped his hands. "Now, let's get this party started. Wait, you never did tell me if you can bake a birthday cake."

"Mister, I can't bake anything, not even an egg."

"You don't bake an egg. You can fry it, boil it, scramble it, or eat it raw, but you can't bake it. Leastways, I don't think so."

"See, what do I know?"

"Pity about the cake, though."

"Yeah, I'm all broken up over that."

"Well, no matter, though it's a sore disappointment. Right, Lily, let's get ready to open the ball."

The woman was shocked. "But . . . but there's dead men here."

"Yeah, I know, but that's all right. They're invited. Hell, woman, it wouldn't be a party without guests, even dead ones."

He filled glasses in their stiff hands, propped them up against the far wall of the saloon, and left them watching him and Lily with open, unseeing eyes. Gabe drank too much, danced too much, sang too many songs, and made himself hoarse. With some success he bedded Lily in her shack behind the saloon and woke with a hammering headache and a parched mouth.

After a gallon of coffee, at Lily's insistence he saw to the disposal of the bodies, three prime specimens of the dead drunk. Grave digging not being in his line of work, Gabe dabbed a loop on each of the dead men and, riding though rain and thunder, dragged them a considerable distance into the brush.

"Did you take them far and bury them deep?" Lily said after the work was done.

"Far enough, deep enough," Dancer said.

"I don't want them close. They'll come back and haunt me."

"No fear of that," Dancer said his slicker dripping water. "Weather and the coyotes will take care of them, ghosts an' all."

"It was horrible, the killing and the burying. The whole thing was just horrible."

"Wasn't it, though," Dancer said.

"Three men dead." Lily snapped her fingers. "Just like that."

"Yup, just like that." Dancer tried to snap his fingers but couldn't.

"Ah well, there's more coffee on the bile," Lily said.

"Suits me. Undertaking is hard work."

It was still thundering as Gabe tightened his saddle cinch and then turned to Lily. "You can come with me if you want. A willing whore with a good attitude and nice personality like your'n can find honest work anyplace."

"I figure I'll stick, see if I can make a go of the saloon." She held a black umbrella over her head that looked like a gigantic bat and she didn't seem well, last night's whiskey punishing her. "You killed the bartender and the blacksmith with the same bullet, Gabe. I'll be shorthanded."

"Sell the cowponies and traps and see what money Flannigan has stashed away. Maybe you can hire somebody."

"Plenty of men looking for work, I guess," Lily said.

"Yup, all kinds of them. Find a ranny who can shoe a horse and pour a whiskey and you'll be set."

"You could stay, Gabe, if you wanted. I'd be good to you. Bake you a cake one day."

"Lady, that's a fine offer and one to make a man hesitate, but I got to be moving on. I ain't much of a hand for staying in one place too long." He climbed into the saddle with rain-stiffened knees.

"It was a fine party, Gabe."

"I'd say that, Lily. Revelry to remember, and no mistake."

"Which way you headed?"

Dancer pointed. "Thataway to take a look-see, on account of how I've never been east of the Brazos afore."

Lily said, "After you cross the river there ain't nothing to see but grass. A hundred miles in any direction and you're on a ranch owned by a woman they call Kate Kerrigan. Biggest spread in West Texas, or so I was told."

"Them cowboys tell you that?" Rain dripped from the brim of Dancer's peaked cap.

"One of them mentioned it."

"Punchers are always tellin' big windies. There ain't no lady-owned ranches in Texas." He touched his hat. "Well, I'll be seeing you, Lily. Good luck."

"Yeah, and you too, Gabe. Here, take this." She handed Dancer a silver ring. "I found this on the floor. Maybe it will bring you good fortune."

"You should keep it your ownself. A whore deserves nice things."

"No, Gabe. I want you to have it."

Dancer placed the ring on the pinkie finger of his left hand. "I'm much obliged, Lily." He touched the peak of his hat. "Maybe I'll see you around someday."

Lily waited until Dancer rode into rain and the gray

day and then she yelled, "Hey, old man, you did all right in bed last night. Did you know that?"

"Damn right I knew it," Dancer called back. He turned his head and grinned over his shoulder. "And so did you."

"I ain't likely to forget it," Lily said.

"Me neither."

"Come back and see me, Gabe. Good luck."

"You too, Lily. Good luck."

CHAPTER NINE

Two three-minute brown eggs in porcelain cups, hot buttered toast, marmalade, and a silver coffeepot with matching cream and sugar servers lay on the tray that Nora placed on Kate Kerrigan's lap. The maid fluffed up the pillow that she'd placed behind her mistress's back and said, "How is the shoulder, Mrs. Kerrigan?"

"It hurts. I've had no sleep." Her voice was cross and drowsy. "It's still dark, Nora. What time is it?"

"Five-thirty, ma'am. Your son Trace and Mr. Cobb are waiting outside the door. They say they were told to wake you before sunup."

"That was before I hurt my shoulder."

Nora gently pushed away the silk of Kate's nightdress, exposing a normally milk-white skin that was covered in black, blue, and sulfur-yellow bruises. "It's doesn't look good at all, ma'am. I'm sure it's very painful."

"Yes it is, and I can hardly move it." Kate tried and winced. "No, I can't move it at all."

"Then you must rest the shoulder for a while."

"I may have no alternative."

Her voice slightly accusing, the maid said, "Mr. Cobb said you plan on riding today. I gave him a piece of my mind."

Kate shook her head. "I can't ride, Nora, not today. I need a few days to heal."

Nora took up a spoon and tapped the top of one of the eggs. When the shell was good and broken, she opened the egg and then added a dash of salt and pepper to the yellow yolk. Handing the spoon to Kate, she said, "You must eat now, ma'am, if you want to keep up your strength and heal quickly. That horrible Blade Koenig person can wait."

"You know I'm going after him?"

"Everybody knows. Jazmine is so beside herself with worry she burned six slices of toast this morning."

"There are men who want my ranch, Nora, men who say a woman has no right to be a rancher. I won't show weakness. What the Koenigs did cannot go unavenged. Blade Koenig and his son will still be lording it on their ranch in a week or so and by then I'll be ready. Besides, what is the saying, something about revenge and a cold dish?"

"Revenge is a dish best served cold," Nora said.

"Yes, that is it," Kate said. Her emerald green eyes flashed. "But I'll heat up the cold dish I serve to the Koenigs with hot lead."

"Oh, Mrs. Kerrigan, you sound so fierce. You make me feel quite afraid."

Kate smiled. "That's what comes of my being around Frank Cobb for so many years. Well, let me just say that the Koenigs will very soon rue the day they violated my home." She winced as she moved her shoulder and was rewarded with a spike of pain. "Pour me some coffee and then take the tray away, Nora."

"But you've hardly eaten anything," the maid said.

"I know. Maybe I'll do better at lunch. On your way out please send in my son and Mr. Cobb."

"I don't want those two hellions upsetting you," Nora said.

"They won't, because I'm already upset."

Frank entered the room first and heard Kate's statement. "Kate, I know you're upset, but what Dunk Jefferson says makes sense. In fact, it's the only thing he's ever said that makes sense."

"No, I won't even consider it, Frank," Kate said. "This is my fight, not his."

Trace said, "But, Ma, it could be weeks before—"

"Before what?" A frown gathered between Kate's eyebrows.

"Before . . . well, before you can ride with that injured shoulder."

"Trace, don't tell me what I can't do," Kate said. "I can do anything I want when I set my mind to it. I'll be well enough to ride in a few days."

Like a man making his way across a floor strewn with thumbtacks, Frank stepped warily. "Kate, Jefferson has a badge and the authority to arrest Blade Koenig and his son and bring them in for trial."

"The KK fights its own battles, Frank. I was the one manhandled by Seth Koenig, not Jefferson. If, and it's a big if, the Koenigs agreed to stand trial for murder and attempted rape Blade Koenig could buy the judge and jury and a whole town if need be. He and his son would return to the Hellfire free men, laughing up their sleeves at the law and at me." Kate frowned again. "Frank, don't you dare tell me I'm wrong, because if you do, I'll know you're lying."

"But damn it all, Kate—"

"No cussing in my home, Frank. Every time Our Lady hears you use foul language she sheds a tear." Kate laid her cup and saucer on the table beside her, moving stiffly, favoring the shoulder. "You're the one who said Jefferson isn't playing cards with a full deck, and we don't really know if he is a marshal."

"Dunk Jefferson is nuts all right," Frank said. "But me, Trace, and half a dozen of our toughest hands will be with him. We'll make sure justice is done."

"Justice will be done when the murderers Blade and Seth Koenig are dangling from a noose," Kate said. "I will settle for nothing less. Now you and Trace and those tough hands of yours will stand down for a few days until I'm fit to ride." To hammer home her point, she added, "My mind is made up. Don't try to change it, because you won't succeed."

Kate read disappointment in the faces of her son and segundo, one she loved and the other she cared deeply about. "This is very personal with me. The Koenigs slaughtered people, one of them just a boy, who'd sought refuge in my home. They injured old Mose and then tried to ravage me and members of my household staff. Now there's an orphaned baby being taken care of by my maids and those cries you hear are the infant calling out for revenge, or so I fancy. This will not stand. My home was attacked, invaded, and I will return the favor with bullets and a rope."

Kate's glossy mane of red hair had fallen over her shoulders, and under the thin stuff of her nightgown her breasts rose firm and aggressive. She looked feminine and combative, like a figurehead at the bow of a man-o'-war, and Frank Cobb fell in love with her all over again.

"Kate, you win. I'll send the men out to cut hay. When you're feeling better we'll ride for the Hellfire."

Trace gave the big segundo a sidelong glance, but, like Frank, there was no argument left in him. Sometimes his mother was an elemental force, a woman to be reckoned with, and it was a bad mistake to stand in her way.

Chapter Ten

Dunk Jefferson didn't show up at the bunkhouse until noon. He came down from the rise behind the mansion with mud on his boots and a shovel in his hand. The first person he saw was Frank Cobb, and he hailed him. "Buried my dead, Frank."

"You plant them boys coyote deep?" Frank said, disliking the man.

"Sure did. Deep enough. I even said a few words, though they didn't mean a damn thing to dead men. Now I got to clean up. Is there grub?"

"Go talk to the cook. He'll feed you."

Jefferson nodded. "I put three good horses in your corral and left revolvers and rifles outside your door. I'll take five hundred for the horses and you can keep the guns."

"I'll inspect the horses and talk with Mrs. Kerrigan," Frank said.

"And when you're talking, tell her I'll bring in Blade Koenig and his son for her."

"She wants to do that job herself."

"And she can. I'll bring them here and she can hang them at her earliest convenience."

"For Kate it's a reckoning, Jefferson. I said she wants to deal with the Koenigs herself and that means from start to finish."

The little man shrugged. "There's no arguing with a woman. All right, then I'll ride with her. When?"

"In a few days. The boss injured her shoulder, and she needs time to heal."

"A man wouldn't need time to heal," Jefferson said. "That's the trouble with having a lady boss. A woman will lie abed every opportunity she gets, unless it's a man doing the askin', and then she'll jump out of the sheets like a scalded cat."

Ignoring that comment, Frank said, "Beef and beans in the cookhouse and maybe there's some bear sign left. Go eat."

Jefferson stared into Frank's eyes. "You still think I ain't right in the head. Isn't that so?"

"You were never right in the head, Dunk, even back in the day."

"I was sane enough to run away from the booby hatch and steal a hoss so I could put a passel of git between me and them brain doctors. A man who can do all that ain't loco. Fact is, he's a goddamned genius."

"So, I was right. You are no longer a deputy marshal," Frank said.

Jefferson put thumb and forefinger on his badge. "This here star says I am. I kept hold of this star, Frank. Even in the insane asylum I kept hold of it. I hid it, Frank, hid it good where them sons of bitches could never find it." His smile was crafty. "Know what I done? I snuck it between the pages of a Bible they give me, right at Isaiah Fourteen and Twelve where it says, 'How you have fallen from heaven, morning star, son of the dawn. You have been cast down to the earth, you who once laid low the nations.' That was wrote for Satan, but it could have been wrote for me." Jefferson's eyes darted to his right and left and his voice dropped to a whisper. "Heard something, Frank. I heard something, a thing you should know."

"I don't want to hear it," Frank said.

"You got to hear it and I'm going to tell it to you. I heard them Koenig boys tried to rape Mrs. Kerrigan. And there's some talk that they succeeded."

Frank's face stiffened but he said nothing.

"Tell her I'll cut them, Frank. Tell her I'll bring back their balls—"

"No, you won't."

"In a poke," Jefferson said.

Frank Cobb sorted out a response in his mind and then said the words. "Jefferson, saddle up and ride on out of here. I don't want you around."

"How come?"

"You're bad news, and I hate your guts."

The little man nodded. "Figured you'd get back to that again. But I'm staying put. The law has been broken, and it's my duty to see that the lawbreakers are brought to justice."

"Damn you, Jefferson, you have no duty," Frank said, his blue eyes showing anger. "You're an escapee from an insane asylum, not a lawman."

"I am a lawman. This star on my chest says so."

"The hell with your star. Now git. Like I told you to."

The stubborn expression on Jefferson's face shut down and left only an expressionless mask. "Frank, you want me gone from here, you'll need to draw down on me to make it permanent." The man's hand was close to his gun. "But I don't advise it. You couldn't shade me on your best day, not then, not now."

Jefferson had supplied the spark and Frank was ready to explode, his anger a terrible thing to see.

Kate Kerrigan saw and quickly put a damper on her segundo's rage. "Frank!" she called from the house doorway. "Let it go! This moment!" For a moment, she thought Frank would ignore her, that she was trying to draw rein on a runaway stallion, but as she walked toward him, she saw the turmoil go out of him, replaced by a slump-shouldered acceptance that it was neither the time nor the place for a gunfight.

Their eyes locked in mutual dislike and hostility, neither Frank nor Jefferson turned in Kate's direction.

Wearing only a dressing gown, her left arm in a sling made from a torn petticoat, she stepped between the two men. A man can tell how angry an Irish woman is by her hands. If they're around your neck she's probably a little annoyed with you . . . but if she's holding a gun, then you can bet the farm that you're in deep trouble.

Kate held a gun—a .455 British Bulldog revolver presented to her by Queen Victoria during Kate's visit to Buckingham Palace. "We trust that this pistol will stand you in good stead after your return to the wild Texas lands," the old queen had said.

Indeed, the Bulldog was standing Kate in good stead. "Both of you, step away." Her heart thumped in her chest. "I don't want to shoot you, but if that's what it takes to restore tranquility to my home, then that's what I'll do."

Frank looked stubborn, but Jefferson defused the situation . . . at least for the moment.

The little man swept off his hat, cut a deep bow, and straightened. "No need for violence, Mrs. Kerrigan, and I apologize most humbly for distressing you so. Mr. Cobb and I were merely trying to settle a disagreement about the hunt for the Koenig scoundrels."

"That will be settled soon, and by me," Kate said. "In the meantime, Mr. Jefferson you look very begrimed. I suggest you wash up and then find yourself some breakfast."

"I buried the Duffy brothers and Platte River Burdett Mohan," Jefferson said. "It was muddy work and grave digging does give a man an appetite. Maybe it's something to do with the smell of dead men. I don't know."

"Then please do as I say," Kate said.

Jefferson gave another bow from the waist. "Your obedient servant, ma'am." He gave Frank a hard look, picked up his shovel, and walked away. A dust devil rose and spun around Jefferson's legs but only for an instant before it collapsed and died.

Kate yelled after the man's retreating back. "And Mr. Jefferson, all the Koenigs succeeded in doing was make me mad."

Jefferson touched his hat brim. "Glad to hear that, Mrs. Kerrigan."

When the man was gone, Kate glared at Frank. "Frank Cobb, I'm surprised at you. How could you match wits with a crazy man?"

Muscles bunched in Frank's jaw. "You shouldn't be surprised, Kate. I've never in my life backed away from a fight."

"Well, this time I'm glad you did," Kate said. "You could be lying dead on the ground right now."

"Or Jefferson could. Don't sell me short."

"Or both of you, killed by stubborn male pride."

"He wants to ride with us when we go after the Koenigs."

"Well, when the chips are down maybe an extra gun will come in handy."

"Kate, Dunk Jefferson is a madman."

Kate frowned. "Yes, Frank, I know, but we'll be going up against madmen. Or had you forgotten?"

"No, what happened here, at your home, is something I'll never forget." He touched his hat. "Now I have to go see how Trace and the hands are doing with the hay cutting or with the not hay cutting, whatever the case may be."

"Frank—"

The big segundo could almost read Kate's thoughts and he smiled. "I'll stay away from Jefferson."

"No, it's not about Jefferson, not really. Frank, you mean a great deal to me and I don't want to lose you."

"Nor I you," Frank said. "So we break even on that score."

When Kate stepped into the house Nora was waiting for her, her face concerned. "Is everything all right, Mrs. Kerrigan? You're shivering and pale and you look affrighted."

"I'm just fine. I know it's early, Nora, but bring me a brandy. And for God's sake make it a large one."

CHAPTER ELEVEN

The last thing Kate Kerrigan needed the evening of Frank Cobb's brush with Dunk Jefferson was a visit from Doña Maria Ana de la Villa de Villar del Aguila and her eighty-strong entourage, including the man with the gun, the feared Mexican pistolero Rodolfo Aragon. Since the noblewoman's retinue had been spotted as soon as it crossed the Rio Grande onto KK range, a puncher on a fast horse had given Kate some warning, but it wasn't nearly enough.

"I don't have time for entertaining," Kate said. "Especially Doña Maria Ana, who complains about everything."

Frank Cobb nodded. "And more especially since she's bringing half the population of Mexico with her."

Kate's sigh was long and dramatic. "Jazmine gave me this dinner menu, Frank. What do you think? It's the best she could do at such short notice."

He smiled. "No beef and beans for the doña, huh?"

"Now you're being silly," Kate said. "Just read the menu and give me your opinion on the fare."

Frank took the paper Kate passed to him and read:

CREAM OF ASPARAGUS SOUP

~

TROUT AMANDINE

~

ROAST CHICKEN, *with* POTATO BALLS

~

HAM TIMBALES, *with SAUCE BEURRE BLANC*

~

GREEN PEAS

~

MOUSSE AU CHOCOLAT

~

FANCY PASTRIES

~

COFFEE

Frank grinned. "Well, I got to say that it sure beats beef and beans."

"It's awful, just an awful meal," Kate said, frowning as she snatched the menu back from Frank's hand. "But, bless her, Jazmine is trying her best. Well, my shoulder is hurting, and I have neither the time nor inclination to bake a sponge cake, so that serves Maria Ana right for not giving me prior notice."

"Yes, indeed," Frank said, his face straight. "It's her loss."

"Nora!" Kate called. Then, after a few moments, her irritation showing, "Where is that girl?"

Nora, looking as flustered as her mistress, opened the door and stepped into the parlor. "Jazmine is worried about her mousse and she's in a terrible dither."

"We're all in a terrible dither," Kate said. "Here, take the menu and tell Jazmine it's just fine, and tell her that her mousse will be wonderful as always."

Nora dropped a little curtsy and stepped to the door.

"And come right back." Kate said. "I need to bathe and dress. The green silk for tonight, please, and the emerald earrings and necklace."

Nora stood at the door for a few moments, obviously pondering her next words.

Kate said, "Out with it, girl."

"Very well, ma'am. Then I'll say it." Nora tilted her chin, her face stubborn. "I think Doña Maria Ana is a snobbish, bossy bitch."

Kate was unfazed and even managed a faint trace of a smile. "Yes, my dear, she's all of that . . . and so much more."

After Nora left, Kate said to Frank, "I sent Shorty Hawkins out on a scout. He says Maria Ana will be here in a couple hours. In addition to her carriage, he counted almost a hundred people on foot and three wagons, one of them piled high with her luggage."

"Hell, that much luggage? How long does she plan on staying?" Frank said.

"I have no way of knowing. Not too long, I hope. Now, if you will excuse me, Frank?"

"Of course." He stepped to the door.

"I'll see you at dinner," Kate said,

"Sure thing," Frank said, grinning. "I wouldn't miss that cream of asparagus soup for the world."

Frank Cobb met Shorty Hawkins as the puncher made his way to the bunkhouse. "Got something to tell you, Mister Cobb."

"About Doña Maria Ana de la Villa . . . and so on and so forth?"

"No, about the gun riding with her," Shorty said. "Tall for a Mex, fancy dresser, sits a silver saddle like he's a king and wears two Colts."

"Yeah, his name is Rodolfo Aragon, and he's been here before," Frank said. "He's the doña's personal bodyguard. Shorty, tell the boys to step wide around him. He's poison."

"You seen him shoot, boss?"

"No, I haven't, but I've heard he's a hundred different kinds of hell on the draw and shoot with the Colt's gun. And I believe it. Son of a bitch never talks, just looks around, missing nothing. They say he dozes upright on his feet with his eyes open, but I don't know about that."

"What about Dunk Jefferson?" Shorty said.

"What about him?"

"Will he tangle with the Mex?"

"Not if he knows what's good for him he won't. Besides, Jefferson has no beef with Rodolfo Aragon. The only time Aragon rides north of the Rio Grande is when Doña Maria Ana is visiting friends or kinfolk."

"He's got a patch over his left eye. Seen it plain," Shorty said.

"I know, but it ain't his shooting eye."

CHAPTER TWELVE

About the same time Doña Maria Ana's party crossed the Rio Grande, a solitary lawman made his way through Hellfire Pass, a rugged, high-walled canyon that saws through the Tres Hermanas Mountains, a trio of peaks that dominate the New Mexico Territory's Luna County. County Sheriff Buford Whelan drew rein on his lanky buckskin and studied his way ahead, the rocky trail partially blocked by mesquite and a few piñons, the only plants of note that managed to thrive in such a hostile environment. In fact, Hellfire Canyon was little more than a narrow, gloomy arroyo, but some forgotten army surveyor had declared it a canyon and the designation had stuck. A wagon train of settlers had been ambushed near there by Apaches and the lone survivor swore he'd seen the devil himself ride out of the canyon on a black horse, wielding a flaming torch as a weapon. From that time onward the place had been called Hellfire Pass, and there were rumors that at a certain time of the year it served as a gateway to hell and hosted the annual Demons' Ball. Wild tales like that were enough to ensure that most people rode wide of the canyon and never stared into its eerie depths.

Whelan, tough and uncompromising, was a man who'd ride into hell if that's what his job required. Once through the pass he'd be facing a different kind of demon in the square, strong form of big Blade Koenig.

It was said that when Koenig crowed it was daylight in New Mexico and for the past twelve years he and his hard-bitten Hellfire riders had lorded it over that part of the territory, unchallenged rulers of two hundred and fifty thousand acres of prime range. As he'd grown in riches and power, Koenig ruled his domain with an iron hand and he gained a reputation as being death on rustlers, nesters, and other undesirables. By Whelan's own count, Blade had hanged and shot at least forty people, but the total was probably twice that many.

The sheriff suspected that the sudden disappearance of the raggedy-assed Tillett family could be tied to Koenig. The Tilletts were as poor as sawmill rats but were neither rustlers nor nesters, since they owned a one-loop spread that adjoined the Koenig cattle empire.

But the Tilletts were not the reason for Whelan's visit.

A farmer's daughter by the name of Caroline Briggs was.

Buford Whelan kneed his buckskin forward. It was time to confront Blade Koenig and make some war talk.

"Out with it, Buford. You didn't ride all the way from Deming to sit in my parlor and drink my whiskey," Blade Koenig said.

"And good bourbon it is, Blade." Whelan smiled. A tall, spare man in his late forties, he had iron-gray hair and weary hazel eyes that had seen and remembered too much. "Well worth the trip, I'd say."

"But you have other business." The big rancher looked wary, like a man who expected bad news. "You were never much of a man for social calls."

When it came, the news was as bad as Blade feared.

"It's about your son," Whelan said.

Koenig closed down. He stared at the lawman with blank eyes, silently waiting for what was to come . . . and it was not long in coming.

"I heard that Seth is sparking a farmer's daughter by the name of Caroline Briggs," Whelan said. "I'm told she's fourteen years old and real pretty. Do you know about that?"

"No, no I don't," Koenig said. "Why are you telling me this?"

"Because if Seth is sparking her I want it to stop," the sheriff said.

Koenig refilled Whelan's glass, playing for time. Finally, he smiled and said, "For a minute there I thought you might be playing Cupid, Sheriff."

"This is no laughing matter, Blade," Whelan said. "There was another girl. Emily Graham was her name and Seth was sniffing around her all the time. That much I know for sure. She left a note for her widowed mother saying that she'd been raped and couldn't live with the shame. She wanted to be a nun, her ma says. You know Dead Mule Wash a ten-mile north of here?"

"I know it. Had a paint mare break a leg up there one time." Koenig's face was as expressionless as a death mask, but the knuckles of his left hand were white on his glass.

"My, this is real good whiskey." Whelan held up his glass and stared into its amber depths. "No burn, real smooth."

Koenig drew a deep breath. "So, Seth was sparking the Graham girl for a spell. He told me about her. He's a young man, Buford. No surprise there. What did she do, run away from home?"

"No, she didn't run away from home, but I guess the only surprise is that Emily Graham is dead. I didn't see the body, but Luke Gorman said—you know him, Blade? Has a horse ranch on t'other side of the mountains?"

"I know him. What did Gorman say?"

"I'll tell you just like he told it to me."

"Then get on with it, man." Blade's voice betrayed his growing irritation.

"Well, sir, Luke and one of his hands were out hunting a cougar when they found Emily's body. She'd been dead for a few days and the coyotes had been at her, but it was still obvious how she'd killed herself. Seems she put the muzzle of her dead pa's Colt Dragoon under her chin and pulled the trigger. Luke says Emily Graham blew the top of her skull clean off."

Blade Koenig's heavy breathing was audible in the quiet room. Finally, he said, "All right, Buford, I admit that we heard that the girl was dead. Seth was . . ."

Seth was brokenhearted about it. But Koenig couldn't bring himself to utter such a dishonorable and nonsensical lie. He shook his head. "It was a terrible thing, an awful thing to happen."

"Why did you lie to me, Blade?"

"I didn't lie to you."

"At first you implied that you didn't know the Graham girl was dead."

"I was protecting my son from a false accusation. You have my word that he didn't rape that girl, Buford."

"It was an awful thing I don't want to see happen again," Whelan said.

Koenig managed to simulate indignation. "After I gave you my word, do you still believe that Seth had something to do with Emily Graham's death?"

"With her death, no. With what led to her death, yes." Before the big man could speak, Whalen said, "Blade, why did the Tilletts suddenly pull up stakes and leave?"

Koenig had an answer ready. "I don't have much truck with their kind. I can tell you that the Tilletts were white trash who didn't know how to run a ranch. They probably sneaked out on a pile of debts."

"That, or something or somebody scared them . . . scared them bad," Whelan said. "Is it possible one of them saw something they shouldn't have seen?"

"Damn it, man, you're talking in riddles," Koenig said. "What was there to see?"

"You tell me, Blade."

"They saw the debt collector, probably," Koenig said.

"Any idea where they are?"

"No, I don't. Why should I? All I can say is good riddance."

"I think I'll scout around, see if I can find them."

"Good luck with that, Buford."

"Maybe ask them Tilletts some questions."

"Like what?"

"I don't know . . . what they seen that scared them, more likely."

"Ask away. It's got nothing to do with me." Blade managed a smile as he rose to his feet. "It's always a pleasure, Buford, but now, if you'll excuse me, I have some ledgers to update."

Whelan stood. "Blade, tell your son to leave Caroline Briggs alone. If I hear that he's walking out with her, I'll take it hard."

"Seth is a grown man," Koenig said. "I can't tell him anything. What he does is his own business."

The sheriff nodded, his eyes suddenly as green and hard as jade. "If anything happens to that girl, anything at all, I'll come looking for him, Blade. Depend on it." Then, as he stepped to the door, "Rape is a hanging offense in Luna County. Maybe you should tell Seth that."

Blade Koenig stood at his open parlor window and watched Buford Whelan ride away. The man sat tall in the saddle, his head turning this way and that, missing nothing. Koenig slammed the window closed as though shutting the lawman out of his life. But he knew more drastic measures were called for. Whelan was smart, very smart, and he suspected too much. That made him dangerous. Koenig nodded to himself. The sheriff had to go.

A high-powered .56-.56 Spencer rifle bullet can do nightmarish things to living human tissue, its 350-grain ball the distilled essence of violent, sudden death. The bullet that slammed into Sheriff Buford Whelan's neck, neatly placed between the top of his celluloid collar and the rim of his plug hat, smashed his spine in the middle of its cervical curve and then ranged upward into his brain case and exited at the top of his skull's parietal bone, blowing a hole the size of a silver dollar.

Whelan was a dead man before he fell out of the saddle and slammed onto the ground.

That fact was obvious to Seth Koenig as he lowered his smoking rifle and grinned. "Damn you, Whelan, when you throw suspicion on a man do it away from an open window."

Seth climbed down from the brush-covered niche he'd found halfway up the canyon wall and walked to the dead man. Whelan lay on his back, his unseeing eyes open to the uncaring, lemon-colored sky. Toeing the body onto its back, Seth studied the entry wound. Good shooting! But as he'd figured, at a range of just thirty yards he'd shot six inches too high. He'd been aiming for a spot between the lawman's shoulder blades. Obviously, the Spencer's rear ladder sight needed adjusting. He'd sight in the rifle at the first available opportunity.

He stripped Whelan of his fancy, nickeled Colt and noticed inlaid on the right side of its grip was a worn, shield-shaped, silver medallion.

SHERIFF BUFORD WHELAN
1 8 7 4
from the grateful citizens
of WAR BOW,
ARIZONA TERRITORY

With his pocketknife, Koenig levered out the medallion and tossed it away. He shoved the Colt into his waistband and mounted the dead man's buckskin. Hellfire Pass was seldom used by travelers, and Koenig looked down at the dead lawman and said, "Lie there and rot in peace, you interfering son of a bitch."

"I could've made him go away," Blade Koenig said. "I could've spread some money around and got him kicked off the job. Damn it, Seth, you didn't have to kill him."

"Whelan needed killing. He was too suspicious the way he was nosing around about that Emily Graham bitch. Rape is a hanging offense in Luna County, he said, and he wasn't bluffing. You want to see me hang?"

"No, I don't want to see you hang."

"Yes, you do, Daddy."

"I want to see you change, Seth. I mean change for the better."

"Too late for that. I'm rotten to the core and that's how I want to be."

"Son, you don't mean that."

"I mean every word of it."

"Why? Why do you want to be—"

"Rotten? Bad to the bone? Because the only person that matters under the sun is me, me, me, the wolf among the sheep. You've heard preachers talk about how heaven is waiting for us all. Well, I want nothing to do with heaven. I'll travel the shortest route to hell a-runnin', kiss ol' Beelzebub right on the mouth and take my rightful place among the baddest of the bad."

"Seth, that's crazy talk."

"It ain't so crazy, old man."

"You're not thinking straight, boy."

"Boy? I'm nobody's boy."

"No, you're not. You're man grown and that's why it's time to change, leave your youth behind."

"What youth? I didn't have a youth, damn you. You worked me like a common puncher, driving me from can't see to can't see, and paid me thirty a month. I wasn't your son. I was just another ranch hand."

"Seth, a man has to learn the cattle business from the bottom up if he wants to succeed. I wasn't driving you. I was grooming you for bigger and better things."

"And when does all that come to me? When you die?"

"Or retire."

"You'll never retire."

"I've been giving it some thought. But I have to know that you're ready to take over the Hellfire."

"I'm ready right now, Daddy, so die real soon, huh? Do both of us a favor."

Blade poured himself a whiskey and after a while said, "None of this would have happened if you'd kept your damned pants buttoned."

"How crude." Seth became defensive. "Emily Graham was asking for it, the way she flounced around in front of me, teasing me with them big tits of hers. I only took what she had on offer."

"That's not how Jed Tillett saw it," Blade said.

"Yeah, well now Jed Tillett ain't seeing anything, is he?" Seth said. "He should've taken the money you offered and kept his trap shut."

"You raped her, Seth," Blade said. "Tillett watched you do it and then you took a shot at him. When he came here with his pa he was half-dead and he didn't want money. He wanted me to have you arrested."

"I told you, the slut was asking for it. How the hell was I to know she'd kill herself? Hell, she'd probably been done by every man in Luna County. Why pick on me?"

"Emily's ma said her daughter wanted to be a nun," Blade said. "I'm guessing she was a virgin. Do you have to be a virgin to be a Catholic nun? I don't know."

"Who tipped off the Tilletts that I was coming after them?" Seth said. "Was it you?"

Blade downed his whiskey. "Of course it wasn't me. I suspect it was one of our punchers with no liking for you."

"If I find him, I'll kill him, lay to that."

"The Tilletts don't matter any longer, we saw to that. Now that's behind you, you should settle down, Seth. Get married maybe. Give me a grandson."

"So you can leave the Hellfire to him? You're spitting into the wind."

Blade's voice speared into his son's sullen silence. "Where's Buford's body?"

"Where I left it, rotting in Hellfire Pass," Seth said.

Blade nodded. "All right. Here's what you do. You get a shovel from the barn and go bury him. It's no small thing to kill a county sheriff, so get rid of the evidence."

"Damn you, let the coyotes bury him."

As though he hadn't heard, Blade said, "I'll send Shield with you to make sure the job is done."

"It's almost dark."

"Take a lantern."

"I don't want that damned Pima anywhere near me."

"Shield goes."

Seth's anger was white hot. He kicked over an embroidered footstool and said, "I don't have the words to tell you how much I hate you, old man. Every passing day I hate you more, and it will be like that until the day and hour I kill you."

"And I should've drowned you at birth, Seth. Like

you said, you're rotten, a bad apple, putrid to the core, but I cling to the hope that one day you'll wake up and see yourself for what you are and then you'll change."

Seth's voice was scornful. "Then lose all hope, Daddy. I'll never change. I like me fine the way I am."

Blade Koenig listened and died another little death, the latest of many. "Go find the Pima and bury Buford. Maybe you can bring yourself to say a prayer for him."

"I was spawned in the lowest depths of hell," Seth said. "A demon doesn't prattle prayers."

"Are you really that, Seth? Are you really a demon?"

"One day you'll find out just how much of a demon I really am, old man. Maybe sooner than you think."

Chapter Thirteen

Doña Maria Ana de la Villa de Villar del Aguilla arrived at the Kerrigan mansion with all the haughty pomp and splendor of the Queen of Sheba come to visit a poor relative.

Kate Kerrigan, aware of how bitchy Maria Ana could be, wore her best, a dress of emerald silk with a huge bustle and a necklace set with gemstones that perfectly matched the sparkling green of her eyes. Her maid had brushed her mane of red hair until it gleamed like spun gold and then piled it high on Kate's head in a mass of curls and ringlets held in place by diamond-tipped pins.

"You look like a princess," Nora had said, a little breathlessly. "As though you just stepped from the pages of a storybook."

By contrast, Doña Maria Ana was dressed from head to toe in Castilian black. Her high-collared riding tunic was split at the front, revealing glossy thigh-high boots, and her frilled blouse was closed at the neck by a black onyx brooch. Her raven hair, as thick and luxuriant as Kate's, fell in tumbling waves from under a black top hat. Doña Maria Ana was six-foot-two-inches tall. The slender heels of her boots added another three inches, and with the top hat she stood almost seven feet tall, towering over Kate's five-nine.

She and Kate met outside the house and embraced.

Maria Ana kissed the air next to Kate's cheek and then stood back. "Now, let me have a look at you." Her accent was more French than Mexican. After her beautiful black eyes roamed over Kate, she said, "Just as I remembered, as lovely as ever. Green becomes you, Kate. I'm sure I've seen you wear that dress before. A few years ago perhaps." She sighed. "Ah well, on the frontier one has to make do with what one has, doesn't one?"

Kate ignored Nora, who stood beside her, her mouth a thin, outraged line, and said, "Do come inside, Maria Ana. How was your journey?"

The woman waited until she was in the reception foyer before she answered. "Tolerable. That is until we crossed the Rio Grande and there was nothing to see. I mean nothing forever, nothing but grass, cows, and cactus. I was so bored. Poor Kate. How do you stand it?"

"I've grown to love Texas. That helps."

"Well, stay out of the sun, dear. We don't want more wrinkles, do we?" Maria Ana's eyes widened. "Kate, I've just noticed that you have a terrible bruise on your shoulder." She smiled and her teeth were very white. "Oh, la, la . . . a jealous lover in a fit of pique, perhaps?"

"No, an oak door. I stumbled and fell against it."

"Oh, how mundane. But that happens to women as

they grow older," Maria Ana said. "They do stumble and fall a lot."

"Tea?" Kate said.

"Something stronger, if you will. I'm all used up from my journey and my fear of that heartless brute, Don Pedro."

"Your husband can't harm you while you're under my roof." After what had happened to the Tilletts, Kate's words sounded hollow even to her own ears.

Maria Ana chose the best chair in the parlor, crossed her long, exquisite legs, and said, "A glass of sherry, perhaps, Kate?"

"I have an excellent bottle of Victoria Regina Amontillado in my cellar, if you'd care to make a trial of it," Kate said.

Maria Ana made a face. "I prefer Oloroso, but I suppose the Amontillado must do. This is Texas, after all."

Kate managed a smile. "During my recent visit to London I learned that Amontillado is Queen Victoria's favorite sherry."

Maria Ana waved a ringed, elegant, and disinterested hand. "Is it really? Well, there's no accounting for taste, is there?"

Nora stood behind Kate's second-best chair, clutching the back with white-knuckled hands, her eyes blazing. "Shall I serve the Amontillado, ma'am?"

"Yes, please do," Kate said. "Two glasses, Nora."

"Clean glasses, girl," Maria Ana said. "Or your mistress will have the hide off your back."

"There is no other kind of glass in this house," Nora said.

"And I do not abuse my servants, Maria Ana," Kate said.

The noblewoman's beautiful eyebrows arched high on her forehead. "You don't? However do you manage them?"

"I manage them just fine," Kate said.

Nora gave Maria Ana one last, scorching look and stepped to the door.

Kate heard the girl give a little yelp of alarm and then "Oh, you took me by surprise."

A tall, lean man dressed all in black stood in the doorway. He wore a short-waisted vaquero jacket with silver buttons and tight pants that were split just under the knee. His roweled spurs were decorated with silver conchos, as was his gunbelt, and each of its twin holsters held an ivory-handled Colt. A huge sombrero completed his attire. The man was dark-skinned and handsome and an eye patch covered his left eye. His visible eye was an amber color and calm, the eye of a man who waited patiently for whatever was thrown his way, knowing full well he could handle it.

Normally Kate would've dismissed any two-gun man as a poseur, but she realized there was nothing of the kind about Rodolfo Aragon. He was self-assured, confident, and easy in his stance, a man who'd ridden some hellfire trails a time or three and had been forged by flame into a dangerous fighting machine. Aragon was exactly what he seemed, a skilled pistolero, a man you crossed at your peril. If he had a weakness it was that he was madly in love with Doña Maria Ana. She didn't know his secret, and Aragon had never revealed it. As the fates would have it, he was destined to carry his forbidden love to his grave.

At Nora's yelp, Maria Ana turned her head and saw Aragon. "Oh, that's my shadow. He's harmless. Well, to my friends, at least. Rodolfo, don't stand there frightening people. Go see that the peons are getting settled without knifing one another and that my luggage is carried into the foyer."

The tall man nodded and left.

Maria Ana said, "He's not long on conversation, Rodolfo, but he's a devoted bodyguard who seldom leaves my side."

Kate waited until Nora brought the sherry and Maria Ana had declared it "acceptable, but barely" before she said, "Now tell me why you left Don Pedro. I must say that I'm surprised."

Doña Maria Ana made a face as though she'd just bitten into a sour apple. "Surprised? You shouldn't be. He's a heartless brute, Kate. He's cruel, selfish, and uncaring. But he's worse than that, much worse. I . . . I just can't find the words." The woman sighed. "All my love for him is now gone, cast up on the cruel, rocky shore of his indifference."

"You must tell me all about it," Kate said.

"It is far too painful to relate."

"We're friends, Maria Ana. Perhaps I can help."

"He doesn't love me, Kate, and he's made it so obvious that he never did. *Mon Dieu*, the man is a monster, a fiend, an ogre . . . a . . . a hobgoblin."

"Poor Maria Ana. Tell me how Don Pedro has mistreated you."

The woman sighed, and Kate, as she always did, marveled at her vivid, startling, and exotic beauty. "Where to begin? At the beginning, I suppose."

"Yes, that's as good a place as any."

"Well, first . . . oh, Lord, I am so overcome I can barely speak . . . first, Don Pedro raised his voice, shouting at me that the expenses of the hacienda were too high, that my personal servant staff was too large, and that I must cut it by half. Then he said I must restrict my trips to Paris and that I could no longer buy French gowns and must adopt the modest garb of a respectable Mexican noblewoman. Kate, can you imagine me dressed like a fat, frumpy señora from the barrio? I think not."

"Cattle prices have been low this past couple years," Kate said. "Perhaps that's the reason."

"Pah! Kate, you sound like my husband. Don Pedro no longer depends on cattle prices. He's as rich as Midas. The trouble is he's a . . . what is the word? . . . ah yes, a miser, a miserable old skinflint." The woman placed the back of her hand on her forehead under the brim of her top hat and groaned. "Just talking about the cruel beast has made me feel so faint I need another sherry."

Kate refilled the doña's glass and then said, "What else has Don Pedro done that troubles you so?"

Maria Ana was shocked. "What else? Isn't what I've told you enough? Doesn't reducing the number of my servants and forcing me to dress like a dowdy hag prove that he's an utter barbarian?" The woman's thigh boots made a *snick-snick* as she uncrossed her legs. "Kate, I'm so distraught that I'm beside myself."

"So, you just up and left him?"

"Yes, I did. I assembled my servants, took my jewelry and the three thousand dollars from Don Pedro's petty cash box, and left," Maria Ana said. "I knew I'd be welcome with you, Kate. You are such a good friend."

"And indeed, you are welcome," Kate said, vowing

to make a good Act of Contrition for that small lie. "And now he'll come after you to take you back?"

"He will, and he'll bring a hundred vaqueros with him, all of them quite as mean as he is." Maria Ana waved a hand. "But I'll be safe with you, won't I, dear Kate?"

"Yes, you're a guest under my roof."

An unwelcome guest to be sure, but a guest nonetheless.

"Perhaps you should retire to your room and rest for a while, Maria Ana," Kate said. "We serve dinner at eight."

"I'd like a hot bath, Kate. Can you arrange for a tub in my room? I brought my own French soap."

"Yes, I can do that. And I'll see that your luggage is brought up. What about your servants?"

"My servants? What about them?"

"Do they need to be fed?"

"No, of course not. They can fend for themselves. I supplied them with a two-week supply of beef, tortillas, and dried apples before we left the hacienda. They won't starve."

"Where was Don Pedro when you were making all those preparations?" Kate said.

"In Chihuahua on business. He said he'd be gone for a week, so that gave me plenty of time to . . . to make a most desperate escape from the clutches of the most hard-hearted, unfeeling creature who ever lived."

"You were very brave," Kate said, determined to be understanding and supportive.

"No, not brave, desperate. I had to flee into the night to escape the clutches of an uncaring husband."

"Maria Ana, do you love Don Pedro?" Kate said.

"I did. That is, I loved him very much until the day and hour he ordered me to never visit my beloved Paris again and to wear the dress of a peasant woman," the doña said. "So now I hate him, hate him, hate him."

"I see," Kate said. But she didn't see at all.

CHAPTER FOURTEEN

"Ma, it looks like half the population of Old Mexico is camped on our doorstep," Trace Kerrigan said.

"Noisy, aren't they?" Kate said.

"Where is Doña Maria Ana de la Villa . . . and so on and so forth?" Frank Cobb said.

"She's resting," Kate said. "She's plumb worn out from her journey."

"How long is she going to stay?" Trace said.

Kate shrugged. "I don't know. Hopefully not long." She looked over Trace's shoulder. "Who's that old man standing by the bunkhouse?"

"We found him out on the range," Trace said. Then by way of explanation, "He was wandering."

Kate waited for more information, and when none was forthcoming, she said, "Does your stray have a name?"

"Calls himself Gabe Dancer," Trace said.

"He's a tinpan," Frank said. "Says he's headed east. I told him he could bed down here for the night."

"Then he must join us for dinner," Kate said.

Frank stared at her. "Kate, he ain't the come-to-dinner kind."

"Perhaps I think he is," Kate said.

Frank looked uncertain. "Kate, he's a rough old man and outspoken . . . and I think he cusses."

"Good. Just what I need," Kate said. "Maria Ana has me all used up and another guest at dinner will be a distraction."

"Ma, I think the doña will be horrified. I mean, we found Gabe on the range. He's just another maverick, and he isn't mannerly."

"Trace is right about him being a maverick," Frank said. "For a spell there, I thought about dabbing a loop on him."

"I'm sure he'll have some interesting stories to tell about his prospecting days," Kate said. "Many of these old-timers do." Despite Frank's misgivings, Kate stepped around him and walked to the old miner.

Dancer touched the peak of his cap and said, "Gabe Dancer at your service, ma'am."

"My name is Kate Kerrigan. Welcome to my ranch."

"It's an honor to be here, an' no mistake," Dancer said.

"Would you care to join us for dinner tonight? The guest of honor is Doña Maria Ana, a Mexican noblewoman. She's very lovely, and I'm sure you will like her."

"To dine with one lady of rare beauty would give me the greatest of pleasure," Dancer said. "To dine with two such will double my enjoyment. I gratefully accept your gracious invitation, dear lady."

"You are too kind, Mr. Dancer. Shall we say eight o'clock?"

"By my watch, I'll be there." He noticed the bruise on Kate's bare shoulder and frowned. "You have suffered a shoulder injury, dear lady. Thrown from your horse perhaps?"

Kate smiled. "No, I had a run-in with a door."

"How unfortunate," Dancer said. "I wish you a speedy recovery."

"Thank you," Kate said. "Then I'll expect you at eight."

Dancer gave a little bow. "I'll be there at eight sharp. And I must say that I look forward to it, ma'am."

Kate walked back toward the house and as she passed Frank and Trace, she said, "I wish all my employees were as mannerly."

Since the corrals were reserved for ranch horses, Frank walked to the barn with Dancer to show him where to put up his shaggy mustang. The old man retrieved a clean plaid shirt from his saddlebags and his rifle from the saddle boot, a well-worn Henry that Frank reckoned had some stories to tell.

They were on their way out of the stable when Dunk Jefferson stepped in their way and raised his hand. "Halt. Stand and be recognized."

Lamps were already lit in the big house and a single sentinel star glittered in the dark purple sky like a diamond stud. The fall air was cool and smelled of horses, leather, and men.

Frank and Dancer looked at Jefferson in surprise as the man said, "What's your name, stranger?"

"You talking to me?" Dancer said.

"None other." Jefferson nodded in Frank's direction. "I already know his name."

"Name's Dancer. Friendly folks call me Gabe and now I study on it, so do some unfriendly folks."

"You on the scout, Dancer?" Jefferson said. "Speak up now. Be bold."

"I just celebrated my seventy-sixth birthday. I'm too old to be on the scout. What's your handle, stranger, if I ain't too forward in asking?"

"Deputy United States Marshal Dunk Jefferson, a sworn officer of the law."

"Right pleased to make your acquaintance, Dunk," Dancer said.

"State your business here."

"My business is my own," Dancer said, a frown gathering on his whiskery face.

"We'll see about that, won't we?"

"I never did have much liking fer lawmen," Gabe said.

"I'm sure you didn't. Did you ever meet the likes of me, a deputy United States marshal?"

"No, I never did. Met some town marshals, though."

"How many times have you written your name on a jail cell wall?"

"None, that I can recall, sonny."

"Mister, you're a cracked bell that don't ring true to me," Jefferson said. "You say *dong* instead of *ding*." He pointed to his right eye with his trigger finger and then at Dancer's chest. "I'll be watching you."

Dancer smiled. "I'm right glad to hear that you'll be watching over me. It makes a harmless old prospector like myself feel safe, since man and boy I've been of a somewhat timid nature."

Frank Cobb didn't believe a word of that. Whatever traits the old man might possess, timidity was not one of them.

Jefferson seemed mollified by Dancer's remark. "Well, just so you know that you are under surveillance. And now I'll give you the road." He brushed past Frank and stepped into the barn.

As Dancer and Frank walked toward the bunkhouse, the old man said, "For many years now, it's been my view that pushy lawmen are a blight on civilization. What's your opinion on that, Mr. Cobb?"

"I guess I agree with you, Mr. Dancer," Frank said. Maybe later he'd tell the old-timer that Jefferson was a dangerous madman.

At dinner that night, the two beautiful women at table glowed a hundred times brighter than the candlelight. Kate had changed her dress and wore a stunning evening gown of bright blue taffeta with a sweep train, half sleeves, and a daring V-neck that revealed her deep and spectacular cleavage. She wore a diamond necklace and earrings, and above the simple gold wedding band on her left hand glittered a ring with a larger diamond surrounded by smaller sapphires.

Dressed in her favored black, Doña Maria chose an under-bust bolero jacket with a high collar and padded shoulders, an embroidered, steel-boned corset that pushed up and flattered her magnificent breasts, and a tight-fitting skirt that was gathered over her hips. A thin black ribbon encircled her neck, and when she fluttered her eyelashes, which was often since there were attractive men present, they brushed her high cheekbones like Spanish fans. Her unbound hair tumbled over her shapely shoulders like dark wine flowing from a midnight fountain.

Kate and Maria Ana were stunning women, but a study in contrasts.

If Kate was a goddess of ivory and gold, then Maria Ana was the flame that burned at her altar.

A still ailing Moses Rice insisted on carrying out his duties. As he seated Maria Ana at the dining table she raised an eyebrow when she saw Gabe Dancer sitting opposite. The old miner had trimmed his beard and donned his clean shirt, and his damped-down hair was neatly parted in the middle. He gave the doña a little bow before he again sat and then he, Frank, and Trace competed for eye space as they ogled the Mexican woman throughout the meal. Dunk Jefferson had refused to attend, saying that he'd rather spend the evening with his horse than people.

To Kate's surprise Maria Ana did not once complain about the dinner or the wine and made agreeable small talk with Frank and Trace. When coffee was served she used a candle to light a slim cheroot and then said, "When one must of necessity dine on rude frontier fare, one longs for French food, especially that served at the Chez Pierre on the Rue de Passy in Paris. Kate, their coq au vin is to die for."

Kate, aware that she had a piece of asparagus wedged between her front teeth, nodded without smiling and said nothing, her tongue working behind a discreet hand.

"Meself, I preferred Pierre's beef bourguignon," Dancer said, all his concentration on the sugar he spooned into his demitasse. "And I told him so a time or two. Of course, his *confit de canard* is also excellent when it's paired with a good wine."

Everyone looked the old tinpan in surprise and

Maria Ana expressed what the others were thinking. "You dined at the Chez Pierre?"

Dancer blew across the top of his cup. "Hot. Yeah I did, Your Excellency. Often. The last time was in '73 afore I lost my last fortune."

Kate finally dislodged the asparagus and said, "Your last fortune? Mr. Dancer, for heaven's sake, how many fortunes did you lose?"

"Not many, Mrs. Kerrigan. Just two. I struck it rich in Georgia in '30 when I was just a younker, lost that fortune, then hit pay dirt again in California in '55, and made a bigger fortune that was all gone twenty years later. Since then I've made a living at prospecting, but I barely scrape by."

Trace said, "Mr. Dancer, how did you lose two fortunes in a single lifetime? Isn't that a bit careless?"

Dancer looked at Kate and then at Maria Ana as though seeking their approval. "I don't want to talk out of turn, but the answer is not carelessness . . . it's women. And gambling and drinking, of course." Then to Trace, "A word of advice, son. Women are just fine in moderation, but women, drinking, and gambling at the same time is a bad mix. That's the road to ruin."

"Do you regret it?" Trace said.

"Regret what?"

"The women and the gambling."

"Hell no . . . begging your pardon, ladies. If I had to do it all over again I wouldn't change a thing."

Maria Ana said, "Mr. Dancer, you are indeed a man of the world."

"Not the world, Your Highness, just a small part of it—mostly America and France, especially Paris."

"Paris in the rain is wonderful, don't you think, Mr. Dancer," Maria Ana said, her eyes shining.

"It is indeed, Your Excellency. And in sunlight. Did you ever try Au Rocher de Canale on rue Montorgueil?"

Maria Ana shook her lovely head, her face bright with interest. "No, I never have." She smiled. "But how intriguing it sounds, Mr. Dancer."

"Then one day you must have their oysters and champagne for breakfast. It is as the French say, *très magnifique.*"

"The next time I'm in Paree I will, Monsieur Dancer. Depend on it." Maria Ana opened a slim, silver cigar case. "Would you care to make a trial of a cigarillo? They're Burmese and very good."

Dancer nodded. "Thankee, Your Majesty. I'm right partial to a Burma or India cheroot, smoked a lot of them in my day."

"Do tell about your adventures in Paree, Mr. Dancer," Maria Ana said. "I suspect you were well-known as a boulevardier and bon vivant along the Champs-Elysees and have delicious tales to tell of those scandalous *Parisienne* women and their *histoires de coeur.*"

"Tales of love affairs? Indeed, I have, Your Excellency," Dancer said. "Why, I mind the time me and pretty young Sarah Bernhardt was strolling along the west bank of the Seine and . . ."

Kate looked around the table. Against the odds, her dinner was turning out to be a great success. A bearded old tinpan in a plaid shirt with his damp hair parted in the middle and racy stories to tell had been her savior.

Chapter Fifteen

Doña Maria Ana complained about the smallness of her room, the view from the window or lack thereof, the firmness of her mattress, and the clumsiness of her lady's maid, an unsmiling peasant girl named Yolanda.

Kate Kerrigan was not well known for her patience, but she made a valiant effort to placate the woman and even sent Nora to help prepare Maria Ana for bed. Nora was about to make the eighty-eighth stroke with a hairbrush of the hundred Maria Ana demanded, when the alarm was raised. Someone pounded on the front door and men's voices were raised.

A shot.

Then silence.

Kate ignored the pain in her shoulder and hurried into her dressing gown and slippers.

As she took to the stairs Maria Ana leaned over the balcony and called out, "What's amiss, Kate? *Mon Dieu, que se passetil?*"

Kate didn't slow her pace. "I don't know what's happening, but I intend to find out."

"Wait. I'll come with you," Maria Ana said.

Kate had reached the foyer and yelled, "No! Stay where you are."

But Maria Ana had already run into her bedroom. Kate opened the door and stepped outside.

Shorty Hawkins greeted her with, "The barn!" and then he sprinted in that direction.

"Shorty, wait!" Kate said, but the puncher had already vanished inside the stable where lamps were being lit.

Kate hurried to the barn and walked inside . . . into the scene of a murder and a shooting, lit by tawny lamplight. She took it all in at a glance.

Dunk Jefferson lay on his belly near his horse's stall, the silver and bone handle of a knife sticking out from between his shoulder blades. The man's head was turned and the frothy blood that filled his mouth told Kate that he was dead. A few feet away, a young Mexican peon, dressed in a white shirt and pants, huarache sandals on his feet, moaned as he tried to stem the flow of blood from a wound in his right thigh.

Frank saw Kate and stepped beside her. "The Mexican's name is Francisco Garcia and we found these on him." He showed Kate what he held in his hands—Jefferson's watch, a silver Masonic ring, and a leather wallet. "There's thirty-six dollars in the wallet. Ain't much to show for a man's life."

"Isn't," Kate said absently. "Did you shoot the Mexican, Frank?"

Frank shook his head. "No." He nodded to the tall, elegant Rodolfo Aragon. "He did. Says he caught Garcia in the act, or almost. The thief was trying to make his escape when Aragon plugged him."

"Why was Aragon here?" Kate said.

"He never gets very far from Doña Maria Ana and he was poking around, making sure she was safe."

"I'll talk with him," Kate said.

"He ain't much of a one for talking, Kate."

"He'll talk to me. He'd better."

Aragon politely bowed his head when Kate approached him. "Señora." The pistolero was tall and slender and distant, a handsome, cold-natured man with more than his share of Spanish hidalgo pride.

"Did you witness the murder?" Kate said.

"No. I saw what happened afterward," Aragon said.

"Please explain."

"When I walked into this"—he waved a hand, taking in the barn—"*granero*, the peon was trying to retrieve his knife from the dead man's back, but the blade was stuck in the backbone and he couldn't pull it free."

"And then he tried to escape?"

"Yes, he tried to escape and I stopped him. I had no need to kill him. The peon was no threat to me."

"Then he is guilty of murder and robbery," Kate said.

"Clearly," Aragon said.

Frank Cobb looked worried. "This is bad, real bad. How do we play it, Kate?"

"We play it according to the law."

"What law?"

"On this ranch, my law, Frank."

"So where does that take us?"

"The Mexican is guilty of coldblooded murder and robbery on my property. Frank, my course is clear. I must hang him."

"Or keep him for the Rangers."

Kate shook her head. "And when would a Ranger pass this way?"

"I don't know. It could be quite a spell."

"Then it falls on me to deal with him."

"Kate, that won't be necessary."

Kate turned at the new voice. Around her the ranch hands stared open-mouthed at Maria Ana. Apart from a few errant strands that blew across her face in the breeze, her hair rippled over the shoulders of her black velvet robe and at that moment she looked as dark and beautiful and vengeful as a fallen angel.

"Kate, this pig is my servant, and it is I who will deal with him," Maria Ana said. "I brought him here, and this outrage is my fault. He has disgraced the house of Villa de Villar del Aguilla, and I don't want his blood on your hands. Let it be on mine."

"Maria Ana, you're not to blame for what happened," Kate said.

"It was I who brought the murderer Francisco Garcia to your home. Yes, the blame is mine." The doña said to Aragon, "Rodolfo, go find Padre Daniel and bring him to me. He will hear Garcia's confession and give him absolution. I will not damn a man to hell with a mortal sin on his soul."

After Aragon left, the condemned man dragged himself to Kate, clutched the hem of her robe, and with tears in his eyes sobbed, "*Misericord, señora, misericord por Francisco.*"

Kate looked at Frank, confused, her eyes asking a question. *He begs for mercy. What do I tell him?*

Frank said, "Doña Maria Ana is right, Kate. Allow the Mexicans to deal with their own."

Maria Ana, her beautiful face expressionless, said, "Listen to your segundo, Kate. This man begs for mercy when there can be no mercy. What mercy did he show to the Americano?" She uttered something in rapid Spanish to Garcia and then explained to Kate. "I told him he sold his soul for a nickel watch and a few dollars and that he is a treacherous dog who has shamed me and the house of Aguilla. For that he must die."

Kate thought she saw a way out of a hanging. "Take him back to Mexico, Maria Ana. Let Don Pedro deal with him."

"Don Pedro? And isn't he as much of a rogue as this one? How can I expect justice there? No, Francisco Garcia has disgraced me and he must pay the price. There is no more to be said."

Aragon returned with a bent and ancient priest who had a black rosary in his hands and a haunted expression on his lined face. Behind the padre walked four sturdy peons, one of them with a noosed rope coiled around his shoulder. Outside in the darkness the wails of mourning women had already begun.

Now that he faced the inevitable, Garcia found courage and dragged himself to a dark corner of the barn, where he confessed his sins to the priest in a low, sobbing whisper. Adding to the tense atmosphere, a high wind picked up and sighed around the barn. Kate crossed herself, struck by the thought that Santa Muerte, the Angel of Death, was mourning Dunk Jefferson, her lethal protégé. Even Frank Cobb seemed uneasy. Half of the ranch hands had already returned to the bunkhouse; the rest were strangely quiet. Gabe Dancer had hurried to the barn when he heard the shot, but he hung back in the shadows and said nothing.

The priest said the words of absolution in the Latin tongue that nobody but him understood and made the sign of the cross over the trembling, sobbing killer.

"Kate," Maria Ana said, "this man tries to evade justice and is not dying well. There's no reason why you should remain."

"This is my ranch. My guest was murdered. It's my duty to see it through to the end," Kate said.

"Very well." Maria Ana turned to Aragon and said in Spanish, "*Cuelgalo.*"

Hang him.

The peon with the rope tossed the noose over a beam and a couple others went for Garcia, who had his back to the barn wall, terrified, saliva stringing from his chin. Outside, the lamenting of his women—wife, mother, sisters—grew in volume and the wailing wind kept up its death song.

"*Misericord, mi señora,*" Garcia whimpered, dragging himself across the barn floor to Maria Ana. Tears stained his face. "*Misericord . . . misericord . . .*"

As unmoving as a pillar, Maria Ana looked down at the man, her face hard. She said nothing.

"Damn it. Get it over with," Frank Cobb said in almost a yell. "Do what you have to do!"

Blam! Blam! Blam!

The racketing roar of three shots fired very fast reverberated through the livery and .44-40 bullets tore great holes in Francisco Garcia's skinny chest and belly. As scared horses whinnied and kicked at their stalls, the impact of the rounds bounced the man around, flopping him this way and that like a ragdoll. Then he rolled onto his back and lay unmoving.

For a moment time stood still, everyone in the barn frozen in place like so many statues.

Then Aragon's hand dropped for his gun and

Gabe Dancer yelled, "I wouldn't try it, sonny." The muzzle of his smoking Henry was pointed right at the shootist's belly. "I swear, ol' Cyclops, I can drill you square from here."

Colt in his hand, Frank swung on Dancer. "Why the hell did you do that?"

"Is he dead?" the old man said.

"Hell, you shot him three times with a .44-40. Son of a bitch is as dead as he's ever gonna be."

"Then it's well. I won't see a man hang," Dancer said. "Seen it once afore, a black feller lynched in a barn up Kansas way. By my watch, it took him twenty minutes to die, choking and kicking and soiling himself the whole time. As long as I live, I ain't never gonna see it again or let it happen."

Dancer's eyes moved from Frank back to Aragon, racked the lever of his rifle, and said to the Mexican, "Well, sonny, is this thing over or do you want to open the ball and we'll have us a hootenanny?"

Aragon seemed uncertain, but he might have gone for it had not Kate intervened. Her temper searing hot, she yelled, "Damn! Damn all of you! I'll hang the next man who shoots a gun in my presence. Maria Ana, call off your dog."

"Rodolfo, the murderer is dead and it's finished. Kate, I am sorry I brought these terrible events down on you."

Kate could not find the words to respond. Taking a deep breath, she finally said, "Frank, you and the hands remove the bodies. Get them out of my barn and out of my sight. We'll bury them at first light." Then to Gabe Dancer, "I'll think about you and what you did here tonight, mister."

"Hanging or shooting, the result is the same, Mrs. Kerrigan, except a bullet is cleaner," Dancer said.

"That was for me to decide, Mr. Dancer. Not you," Kate said.

"Did I do wrong, Your Excellency?" Dancer said to Maria Ana. "What's your opinion on it?"

"If this had happened at my husband's hacienda, he would have hanged you alongside Garcia, Mr. Dancer," Maria Ana said. "On his own land, Don Pedro—he alone—is judge, jury, and executioner."

"But you, Your Highness . . . what would you do if this was your own land?" Dancer said.

Maria Ana waited until Dunk Jefferson's body was carried past her and then she said, "Dead or not, I would have hanged Francisco Garcia and you alongside of him."

Dancer seemed shocked. "Well, that's as plain as the ears on a Missouri mule, ain't it?"

"You asked me and I told you," Doña Maria said.

In the silence that followed, Frank Cobb's words dropped like pebbles into a pond. "It's a hard thing to see a man hang."

"You seen it afore, sonny?" Dancer said.

"More times than I care to remember."

"Then you know what I done was right."

"I don't know if what you done is right or wrong, Dancer," Frank said. "And I don't plan to study on it."

"It's not a question a decent man should ever have to ask himself, Mr. Cobb," Maria Ana said. "I'm sorry I brought this to you."

"I think it's high time everyone went back to bed," Kate said. "That includes you, Mr. Dancer."

The old man nodded. "I would do it all over again, Mrs. Kerrigan. I wouldn't hesitate."

"Perhaps, but there won't be a next time. Not on my land."

The following morning in a drizzle of misty rain, two men—a murderer and a madman—were buried on the rise to the north of the house. The Mexican women wailed for their dead, as was their custom, and Padre Daniel spoke the words, but no one else had anything to say.

Doña Maria Ana, dressed in black, watched from afar, Rodolfo Aragon at her side.

Chapter Sixteen

"I got something to say."

"Then say it," Blade Koenig said.

"We left unfinished business at the Kerrigan ranch," Seth said. "Buford Whelan was getting close, and now I ask the question, How much does Kate Kerrigan know?"

"She's found the bodies of the Tilletts by now, that's for sure," Blade said.

"But has she spoken to the Texas Rangers? If she has, we could be in big trouble."

"Maybe we scared her."

"Don't even consider that, because she doesn't scare worth a damn. She took pots at me when I was leaving her house, remember? If you hadn't butted in when you did, I would've killed her then."

"Maybe, or she would've killed you." Blade Koenig stepped to the parlor window and glanced outside. The ranch was deserted, all the hands out cutting and stacking hay against the coming winter. He turned to face his son. "Jed Tillett saw you rape—"

"I told you already. I didn't force her," Seth said, his face reddening.

"Saw you rape Emily Graham. He tried to stop you and you shot him, and you couldn't even do that right. You only wounded him and didn't go after him when he ran away. Right then, you figured that the Graham girl needed all your attention."

"Well, I got Tillett in the end, didn't I, Daddy?" Seth said, his face twisted in an ugly scowl. "I gunned that piece of white trash and his wife and his son." He grinned, his tone mocking. "The Tillett filth won't go around spying on me again."

Blade Koenig said, "Yes, Seth, you killed the Tilletts and then Buford Whelan, a good man. And now you want to do the same to Kate Kerrigan and everybody who works for her. That's a lot of killing. Hell, boy, how much do you think your life is worth?"

"Nothing to you, old man, but helluva lot to me. I want it all, money, women, power, and everything else wealth can buy, and I'll kill and never stop killing until I get it . . . if that's what it takes."

Suddenly Blade Koenig looked old. "Seth, I'll keep on living to spite you. Sure, I think you're a monster whose shadow shouldn't fall on the earth, but you can change, renew yourself, and, if you'll let me, I can help you change, make you the son I've always wanted. We can start right now by forgetting about the Texas woman. We scared her so badly she won't dare talk to the law. By now Kate Kerrigan is afraid because she knows only too well what destruction we can bring down on her. You've covered your tracks well, Seth, and you're safe. You hear me, son? You're safe."

"Pa, the only true thing you said in that speech is that I'm bad to the bone and you're right, I am. Know something else? I enjoy it. It suits me fine because power never rests with good men, only with those who have an evil streak. Here's where things stand—if you won't ride against the Kerrigan woman, I'll find another way to destroy her and all she stands for . . . and in the end, very soon now, I'll destroy you."

Seth Koenig got to his feet. "Draw!" His gun came up fast.

Startled, his father took a step back, his face ashen.

"Bang! You're dead," Seth said. "And I'm the new owner of the Hellfire."

Laughing, he turned and left the ranch house. He was still laughing when he consulted his watch and then mounted his horse. His spurs raked the animal's flanks as he rode away at a gallop.

Hidden in the shadows under a wild oak that grew near the corral, the Pima watched Seth go, his broad face unreadable.

Blade Koenig saw the Indian from the parlor window but decided that Shield, as secretive as a lobo wolf, would not acknowledge his presence. He turned away, sat down heavily in his chair, and buried his face in his hands.

Chapter Seventeen

Seth Koenig rode north in the shadow of the ten-mile length of the Tres Hermanas Mountains before the peaks faded away to a few hills that soon became one with the brush flats. Andy Moran, a Hellfire puncher who'd once ridden with Sam Bass and Joel Collins and that rough bunch, had arranged a secret meeting at a dry wash a mile northeast of the mountains.

"Seth, Davis Salt says to tell you he'll wait at the wash for three days," Moran had warned. "If you don't show by then, he won't linger any longer."

"I'll be there," Seth had said. "How many men has he got?"

"I have no idea. They come and go. But when he hit the army payroll wagon that time last year he had thirty, enough to leave the paymaster and four cavalry troopers dead on the ground."

Seth had smiled and hooted. "Yee-hah! He's the kind of ranny I need."

* * *

As he rode toward the wash on the second day he knew that Davis Salt would be there.

The banks of the wash were broken down by cattle, but Davis Salt had set up camp in a bend that was somewhat sheltered by a few mixed trees, mostly piñon and juniper. The monsoon season had played out in late September, but iron gray rainclouds hung in the sky and the west wind blowing off the mountains held a fall edge.

Seth Koenig smelled mesquite smoke and coffee in the air and slowed his horse to a walk, keeping his hands in view, but even so his welcome was less than cordial. Two riflemen appeared from the wash and walked toward him.

When he rode within talking distance, he drew rein and placed both his gloved hands on the pommel. "Howdy boys. Name's Seth Koenig and I'm here to see Mr. Salt."

One of the riflemen, a grim-looking man with a tight, thin mouth as clamped shut as a steel purse, turned to his young, red-haired companion. "Tell Davis we got company."

The man nodded and left, taking his time.

"Looks like rain," Seth said. "Maybe so, huh?"

Thin Mouth said nothing, his eyes fixed on the V-neck opening of Koenig's shirt. A timorous man would have worried that it was there the outlaw planned to place his first bullet, but Seth Koenig had no such thought. Davis Salt had the undeserved reputation of being a gentleman outlaw, but nonetheless he was greedy and avaricious, a bandit businessman who would readily see that a profit was to be made from the death of Blade Koenig and the destruction of Kate Kerrigan's ranch.

The carrot-topped rifleman stepped up from the wash and waved a hand. "Come in, you," he yelled. "Give your pistol and saddle gun to Jasper."

Seth smiled and said to the man called Jasper, "Salt ain't a trusting man, is he?"

"That's why he's lived so long." Jasper took Seth's gunbelt and rifle and then said, "And now the hideout."

Seth's smile slipped as he reached under his shirt. From his waistband he pulled a .41 caliber derringer with ivory grips and amateurish engraving and passed it to Jasper.

"Fancy," the outlaw said.

"How did you know I had it?" Seth said.

"You look the type," said the outlaw, a man of grit, spit, and gravel.

Davis Salt was once a handsome man, but he'd been stricken with smallpox during the Deadwood epidemic of '76 and the lesions had destroyed his features. Calamity Jane had nursed him back to health. Since then, the outlaw, a man of few loyalties, would never allow a bad word to be said about her. He'd killed a man in Abilene for calling her "a drunken whore" and as far is known, no one ever again mentioned Calamity's name in his presence. John Clum, the first mayor of Tombstone, would later write that at the suggestion of Calamity, Salt sometimes wore a black velvet mask to hide his grotesque disfigurement. But the Earp brothers, who had business dealings with him, never mentioned the mask nor, apparently, did anyone else in Tombstone.

What is known is that Davis Salt's appearance was a shock to those meeting him for the first time, many of who took him for a leper.

Seth Koenig was no exception.

Salt met him in the wash and told him to light and set. Seth could only stare at him, his expression a mix of amazement and horror.

"You'll get used to it," Salt said. "Now climb down and state your business."

Playing for time to collect himself, Seth stepped from the saddle. "Smelled your coffee, Davis. I could sure use a cup."

Salt told one of his men to get Seth coffee and then fixed him with a stare. In contrast to his face, the outlaws' eyes were startling, golden brown with green highlights, the lashes long, black and thick, eyes that would be the envy of a beautiful woman.

After he tested his coffee and lit a cigar, Seth recovered enough composure to say, "Got a proposition for you, Davis. I think you'll like it."

Salt's cold stare was unrelenting. "Koenig, you can call me Mr. Salt. Hell, you can call me plain Salt, but I'll tell you when you can use my given name. Now state your business and your intentions."

"Yes, sir, Mr. Salt. But what I propose involves killing." Seth was uneasy. At that moment, the tall, lanky outlaw looked dangerous, almost disdainful, like a man who doesn't like what he sees.

"I've killed before," Salt wore a full dragoon mustache, the better to cover some of his scars. His pockmarked skin was tight to the skull of a strong-boned, domineering, bold face.

"Have you heard of the KK ranch in West Texas?" Koenig said.

"I've heard it mentioned a time or two. Owned by a woman, isn't it?"

"Yeah, her name is Kate Kerrigan."

"What do you want me to do that involves this woman?"

"Like I said, there's killing to be done."

"You want this Kate Kerrigan dead?"

"Her? No, she's a red-haired woman and I want her alive . . . but kill everybody that works for her—men, women, children, her dog, I don't care. Kill them all." Seth decided to make a good joke. "Salt, pepper them with lead."

"We're talking business here, Koenig. Don't make funny remarks. Speak to me like a man."

"Sorry, I sure will. Yes, I want the Kerrigan woman, but destroy everyone else. There, I've said it plain."

"Tall order," Salt said. "A ranch that big is bound to have some tough gun hands on the payroll. They usually do."

"I know, and that's why I came to you, Mr. Salt." Seth looked around him. "I see six men here. How many more can you muster?"

"Enough."

"How many is enough?"

"I'll decide that."

"They've got to be top gun hands."

"All the men I hire are top gun hands."

"You have to make this enterprise look good."

"How good?"

"Well, here's the nub of the thing. We'll force Kate Kerrigan to sign a predated bill of sale, turning her ranch over to me."

"Suppose she refuses?"

"She won't refuse. Not when I've finished with

her. And then, when everybody is dead, make it look like Mexican banditos crossed the Rio Grande and attacked the house. One thing . . . I like that house and plan to live there, so see that it isn't damaged too badly."

"You want the house?"

"Yeah. Hell, I want the whole ranch."

"Got it all figured out, haven't you, Koenig?" Salt said.

"Yeah, I got it figured. I even know where you can shoot some Mexicans and scatter their bodies around so it looks like they were killed in the attack. There's a Mexican village just across the Texas border, a cantina and some adobe hovels around a central plaza. It ain't much, but at any given time there's thirty, forty males there, tenant farmers and the like who don't know how to fight. Plenty enough greaser bodies for our purpose."

"No, that becomes too untidy. I'll figure another way."

"Suit yourself." Seth grinned. "But nobody gives a damn about greasers, especially dead ones." He offered Davis Salt a cigar.

The man refused. "Your Pa owns the Hellfire spread, huh?"

"Yeah, but not for long. I'm taking over."

"What does Blade say about that?" This from one of Salt's riders, a sour-faced man who carried a Smith & Wesson .38 in a canvas shoulder holster.

"Leave Blade to me," Seth said. "That old man has walked the earth long enough."

The sour-faced man spat. "Big talk, but it's empty, and empty talk comes cheap."

"I talk the talk and I can walk the walk," Seth said, his face ugly. "Maybe you want to try me some time?"

"Ben, let it go," Salt said, talking to the sour-faced man. To Seth he smiled, showing good teeth. "So, if all your plans come to pass, you'll own the Hellfire and the KK. Hell, man, that's half the cattle country."

"And it's still not enough, not for a man like me who's destined for great things. But it will do for a start."

Salt sat in silence for a while and then said, "Koenig, you could be talking about thirty, forty dead people and maybe a sight more."

As the shock of seeing Salt for the first time wore off, Seth Koenig's self-confidence reasserted itself. "The only person still breathing when we're done will be the Kerrigan woman and only because I want her for myself. Well, at least for a while and then I'll dispose of her. But if the job is too big for you, Salt, I can find someone else."

"Never said the job was too big, but it will be costly," Salt said. "I mean, costly to you."

"Once the business is done and the beautiful widow is in my bed, I'll own the Hellfire and the KK ranch. Mr. Salt, I won't only pay you, I'll make you rich."

"How rich? Put a number on it."

"Hell, man, I haven't counted the money yet but I'm talking thousands. I'll put you on a retainer for life. Yeah . . . that's what I'll do, a retainer for life. Think about it, all the whiskey and whores you could ever want for the rest of your days."

Salt stared into Seth's face for long moments and then said, "Koenig, are you familiar with the works of Fyodor Dostoyevsky, *Crime and Punishment* or *The Brothers Karamazov*?"

"Hell, no," Koenig said. "Never heard of him. Sounds like a damned foreigner to me."

"How about Alexandre Dumas? Does *The Count of Monte Christo* ring a bell?"

Koenig shook his head. "No, and I'm not catching your drift, Salt."

"I didn't think so," Salt said. "All right. I'll confine our future conversations to whiskey and whores. You understand those, huh?"

Seth grinned. "Damn right, I do. I'm partial to both."

Salt nodded. "I took you for a whoring man." He rose to his feet from where he'd been sitting on the trunk of a dead cottonwood. "Ten thousand. And I'll need a week to round up about thirty more men. Attacking a ranch as big as the Kerrigan spread is like invading a country. It will take planning and manpower."

Seth smiled. "I find those terms acceptable. By the time you're ready to destroy the Kerrigan bitch, I'll have the Hellfire." He stuck out his hand. "Partners."

Salt ignored the proffered hand.

"Ah, well, so we won't shake on it until the job is done. Can I at least call you Davis?"

"No, you can't."

BOOK TWO

The Murderous Range

Chapter Eighteen

Hiram I. Clay, president of the West Texas Cattleman's Association as well as Kate Kerrigan's most passionate suitor, drove up to the mansion with his personal physician in tow. A couple tough hands rode along as outriders.

Clay, his ardent face brick red, eyes bright with worry, jumped out of the surrey, grabbed Dr. Zebulon Farrell by his thin shoulder, and dragged him to the door. He urgently slammed the brass knocker several times and when Moses Rice opened the door he yelled, "Quick! Tell Kate that her Hiram is here!"

Moses, his white butler's tunic awry, suggesting that he'd dressed hurriedly, blinked in the dawn light. "Miz Kerrigan is still abed, Mr. Clay."

Between its bookends of heroic muttonchop whiskers, Clay's face took on a stricken expression. "Is it ever thus? I am blighted. I am wrecked. In short, my good man, I am undone. As we speak, Kate lies abed with her terrible injury while her Hiram stands at her door as useless as a needle without an eye. Go then,

Moses, named for that great lawgiver and trail scout of old, and tell Kate that, although lost in heartbreak, I am close at hand."

"Then I'll show you the way to the parlor," Moses said, a twinkle in his black eyes.

"And see if you can rustle us up some decent coffee," Dr. Farrell said, Clay's pompous pontificating irritating him as it so often did. "I've been drinking cowboy swill made with Arbuckle's and gunpowder for the last three days."

As he stepped through the door, Clay said, "Coffee! There speaks a man who has never been in love." Then after a few moments of thought, "Mind you, I could use a cup myself and perhaps, if Mrs. Salas is up and about and it would not be too much of an imposition, a few of her excellent biscuits and a small pile, well, a medium pile, of bacon would not go amiss."

Moses told a housemaid, who told the parlor maid, who told the lady's maid, who told Kate that Hiram Clay presented his compliments, had brought along his personal physician to treat her injury, and was most desirous of beholding her lovely countenance once again.

Kate groaned and with both hands pushed her hair off her face. "Oh my God. Hiram Clay . . . and I haven't had my coffee yet."

"Ma'am, Jazmine is cooking breakfast for Mr. Clay and the doctor, so you have plenty of time for coffee," Nora said. "I'll bring a tray."

* * *

Kate was drinking her second cup when Nora announced that Dr. Farrell wished to examine her. "There's no need to get up, ma'am. I'm sure the doctor can examine your shoulder just fine from there." She smiled. "My, you look so beautiful this morning."

"I look terrible because the pain in my shoulder kept waking me," Kate said. "But that was a nice thing to say, Nora, so thank you."

Dr. Zebulon Farrell was a stern man who smelled dusty, perhaps, Kate guessed, from reading musty old medical books. His bedside manner was brusque, but his touch as he examined Kate's shoulder was gentle, almost feminine, his blunt fingers barely touching, moving over the purple and yellow bruise like so many feathers.

After a while he sat back on the chair he'd pulled next to the bed. "It's a deep bruise and very extensive." Then he gave a rare smile. "But you already know that."

"Yes, I do, Doctor. The pain is a constant reminder of how extensive it is." The Koenig father and son uppermost in her mind, she said, "When can I ride again?"

"You can ride now, Mrs. Kerrigan, a short jog around the house, but I don't advise it. Wait a week to let the shoulder heal. In the meantime, I'll give you something for the pain and to help you sleep."

"A week? I thought I'd heal up faster than that."

"You're a strong, healthy woman and you might, but we must err on the side of caution, Mrs. Kerrigan."

Kate thought about that for a few moments and then frowned. "Then I must follow doctor's orders, I suppose."

"You must, if you don't want to further injure that shoulder," Dr. Farrell said.

The physician would have said more, had not a stentorian voice from the other side of the door said, "Hark! Kate, do you hear that noise? It's the sound of your poor Hiram's heart breaking."

Kate pulled her nightdress back over her shoulder and said, "Do come in, Hiram."

Clay was not alone. He was preceded by a kitchen maid carrying a tray heaped with biscuits, strips of bacon, and a pot of coffee.

"Just put the tray down on the little table over there, Luella." He watched with some trepidation until the tray was safely deposited. "Thank you. That will do nicely." Only then did he step to the bottom of Kate's bed, spread his arms wide, and say, "Hiram is here!"

Kate smiled. "How nice of you to come." She extended her hand and Clay kissed it.

"Wild horses, my dear one! As soon as I heard of your dreadful injury, wild horses could not keep me away." Clay turned to Dr. Farrell, his voice dropping to a concerned whisper but loud enough for Kate to hear. "How is she?"

Before the doctor could answer, Kate said, "I'm on the mend, Hiram. It's only a bruise and a sore shoulder joint. Dr. Farrell says I'll be back to my old self in a week."

"Happy, happy day!" Clay said. "Now, Dr. Farrell, I believe the fair Mrs. Salas has your breakfast ready in the kitchen, and I will take your place at the bedside of the beautiful invalid."

Before he took the doctor's vacated chair, Clay scooped up the plate from the table and carried it to

Kate's bed. He delicately wedged a thick slice of fatty bacon into a biscuit and held the reeking sandwich under Kate's nose. "Would you care to partake, my dear? To build up your strength, like."

Thoroughly nauseated, Kate's eyes widened as she shook her head.

Clay held up his porcine creation and shook it, as a man would shake a rattle over a baby. His face full of trepidation, he said, "But you don't mind if I do? Enjoy a bite of two of this small repast, I mean?"

"Not at all," Kate lied. "You must be sharp set after your long journey."

"Indeed, I am," Clay said. "The trail was long and dreary and your Hiram's heart was full of foreboding. Ah, my dear, you are always so considerate of them in need and that makes me adore you all the more."

Famed in Texas as a mighty trencherman, Clay bent to his pile of biscuits with a will, taking time between bites to talk of weather, range conditions, cattle prices, and his undying devotion to his "precious Kate."

As Clay talked, Kate answered only with the occasional, "Uh-huh," or a nod, but her mind was racing.

How easy it would be . . .

Hiram, Blade Koenig and his son invaded my home and abused my staff, and Seth Koenig tried to rape me. They murdered the guests that had sought protection under my roof and left their bones on the prairie to be scavenged by coyotes.

How predictable would be Hiram Clay's reaction . . .

Indignation, anger, the mobilization of the cattleman's association, and an onslaught of a hundred and more riders on the Hellfire. Blade and Seth Koenig would be hanged from the same tree and justice would be done.

How easy it would be . . .

Kate dismissed the idea from her mind. She would not shelter behind the power of the cattleman's association, nor let others do her dirty work and die fighting her battles. The KK fought its own fights, and Kate Kerrigan would not beg anyone for help.

"Well, that was most satisfying." Clay sighed and took a somewhat rueful glance at his empty plate. Using the tip of his little finger, he picked up an atom of bacon and popped it in his mouth.

"I'm so glad you enjoyed it, Hiram. I do like to watch a hungry man eat."

"And may you watch me eat many more times in the future," Clay said with dubious gallantry.

"It would be such a pleasure, and listening to you eat as well."

"What a romantic you are, dear Kate. Yet another reason why Hiram adores you."

Kate smiled and said nothing. Suddenly she felt tired.

Clay laid his plate aside and said, "You seem distracted, my precious Kate. Is there something troubling you?"

How easy it would be . . . "No, nothing is troubling me, Hiram. The pain in my shoulder has made me a little tired, is all. Perhaps I should take a little nap."

Clay's face lit up. "Yes, that's the ticket. Rest is a great healer."

"You don't mind, Hiram? I feel cruel sending you away when your presence means so much to me."

Clay sprang to his feet, a starry-eyed Humpty-Dumpty who Kate Kerrigan knew was one day destined for a great fall. "Yes, you should rest, and perhaps you will dream of your faithful Hiram."

Kate smiled. "Those will be pleasant dreams indeed."

Elated, Clay gave a little bow and tiptoed out of the room, taking his plate with him. He closed the door very quietly, and Kate let out a sigh of relief. She sank back on her pillow, resigned to what was to come. The violent showdown with Blade Koenig and his degenerate son was approaching rapidly, and on both sides, men who rode for the brand would die, a fact that troubled her deeply.

She knew that Hiram Clay was still very much in love with her, that much was obvious . . .

Yes, it would have been so easy to tell him all, play the helpless woman, and ask for his help.

But that was not the road Kate Kerrigan was willing to take, not then, not ever.

Chapter Nineteen

"Something wicked this way comes . . ."

The old Creole woman Ezora Chabert shivered in anticipation as she felt the nearing presence of a soul as evil as her own. She smiled. She had known for days that the handsome blond white man with the satanic eyes would visit her, and she had made all ready to greet him. But not for this man a love potion or a spell for wealth or an amulet to protect against the evil eye, but something darker, more elemental, the acquisition of the truly wicked . . . the powder that paralyzes or the poison that kills.

Ezora had both, and more, should the customer require it.

The woman who watched Seth Koenig from the window of her shack ten miles southwest of Deming was small, thin, bent, the very image of the old crone, the foul witch of legend. Once, as a young woman in her native New Orleans, she'd been beautiful, or so the city's police records have it, but she'd poisoned a rich and old husband, then another, and then the wife of a man she craved. As she prospered in her murders, something evil crept into Ezora's soul like a dark mist into a swamp and all that was beautiful in her withered and died, leaving a malformed, hideous husk. She fled New Orleans to escape the hangman's noose and by the time Seth Koenig came to call she was wanted for murder in half a dozen states, cited in several court records as a "supplier of poisons and other noxious drafts."

She was wickedness personified and a fit match for the man who was there to ask her help.

Seth dismounted outside the old woman's cabin, a former prospector's shack set among trees at the base of a stunted limestone ridge. The tinpan had lain dead inside for several years before his mummified body was discovered. The local punchers avoided the place, and no one had occupied it until Ezora moved in, three years before she opened the door to Seth.

The woman read the surprise on the man's face and said, "No need to announce yourself. I've been expecting you." Her voice was midway between a hoarse whisper and a raven croak. "Come inside."

"How did you know I was coming?"

Ezora's smile was toothless and ugly. "I see things. And I smell things. Evil has a stink that carries in the wind."

"And you have a stink that's all your own, hag," Seth said.

"I stink, you stink, because we share the same darkness of soul. Come now, a riddle. Whose soul is blacker, the witch or the parricide?"

"Parricide? What the hell does that mean?"

"It means father-killer. Ha! I see the guilt in your face."

"I have no guilt, crone. Now step away from me. You smell like a gut pile." Seth looked around him.

The gloomy cabin consisted of one room with a dirt floor and was furnished with a cot and a rocker pulled up to a stone fireplace. A blackened pot hanging from an iron hook bubbled above the flames and smelled of boiling meat. The wall to the right of the door supported three shelves that were covered in clay pots of varying shapes and sizes, and bunches of dried herbs hung from the roof beams. On the floor, a steel cage the size of a steamer trunk held half a dozen brown rats that scrambled and squeaked and scratched, and nearby an oil lamp stood on a three-legged stool.

Ezora wore a shapeless dress that was once white and a black shawl that she drew closer around her skinny shoulders. "What do you want from me?"

Seth grinned. "I thought you knew everything."

"Nothing is closed to me," the old woman said. Her hair was gray and thin and very dirty. "But I need to hear it from your own lips. It is the way of the witch."

"I want to kill a man."

"Yes, I know. You wish to kill your father."

"My father. Yes, he is the one that must die."

"But you don't want to shoot him."

"No. His death must look natural, like his ticker stopped and he keeled over."

"Do you want this man to die quickly or slowly in great pain?"

"Quickly enough that he doesn't have time to draw his gun," Seth said

"Ah, then you need a poison that kills fast."

"Yeah, something I can put in his whiskey."

"Then I have something special for you."

"All right. Then give it to me."

"Patience. First describe this man," Ezora said. "Describe your father."

"Why the hell do you want to know that?"

"The strength of the poison depends on the strength of the man."

Seth saw the logic in that and said, "As tall as me, maybe twenty pounds heavier."

The old woman nodded. "Yes, I can see your father. What a big man. But you do not wish to wait a day longer for your inheritance . . . so he must die."

Yes, he must die and so must you, old witch. "You're right. He's my fond papa, and I want his money," Seth said, grinning. "He's lived too long."

"Then so be it," Ezora said. "You have coin? Silver and gold?"

"If you help me, I'll pay your weight in silver."

"You are very generous."

"When I want a thing, I'm willing to pay for it."

"I can help you in your endeavor . . . as I've helped many before you," the old woman said. "But first listen to me. Poisons, even my venoms, do not kill instantly. Often the victim will scream and groan and foam at the mouth as he clutches his belly and rolls on the floor. It can be an exquisitely painful death and may arouse suspicion."

Seth did not receive that bad news well. "Hell, you crazy old slut, that will give Blade time to draw his iron and plug me."

"And you have no wish to die."

"Damn right, I don't. I'm destined for great things."

Ezora smiled. "You will fulfill your destiny, never fear. I told you I have something very special and it is true, I have. Many years ago, the making of it was taught to me by a voodoo priestess in New Orleans. It is very ancient and very powerful."

Seth smiled. "Then let's have at it."

It was stifling hot in the cabin. Fat black flies buzzed around his head and the rancid smell of boiling meat was overwhelming. The rats in the steel cage squeaked and scuttled.

"The powder I will show you has killed many," the old woman said.

"Yeah, yeah, I know. Then let's get at it. The stench in this damned hovel is making me sick to my stomach."

"Very well. I'll reveal the powder's secrets."

The old woman crossed the floor to the shelves and picked up a leather wallet that contained three glass vials. As he watched, Ezora opened one of the vials and sprinkled its contents, a fine white powder, on the palm of her left hand.

"What is that?" he said, stepping toward her.

"No, stay back," the woman said. "Watch from there where it is safe."

She stepped to the cage on the floor and grabbed a rat. The animal wriggled and squeaked . . . until Ezora lifted her palm to her lips and blew the white powder into the rat's face. Instantly the rodent stiffened and all movement ceased, like a doorstop in the shape of an iron rat.

Seth Koenig was stunned. "What the hell?"

"The powder paralyses and then death follows, hours or perhaps days later, but it comes," Ezora said. "Your father will die two deaths, one by powder, one by poison." She cackled. "And you will become a rich man." The old woman stepped to the fire and dropped the rat into the boiling pot.

Seth was horrified. "You're going to eat that?"

"I live on soup," Ezora said. "It is my only food."

He felt his gorge rise. "Give me what I need. I got to get the hell out of here."

"Young man, murder in cold blood is never a pleasant road, especially the murder of a parent. You know you will burn in hell for what you do?"

"Let me worry about that. I only want the poison, not the damned powder. And I'll take my chances on hell."

The woman nodded. "Very well. Who knows, perhaps your father will die quickly from the poison."

Seth smiled. "Make the stuff strong, hag. A dose that will kill an elephant will kill a man fast enough."

"Have you ever seen an elephant?" Ezora said.

"No. I never have," Koenig said.

"It is large and powerful, the true king of the beasts."

"Just like my pa."

Ezora Chabert poured a measure of clear liquid into a glass vial the size of a man's thumbnail and handed it to him. "Death in a thimble, yet enough to kill the biggest and bravest. Pour this into your father's whiskey and then sit back and watch him die."

Seth smiled. "It will give me the greatest of pleasure."

"You must hate him very much. I have seen many strong men die from poison, and their deaths were terrible."

He grinned. "Like I give a damn."

"Is there anything else I can do for you?" Ezora said. "A love potion, perhaps?"

"I don't need love potions. I want women to fear me, not love me."

"Then our business is finished. Now pay me my weight in silver as you promised," Ezora said.

"I don't have that much." He pressed a silver dollar into the old crone's veined hand. "I'll make up the difference in lead."

He drew and fired.

The .45 bullet hit Ezora's chest and she staggered back against the far wall. He kept shooting, nailing the old woman to the timbers like a grotesque trophy. His revolver finally ran dry, and he watched Ezora slide slowly to the ground, leaving behind a glistening snail trail of blood.

Grinning, feeling good as he always did after a killing, he worked quickly. He smashed the oil lamp on the floor and then grabbed a burning brand from the fire and set the spreading kerosene ablaze. The cabin was tinder dry and the fire spread quickly, forcing him outside, where he stood and watched the building burn. A column of black smoke rose into the sky but was quickly shredded by the prevailing wind. Within minutes all that was left of the cabin was a pile of ashes and a few blackened spars of wood, flames clinging to them like scarlet moths.

Seth Koenig was mighty pleased with himself as he swung into the saddle and headed south for the Hellfire. He patted the poison vial in his shirt pocket where it rode alongside his tobacco sack. He had the means to kill Blade and make it look good to the ranch hands. For all the world, it would seem like Pa's heart had given out and he'd just keeled over. Of course, Seth would put on a show of grief in keeping with the sad situation.

If he'd been a singing man, he would've sung a happy song as he crossed the flat scrubland, but since he wasn't and didn't know any happy songs anyhow, he contented himself by imagining Blade's horrified expression when he whispered into his ear that he'd been poisoned. Seth tilted his face to the sky, his arms outstretched, and laughed out loud at the pictures that took shape in his mind.

Damn, life was good . . . and getting better.

Chapter Twenty

Hiram Clay and Dr. Zebulon Farrell spent the night at the KK and left early next morning amid many declarations of love and admiration for Kate from the rotund rancher and a promise to return "ere another month passes."

Rousted out of bed in the dawn light to say her farewells, Kate decided to have coffee in the warm kitchen . . . and ran into a major problem.

It took a while before Kate noticed that Biddy Kelly, the young Irish kitchen maid, had been crying, her eyes red and swollen. Rather than question the girl directly, Kate asked Jazmine Salas what was the matter.

"She won't tell me, Mrs. Kerrigan," Jazmine said. "She says she doesn't want to cause more trouble for you and the ranch."

"Is it a young man?" Kate said.

Jazmine shook her head. "She's not walking out with anyone, at least as far as I know."

"It's not like Biddy to be sad."

"I know. She's forever singing and dancing around the kitchen." Jazmine smiled. "Drives me crazy sometimes when I'm busy."

An unhappy kitchen maid could be a problem, and Kate was determined to get to the root of the mystery. As was her nature, she determined to tackle the problem head-on. When Biddy poured Kate another cup of coffee, her tearstained face turned away, Kate said, "Sit down beside me, girl, and tell me what's troubling you."

Her chin sunk on her chest, Biddy shook her head. "I'd rather not, Mrs. Kerrigan. Begging your pardon, but I don't want to cause trouble."

"We all have to do things we'd rather not do," Kate said. "Now sit and tell me true . . . what can the matter be? Is it a young man?"

Another shake of Biddy's head and then, "No, ma'am, nothing like that. Oh, I can't tell you. I can't, I can't."

"Then tell me *now*, Biddy, and stop that babbling or I swear I'll box your ears," Kate said, irritated at the girl's reticence.

Biddy took a seat at the kitchen table and perched on the very edge of a chair. She dabbed a scrap of handkerchief to her nose and sniffed. "I don't want to get anyone into trouble, Mrs. Kerrigan. Me mother would take a stick to me if I got someone shot or hung."

"Your mother lies in Ireland, Biddy, so it's not likely she'll take a stick to you, is it?" Kate said, pretending to be more severe than she felt. She stared at the seventeen-year-old, a girl neither clever nor pretty but a hard and willing worker. "Well, I'm waiting, missy."

Biddy took a deep, shuddering breath and said, "Ma'am, do you remember I told you about me silver claddagh ring?"

"Yes, the one taken off your martyred father's dead

finger by the Black and Tans of cursed memory," Kate said. "Then British soldiers gave it back to you in a rare act of compassion . . . or maybe it was guilt."

The girl nodded. "I don't know why they gave it back, but I saw the ring yesterday."

"Where?" Kate was surprised and horrified. Biddy hesitated, and Kate said, "Where did you see it?"

A deep gulp of breath and then the kitchen maid said, "On the little finger of Mr. Dancer."

"Gabe Dancer! But he wasn't with the Koenigs when they invaded my property. Are you sure it's the same ring?"

"Yes, Mrs. Kerrigan, I'm sure. Mr. Dancer came into the kitchen yesterday for coffee. He said Mr. Ogilvy's coffee is swill and that he refuses to drink it. I got a good look at the ring and it's me da's all right."

Kate's chin took on a determined set. "Well, there only one way to find out. Jazmine, will you ask Mr. Rice to find Gabe Dancer and bring him here, instanter!"

The cook nodded and left, and Biddy began to quietly sob again.

Kate put her arm around the girl's shoulder and held her close. "Don't cry, Biddy. We'll get all this sorted out and if the ring is yours, it will be returned to you."

"I don't want to get Mr. Dancer into trouble, Mrs. Kerrigan," Biddy said. "He seems such a nice old man and sometimes he talks pretties to me."

"He's too old to be talking pretties to a young girl like you. Biddy, nice old man or not, if Gabe Dancer has anything to do with the Koenig bunch he's in for more trouble than he's ever seen in his life."

"See, that's why I didn't want to tell you. Now I feel so sorry for him. I don't want you to shoot him."

"You did the right thing, Biddy," Kate said. "If we substitute compassion for justice, civilization will fall apart. Do you understand that?"

Biddy nodded. "Yes, Mrs. Kerrigan. I . . . I think so."

"Do you feel sorry for the Black and Tans who murdered your father?"

"No, I don't. I hate them."

"Should they be brought to justice and face trial in an Irish court with Irish patriots on the jury?"

"Yes, yes they should."

"And if they're found guilty should they be stood up against a wall and shot?"

Biddy was silent.

"Well?" Kate said.

"Yes, they should be shot."

"Then if Gabe Dancer was with the brigands who invaded my home and murdered my guests should he hang?"

After a while Biddy said, her voice small, "Yes."

"The West has no rules, Biddy, except one—the rule of law. And the law says a man who commits murder or who stands idly by doing nothing while murder is being committed should hang. Do you agree with that?"

"Yes, I suppose I do," Biddy said. "I never think about things like that."

"Then save your pity for the more deserving," Kate said.

At that moment Moses Rice stepped into the kitchen and formally announced the presence of "Gabe Dancer, Esquire."

Kate dismissed the butler and told Dancer to sit.

After he took a chair, Dancer said, "How are you this morning, Biddy me darlin?"

The girl lowered her head and said nothing and the old man seemed disappointed.

Then he said, "I was summoned into your presence, Mrs. Kerrigan. To what do I owe this great honor?"

Her voice clipped, Kate said, "Show me your hands."

"My hands?"

"Yes, show them."

"It's a strange request, but I guess I've heard stranger." Dancer shrugged and placed his gnarled hands palms down on the table, fingers spread. "They ain't pretty. All scarred up, like."

Kate pointed to the silver ring on Dancer's little finger. "Let me see that."

"It's only a cheap little silver ring," Dancer said.

"Nonetheless I want to see it," Kate said.

Dancer shrugged, slipped off the ring, and passed it to Kate. "Got two human hands on it. Maybe it's Navajo. Or maybe Apache, but I don't think so."

Kate passed the ring to Biddy. "Is it yours?"

The girl turned the ring around in her fingers. "Yes, it's me father's ring, all right. See there, Mrs. Kerrigan, in the inside. Those are his initials, *PK* for Patrick Kelly."

The eyes Kate turned to Dancer were cold as green death. Slowly, emphasizing every word, she said, "*Where . . . did . . . you . . . get . . . this*?"

Dancer looked puzzled. "It's a story long in the telling."

"Then shorten it," Kate said. "I'd hate to hang a man with half his story still untold."

"Hang? Hang for what?" Dancer said. "Wait . . . here now, Mrs. Kerrigan, are you kin to one o' them rannies I killed up in the Yeso Hills country in the New Mexico Territory?"

"No, I am not," Kate said. "Tell me about the ring."

"Well, and this is back about a week ago or more, up in the territory. I planned to blow my poke to celebrate my birthday at a saloon called the Golden Nugget," Dancer said. "One time I knew a fancy woman there, but that was years ago."

"Go on," Kate said, her eyes never leaving Dancer's face.

"Well, I'm headed for the saloon . . . up in the Yeso Hills country, did I tell you that?"

"Yes, you did. Now go on."

"Sorry, I forget things," Dancer said. "Well, anyhoo, up comes this decent-looking feller and says he, 'Halt! Are you headed for the Golden Nugget?' Says I, 'Yes, I am.' And the feller says, 'Don't go there.' And I says, 'Why not?' and says he, 'Because there's a couple punchers in there from the Hellfire and they got a fallen woman with them and they're on the prod. Be warned, they'll do you harm.'"

Kate's interest perked up. "Did he mean the Hellfire ranch?"

"Yeah, he did."

"Go on."

"Well, says I, 'It's my birthday and a couple o' unsociable waddies won't spoil my celebration.' 'Well,' says the feller, he was a rancher and real nice, 'you've been warned.' Says I—"

"Cut to the point," Kate said. "What happened in the saloon and how did you come by the ring?"

"You mean make a long story short?" Dancer said.

"I strongly advise it. At times my temper can be short."

"Well, them two waddies was pistol fighters and as mean as eight acres of snakes. 'Give us your poke,' they says. "No,' says I. 'Then die,' says they. Then all hell broke loose and after the smoke cleared, the two waddies lay dead on the sawdust and my rifle barrel was hotter 'n the hinges of hell, but I was still alive and as eager for a shindig as ever. Well, me and the fallen woman had us our birthday party and when I'm leaving in the morning she says, 'Here, take this ring. I took it off one of them dead fellers.' That fallen woman thanked me for all I'd done for her and said the ring would bring me luck." He shook his head. "But that don't seem to be the case so far."

Kate was inclined to believe Dancer's account, but she probed a little deeper. "Do you know Blade Koenig, the owner of the Hellfire?"

"Like everybody who's spent some time in New Mexico Territory, I've heard the name, but I've never met him," Dancer said. "And after meeting up with a couple of his riders I'm not sure I want to."

Kate and Biddy's eyes met, and the girl said, "I believe him."

"I do too," Kate said. "Mr. Dancer, you may go, but the matter of the shooting of Francisco Garcia still stands between us and must be resolved."

"I await your convenience, dear lady," Dancer said. "I admit that it's crossed my mind to winter here."

"Perhaps. That is if I don't hang you, and Frank Cobb says you can make yourself useful about the ranch."

"Well, on that account, I've already spoke with your blacksmith, and he says I can help him around the forge since I done some smithy work afore as a younker," the old man said. "As for the hanging, that subject didn't come up in our polite conversation."

Dancer turned to leave, then stopped and smiled at Biddy. "Wear the ring in good health, young Irish lady."

The girl blushed but said nothing.

When Dancer was gone, Jazmine refilled Kate's coffee cup. "Ma'am, my husband speaks very highly of Mr. Dancer. Would you really hang him?"

"When he had the shoot-out in the Golden Nugget saloon he reduced the number of my mortal enemies by two. Now I don't know if I want to hang him or hug him," Kate said.

"I'm glad, because I really like Gabe," Biddy said.

Kate and Jasmine looked at her in surprise.

Chapter Twenty-One

After a couple days cooped up in the house, Kate Kerrigan had had enough of idleness. She decided it was time to ride and test her injured shoulder.

"I'm so glad you agreed to let me come with you, Kate," Doña Maria Ana said later as she and Kate stood together in the barn. "Small houses always make me feel so closed in and restless."

Kate ignored the jab at her spacious, four-pillared mansion and smiled. "It will be a pleasure to ride with you. What about your shadow?"

"Rodolfo? I told him he must remain at the ranch, that this was a trip for women alone. He didn't like the idea, but he's staying. Kate, I suggest we head toward the Rio Grande and see if there's any sign of Don Pedro. It's been a week, and my heartless beast of a husband still hasn't come looking for me."

Kate watched Shorty Hawkins tighten her saddle cinch, his knee pressing into the roan's ribs, and then said, "I thought you never wanted to see him again."

"I don't," Maria Ana said. "But by now, I expected he'd be here on bended knee begging me to come back to him." Her dark eyes flashed. "Men are such cold, unfeeling brutes, and Don Pedro is the worst of all. I hate him."

Kate wore her usual range clothing: a plain gray shirt, suede riding skirt, scuffed boots, and a battered, shapeless hat.

Doña Maria Ana, on the other hand, looked ready for a canter along London's fashionable Rotten Row bridle path. As she had done so many times in the past, she reminded Kate that her riding companions included the Prince of Wales, the divine Sarah Bernhardt, a friendship she shared with Gabe Dancer of all people, and the notoriously rich Alva Vanderbilt, who, even when riding, wore the pearls that once adorned the neck of Catherine the Great.

In contrast to her usual black, Doña Maria Ana wore a bright red but severely tailored riding habit consisting of a hussar-style pelisse trimmed with gold bullion lace. The front of the jacket featured parallel rows of frogging and loops with two rows of gold buttons. Her skirt was unadorned and full, split at the front for riding, revealing polished red thigh boots. She wore a red top hat with a black veil that covered her eyes and cheekbones and carried a red leather riding crop.

Comparing herself to that gorgeous creature, Kate felt quite dowdy, before reminding herself that the vast West Texas range was far removed from the civilized bridle paths of Europe. Still, as she and the stunning Maria Ana rode sidesaddle out of the stable, attracting admiring and other looks from the hands, Kate felt like a frump.

The two women rode south through a cool, sunny morning that was coming in fresh and clean.

By one o'clock, when Kate judged that they were halfway to the Rio Grande, she suggested they stop for lunch. Jazmine had provided a picnic basket that Shorty Hawkins had strapped to the back of Kate's saddle.

Kate opened the basket under the thin shade of a mesquite, a plant she normally considered a noxious weed because its thorns injure cattle, horses, and cowhands and its extensive root system demands more than its fair share of water. But in West Texas shade is shade, and for now she'd live with it.

She kneeled and sorted out the contents of the basket.

Maria Ana, heedless of her scarlet finery, plopped herself down on the sparse fall grass and said, "Let's eat lunch, Kate. Suddenly I'm hungry." She reached into the pocket of her skirt, produced a small, brass telescope, and scanned the land to the south. After a while she angrily palmed the telescope shut and said through a deep sigh, "Nothing. Still no sign of that wife-abuser, the unspeakable Don Pedro. He's abandoned me to my fate, and soon I must surely starve to death."

Kate smiled. "I won't let you starve, Maria Ana. Let's see if Jazmine has done us proud. Ah . . . ham, beef, and . . . let me see . . . yes, chicken sandwiches, pickles, a bottle of Jazmine's cold tea that she flavors with sugar and lemon. And for dessert . . . Huzzah! . . . gingerbread. Are you ready to make a trial of everything?"

Doña Maria Ana most certainly was, and while she ate, she kept up a running narrative about the sundry cruelties she'd suffered at the hands of Don Pedro.

"Can you believe it, Kate? He even insisted I abandon my longtime chaplain, the aristocratic Padre Alfonso Daniel, and confess my sins to the resident hacienda priest."

"Why would Don Pedro do such a thing?"

"Because, Kate . . . listen to this . . . he said Padre Alfonso was so old he kept reminding him of death and Judgment Day. And then he said, my husband said, mind you, that reciting twenty rosaries was too severe a penance for squeezing the tit of a servant girl. And he said, "It was a small tit. Imagine how many rosaries I would've had to say for a big one."

"He said that?" Kate was shocked.

"Yes, and despite my tears, he then threatened to banish Padre Daniel from our lands forever."

"Forever?" Kate said.

"Forever," Maria Ana said. "Never to return."

Kate crossed herself. "Imagine banishing such a holy priest forever. Jesus, Mary and Joseph, and all the saints in heaven protect us."

"Yes, Kate, and now you know what a selfish . . ."

"Lecherous."

". . . fiend Don Pedro really is. Mmm . . . the chicken sandwich is really good."

"And you must try the gingerbread." Kate's eyes fixed on movement in the distance. "Maria Ana, I thought you said you saw no sign of riders."

The doña's face lit up. "Is it Don Pedro?"

"I don't know. Two men, I think, and they're headed in this direction."

"My telescope isn't very good, yet another of Don Pedro's tawdry gifts."

Kate stood and watched the riders as they came

closer. They were on Kerrigan range but all kinds of travelers used it as a throughway to the New Mexico Territory or the Nations. The riders could be punchers hunting work or just a pair of wandering Mexicans, but an insistent alarm bell rang in Kate's head. They could also be outlaw border trash on the scout.

Maria Ana read Kate's stiff posture and sensed her tension. "Kate?"

"It may be nothing."

"Or it may be something," Maria Ana said.

"Yes . . . or it may be something."

"We best keep an eye on them."

"I intend to do just that." Kate's hand dropped to the British Bulldog in her skirt pocket, taking reassurance from its cool steel. She knew she might be overreacting, but in West Texas any strangers met on the range were treated as potential enemies until they proved otherwise by sociable talk and honorable intentions.

"Maria Ana, are you armed?' Kate said.

The woman shook her head. "No. I never had the need while Rodolfo was around. Kate, are we in danger?"

"I don't know."

"Well, I hope not."

"So do I."

"I hope they don't spoil our picnic. I haven't even tasted the gingerbread." Maria Ana dropped her half-eaten sandwich into the picnic basket and stood next to Kate. "Well, if worse comes to worst, I have claws and teeth. I will be a tigress in a fight."

Kate nodded and smiled, Maria Ana rising in her estimation. Whatever else she might lack, the woman had sand.

"We could mount up and outrun them," Kate said. It was more question than statement.

"Doña Maria Ana de la Villa de Villar del Aguila does not run from danger. From an ogre of a husband, yes, or the jealous wife of a lover, but never from common brigands."

"Kate Kerrigan doesn't run either. Besides, we don't know that they are common brigands or any other kind of brigands."

"Time will tell, won't it?" Maria Ana glanced at the burned-out sky. "Hot, isn't it?"

"Odd for this time of year," Kate said, her eyes on the riders.

"Paris in the fall is . . . how do you say it? Ah yes, *magnifique*."

"I was in London in the fall," Kate said, her growing anxiety clouding her smile. "It was cold, damp, and foggy." She looked up at the riders, two bearded, rough-looking men astride good horses that looked like they could run. Outlaw mounts, she was sure.

Beside her Maria Ana said, "A rough-looking pair."

"Outlaws by the look of them."

When the men rode close and drew rein, Kate said, "Howdy."

The older of the two men touched his hat, a good sign. "Howdy, ma'am. Picnicking, are we?"

"Seems like." Kate smiled. She kept her hand in her pocket and was sure the older man knew why.

"Hot to be out."

"Yes, isn't it? I mean, for this time of the year."

From Maria Ana came a long, drawn-out shriek. "What have you done to him?"

It was only then, previously hidden by the legs of the horses, that Kate noticed a slat-sided, tan and white dog attached to the younger man's saddle by a length of thin, hairy string. The dog, its tongue lolling, lay down with his scarred muzzle on his paws, the string biting deeply into his muscular neck. She thought the mutt looked like a tough customer until Maria Ana kneeled beside him and the dog laid his head on her lap and allowed her to stroke his head.

"What have you men done to this dog?" Maria Ana said. "He's got scars all over him."

"That's because he's a fighting dog, lady," the younger man said. "We paid fifty dollars for him in Old Mexico and figure to unload him for ten times that much up El Paso way."

"He's thin," Maria Ana said, her brown eyes hard and glittering. "This poor dog is half-starved."

"Yeah," the man said. "Makes him meaner and a mean mutt is a fighter."

"Kate," the doña said, "bring me a couple sandwiches. I'm going to feed this poor, starving animal."

"Don't feed that dog," the man said.

"He's hungry," Maria Ana said.

Suddenly the younger man's expression turned hostile, scowling, his mouth thinning to a tight gash. "I told you not to feed him. Listen to what I'm telling you, lady."

"You go to hell." Maria Ana gently lifted the dog's head off her lap, rose to her feet, and stared defiantly at the man. "This dog will never have to fight again. He's coming home with me." Then, turning, "Kate, do you have a knife? I need to cut the string off Toro's neck." She smiled. "From now on that's his name because he looks like a little bull."

The older man spoke directly to Kate, and his tone

was ominous. "Lady, we came up on your picnicking and we was prepared to be sociable and maybe partake of the delicacies, but that's all changed. So, heed me. Rein in your friend or—"

"Or what?" Kate said.

"Or something real bad might happen to her."

"Kate, do you have a knife?" Maria Ana asked again. Her eyes were large and bright, betraying no fear.

Her gaze moving between the two men, Kate said almost absently, "There's a knife in the basket."

Maria Ana found the knife and walked back to the dog, who was watching her intently. She kneeled beside Toro, who wagged his tail and butt as though she'd been gone for hours.

Things went downhill from there. And mistakes were made.

As Maria Ana opened the blade of the knife with an almond-shaped scarlet fingernail, the younger rider slid the Winchester from the boot under his knee and reversed it, planning to use the rifle stock as a club.

Kate watched in alarm as the man growled in his throat, leaned from the saddle, and raised the rifle above him like a headsman's axe. She frowned. *Well, that tears it!*

Kate drew the Bulldog and triggered its bark.

The big .455 slammed into the younger man's right forearm midway between elbow and wrist, smashing bone. The man screamed and the Winchester cartwheeled out of his hands.

Time accelerated for Kate. Her entire body throbbing in alarm, she swung the Bulldog on the older man, expecting him to make a play. There was none.

Calmly, evenly, both hands on the saddle horn, he said, "I don't draw down on ladies."

Half deaf, her ears ringing from the report of the Bulldog, the .455 a notoriously loud cartridge, Kate heard her voice as though it came from the far end of a tunnel. "I'll shoot you if I have to." Looking back on it later, she realized she'd told the older rider nothing he didn't already know.

The wounded man was more vocal. He grabbed his bloody arm and cursed at Kate and Maria Ana, the words *bitches* and *whores* repeated often.

Her hearing slowly returning to normal, she said to the older man, "Ride on out of here and take your profane friend with you."

The man smiled. "A heller in a skirt, ain't you, lady?"

"Mister, you better believe it."

"And we're keeping the dog," Maria Ana said.

"Hell, where did a beautiful lady like you learn to shoot like that?" the older man said.

"The slums of New York city and later right here in West Texas. And I've had some mighty good teachers. Now get out of here."

The older man said to his groaning companion, "We're moving on. You need a doctor to attend to that arm."

"Head east a couple days and you'll come up on the Clay range," Kate said. "You'll find a doctor there."

The younger man spat out his words. "Hell, a couple days I could lose my arm."

"You should've thought about that when you were fixing to brain my friend," Kate said. Her gun still in her hand, she picked up the man's fallen Winchester, racked it dry, and then shoved it into the boot under his knee. "Like you say, mister, time is a-wasting. When you get to the doctor, tell him to wash out your mouth with soap. It sure needs it."

* * *

Kate didn't slip the Bulldog back into her pocket until the two men were out of rifle range.

Maria Ana sat with the hungry dog, feeding him the last of the sandwiches. "Kate, who do you suppose those two were?"

"Nobodies," Kate said. "But they're the kind of nobodies who will steal what they can if they think they can get away with it."

"They rode blood horses."

"And probably stole those. Outlaws are mighty picky about horseflesh. They need mounts that can run fast and far."

"Well, we did a good deed," Maria Ana said. "We saved Toro. He's got bite scars all over him, poor thing. May I have a piece of gingerbread?"

"For the dog?"

"No, for me, silly."

"I'm sorry our picnic was spoiled." Kate laid a thick slice of gingerbread on a plate and handed it to Maria Ana."

The doña looked startled. "Spoiled? My dear Kate, it was wonderful, a great adventure. Who knew you could shoot a pistol like that?"

"I did," Kate said.

"And I saved this mistreated dog, abused in the same way Don Pedro the Cruel abuses me," Maria Ana said, chewing gingerbread. "Although I will say that he loves dogs, horses, and children. It's only his wife he has a problem with."

Kate said, "What are you going to do with him?"

"Don Pedro?"

"No, the dog."

"Well, if you don't mind, I'll take Toro back to the ranch. When I leave, he'll leave with me."

Kate smiled. "Well, thanks to my sons and Frank Cobb, we have a dozen dogs at the ranch, twice that many cats, and a three-legged raccoon. I suppose another dog won't make any difference."

"Toro will be very well-behaved, I promise. He doesn't want to fight anymore."

"Did he tell you that?"

"Yes, he did." Maria Ana held a piece of gingerbread to the dog's nose. "Here, Toro-kins, this is for you."

The dog ate the gingerbread, licked his lips, and smiled.

Chapter Twenty-two

"The dog ate the gingerbread, licked his lips, and smiled," Kate said.

"Dogs don't smile, not really," Frank Cobb said.

"Believe me, this one smiles, really," Kate said.

"I'd smile too if Doña Maria Ana let me rest my head on her lap and fed me gingerbread," Trace Kerrigan said.

Kate frowned at her son. "Trace, do you know that every time a young man has an impure thought, Our Lady sheds a tear?"

Frank grinned. "She must cry buckets around this place."

Kate's frown deepened. "And she also weeps when a certain segundo makes fun of her."

Frank let that go. "All right. Tell us about it. I mean, all of it."

"I've already told you all there is to tell," Kate said.

"Did you recognize either of them?"

"Of course not."

Trace squirmed in his chair as the parlor rapidly

filled with dusk shadows. "Where was that Aragon feller?"

"Maria Ana left him at home." Kate glanced out the window into the growing darkness. "Winifred is neglecting her duty. It's time to light the lamps."

"I wish I'd been there," Frank Cobb said.

"If wishes were fishes starving men would dine." Kate smiled. "I'm sorry, Frank, I'm being silly. I wish you'd been there, too."

"The wounded man needs a doctor, so I doubt he'll return," Frank said. "But just to be sure, I'll have the hands take turns to watch the house for the next few nights." He leaned forward in his chair. "How did the shoulder hold up?"

"Fine," Kate said. "It's a bit stiff now, but not as painful as it's been."

What lay unspoken between her and Frank was a date for the vengeance ride. Trace was also aware that the subject crouched in a dark corner like a black dog.

The entry of Winifred, a lighted spill in her hand, banished the topic, at least for now.

As the maid began to light the lamps, Kate rose to her feet. "I feel like I was born in riding clothes. I must bathe and change before dinner."

Frank and Trace followed her lead and stood.

Frank said, "Kate, you done good today. Where is Maria Ana?"

"Playing with her dog, I guess."

"She stood up, held her ground," Frank said. "You told us that."

Kate nodded. "Yes, she did. She's got spunk."

Frank smiled. "That lowdown border trash must be sorry they met up with two such formidable ladies."

"Well, one of them is for sure," Kate said.

* * *

Against her better judgment, but because Mrs. Kerrigan had experienced such a traumatic day, Jazmine Salas cooked boiled salt pork and cabbage for dinner, Kate's favorite dish from the old country. She accompanied what Kate praised as "a fine feast indeed" with a silky parsley sauce and glasses of Irish stout from a fresh barrel.

Predictably, Maria Ana was horrified, but after tasting the dish, her face lit up, and she said to Jazmine, "My compliments to the chef. This is even better than your gingerbread." She also waxed eloquent about the bread and butter pudding with Irish whisky sauce that followed and insisted that her precious Toro should have a taste.

Trace and Frank, when they heard what was on the menu, decided to eat beef and beans with the hands, though Gabe Dancer once again combed his hair and dined with the ladies.

The next couple days settled into a tense and somewhat edgy routine. Out on the range more hay was cut and stacked. Shorty Hawkins had a wisdom tooth extracted by Marco Salas the blacksmith and squealed like a baby pig caught under a gate. Maria Ana continued to search the horizon for her wayward husband, and Toro bit Tom Ogilvy the ranch cook. At first Frank took the bite very seriously, warned that there could be serious repercussions, and whispered darkly about a possible execution or at the very least, banishment. But then a puncher gave an eyewitness account of the offense, and it transpired that Ogilvy had teased the dog with a piece of bear sign before Toro decided that enough was enough and tried to take a chunk out of the fat man's hand. At the pleading of Kate and Maria Ana, Frank wrote off the unhappy affair as a misunderstanding, but Toro was banned from ever again entering the cookhouse, and he and Ogilvy became mortal enemies from that day onward.

Kate's shoulder had healed enough that it no longer pained her. The problem that agonized her was the attack on the Hellfire. She had declared war on a strong enemy and in such a war men die. The deaths of such men, especially her own punchers, would be on her head and on her conscience.

"An unjust peace is better than a just war." Cicero had said that.

Kate had read the quote somewhere, and at the time it had resonated with her. But the old philosopher was a Roman and Rome wasn't West Texas, where accepting an unjust peace was a sign of weakness and plenty of predators were waiting to pounce. Every night before bed she prayed for strength and courage to see this war through to its bitter end. And then, after the last amen, she'd remember what had happened to her and the tragic Tilletts, and her prayers and good intentions went out the window and her thirst for revenge returned.

That thirst returned again as she watched her son and the rest of the tired hands ride in from the range. Wait . . . perhaps she could make some excuse and send Trace away from the KK to safety. As soon as that thought entered her head, Kate dismissed it. Her husband Joseph Kerrigan had not fled to safety from the Battle of Shiloh, and Yankee cannons had taken his life. Joe would expect his son to stand his ground and fight and not turn tail and flee. Suddenly Kate felt ashamed, not only for the treacherous thought she'd had but also at the betrayal of her own principles.

Trace smiled at Kate and waved, a handsome young man in the prime of his youth. She knew when the guns began firing and the battle joined, he'd be as brave as his father.

How could a Kerrigan be any less?

"Hey, Kate, what's for supper?" Frank Cobb called out, grinning as he rode in the direction of the livery.

"Ask Jazmine. she's the cook," Kate called back.

Frank turned his head. "Can't you take a guess?"

"Salt pork and cabbage," Kate said.

Frank shook his head and yelled. "Hell, Kate, I'm not that hungry."

Kate smiled. She felt strong again.

Chapter Twenty-Three

Now would be a fine time to kill them, every man jack of them, while they were out in the open cutting and baling hay against the coming winter. The man with the field glasses shook his head. Pity. It was a lost chance. Ol' Salty hadn't gathered enough men yet, and he wouldn't strike the ranch until he held the advantage in numbers.

Well hidden among a stand of catclaw in a deep cut at the northern border of the Kerrigan range, Archie Lane had seen enough. Bending low, he faded back into the wild oaks where he'd left his horse and swung into the saddle. His job was to scout the Kerrigan ranch house and its outbuildings and look for weaknesses.

When he attacked, Davis Salt wanted an edge, something only a reconnaissance could give him. He'd chosen Lane for the job, because for a spell the man had run with Jesse and Frank and them, and he knew how to scout a town and its bank and figure the best way to take the place. An additional qualification was that Lane was good with a gun and could take care of himself. He'd spent two years in Yuma for gunning a pimp and pistol-whipping his whore and vowed he'd die before returning to Yuma, or any other federal prison. To avoid arrest he'd killed four lawmen and made himself a luminary of the frontier's most wanted list. Keeping a heap of git between himself and the next hanging posse made Lane a desperate man . . . and in Salt's opinion desperate men made excellent business associates.

Lane looped wide around the Kerrigan range and then headed south, finally riding up on a low rise that overlooked the ranch house. The outlaw dismounted, made his way to the top of the rise on foot, and found himself in a small cemetery with a few fresh graves. Lane was as superstitious as any cowboy, and the cemetery, especially the newer graves, made him uncomfortable. He considered finding another viewpoint. But the boneyard offered cover, and it was unlikely that anyone would go that way. Lane fished in the pocket of his shirt for the beef jerky he'd stashed there and chewed on a piece as he used his field glasses to study the big, four-pillared Southern mansion, small cabin, bunkhouse, stable, corrals, and a cluster of other buildings, including a smokehouse and what looked like a toolshed. The place was well laid out and meticulously maintained, and seemed to be prospering, judging by the blood horses in the corrals and the sleek Hereford cattle grazing nearby. A fat man in a stained apron, a bandage on his right hand, stepped out of the cookhouse, emptied a dishpan, looked around, and walked back inside.

Then Lane's heart raced faster.

A raggedy-looking dog appeared from somewhere near the cookhouse door, stared hard at the rise, and

then cocked his head to one side, thinking thin
over. Lane watched the mutt with growing apprehe
sion. The last thing he needed was a barking cur
raise the alarm. To his relief, the dog decided th
there was nothing of interest on the rise to justify suc
a long walk. He found a patch of sun, lay down, ar
put his chin on his paws, his gaze fixed on the coo
house door.

Archie Lane breathed a sigh of relief and raised th
glasses again, but he never got them to his eyes. Som
thing hard slammed into the back of his head and h
tumbled into a bottomless well of darkness.

Lane opened his eyes to the blur of a bearded fac
just inches from his own. He blinked, blinked agair
and stared into a pair of faded blue eyes.

"Howdy, young feller," Gabe Dancer said.

"Wha . . . what the hell?' Lane said.

"You've been sleeping like a baby for nigh on twent
minutes, sonny. Hell, for a spell there I thought I'd kil
you for sure."

Lane heard a woman's voice say, "Oh, thank God
Gabe. I thought you'd killed him too. Is he all right?

"He's fine. Got a hard head, I guess."

The outlaw groaned and fixed Dancer with colc
eyes. "Did you hit me, old-timer?"

"Sure did. With this." He slapped the stock of his
Henry. "Made quite a clunk."

Lane's hand slid down to his Colt and closed on ar
empty holster.

"Looking fer this, sonny?" Dancer said, holding up
the revolver.

Lane's fingers massaged his temples. "Why did you hit me, you crazy old coot?"

Biddy Kelly, dressed in a brown cotton walking-out dress with a white collar and cuffs, kicked Lane's booted foot. "Don't you talk to Mr. Dancer like that. It's not polite."

"That's all right, Biddy, my darling. The gent just regained consciousness and don't know what he's saying." Dancer prodded Lane's belly with the muzzle of his cocked rifle. "You're a spy. That's why I hit you, and if you call me a crazy old coot again I'll blow your belly button into the next county, just to prove how crazy I can be."

"Damn you, I'm not a spy," Lane said. "I'm just passing through."

"Going where?"

"I don't know. Anywhere."

"If you ain't a spy, then what are you, sonny?"

"A . . . a . . . birdwatcher."

"No, you ain't."

"Yes, I am. I watch birds."

"What kind of birds?"

"All kinds, big birds, little birds."

"You ever see a red-breasted—forgive me for saying that word in your presence, Biddy—pickle tit—and for that one too—around here?"

"Yeah, sure I did. I watched two of them not long ago."

"Partial to graveyards, are they?"

"That's what I heard. Something to do with the quiet."

"You're a damned liar," Dancer said. "There ain't no such bird as a red-breasted pickle tit—sorry again Biddy. I just made it up."

The girl seemed a little irritated. "Mr. Dancer, don't keep apologizing all the time. I've heard both those words many times before. And remember we're talking about a bird, not a . . . a . . ."

"Bosom," Dancer said.

"Yes. That."

"Saw your hoss down below," Dancer said to Lane. "Not many big American studs around these parts. Mister, you're an outlaw"—he held up the field glasses—"and a spy. You know what happens to spies? They get shot."

"No, I'm not any of those things," Lane said.

"You got an outlaw's eyes, like looking into a nest of vipers, and you got a gunman's hands. Look at them, as well kept as a woman's, clean fingernails an' all. You've never done an honest day's work in your life."

"A man doesn't need hard hands to watch birds."

"Is that a fact? But around these parts he needs a hard head, as you discovered."

"You go to hell." Lane groaned and placed his palm on his forehead. "Damn you, old man. I think you scrambled my brains."

"Sonny, you don't have any brains to scramble. All the outlaws I've known were as dumb as snubbin' posts." He motioned with the Henry. "On your feet. I'm taking you to Mrs. Kerrigan, and you got some explaining to do."

Lane stood, a tall, loose-geared man dressed in dusty range clothes. His boots and gunbelt were of good quality, and a silver watch chain crossed his flat belly. He looked lean and dangerous, and Dancer did not take any chances with him as they left the rise and walked to the house.

CHAPTER TWENTY-FOUR

"By the cut of your jib you ain't a puncher," Frank Cobb said. "So, what the hell are you?"

"A spy," Gabe Dancer said. "That's what he is."

"I'm asking him," Frank said.

"Go to hell," Archie Lane said.

"What do they call you?"

"John Smith."

"Why the field glasses?" Frank said.

"Like I told the crazy old coot, I'm a birdwatcher," Lane said.

"From where?" Frank said.

Lane's eyes moved rapidly, as though they were trying to escape their sockets. Finally, he said, "Deming."

"You came all the way from the New Mexico Territory to watch birds on Kerrigan range?" Frank said.

"Yeah. All the way."

Lane's arms were stretched above his head, his wrists tied to a stable beam. Adding to his discomfort, he'd been lifted just high enough so that he was forced to stand on tiptoe, painful for a man wearing hand-sewn boots made on a narrow last.

"Boss, you want me to beat the truth out of him?" Shorty Hawkins said, slamming his fist into his palm. He looked aggressive and angry.

"It might come to that, Shorty," Frank said. Then, "Smith, you ever heard of a man in the territory by the name of Blade Koenig?"

"Hell, I bet his name ain't Smith," said a puncher, one of the eight crammed into the barn to watch the fun.

"Smith will do for now," Frank said. "Answer me, have you heard of Blade Koenig?"

"I don't know the man," Lane said. "Never heard of him."

"You're from Deming, but you never heard of Blade Koenig, the biggest rancher in that part of the New Mexico Territory?"

"No. Never even heard the man's name mentioned."

"You're lying to me, Smith," Frank said. "Somebody sent you to scout this ranch. What's his name?"

"I told you. I was birdwatching," Lane said.

"Frank, that's enough." Kate stood in the doorway, listening to Frank's interrogation and realizing it was going nowhere. "I'll get the truth out of him."

It was time to play her ace—in the stocky, soot-stained form of Marco Salas, the ranch blacksmith. He held a pair of fire tongs that still glowed cherry red from the forge.

"One of you men take down his britches," she said. And then to Marco, "You know what to do. They'll crush easily, and when they're just a pair of cinders they'll drop off. Understand?"

"*Sí, señora*. The tongs are still hot. Squeeze and then they drop off, *esta bien*?"

"*Sí, Marco,* that is right," she said.

Archie Lane's eyes took on the size and sheen of silver dollars. "What the hell are you doing, woman?" he said, his naturally high-pitched voice spiking.

"Me? I'm doing nothing." She nodded at Marco. "He's the one doing."

"Doing what?" Lane squeaked.

"He's going to geld you, castrate you, eunuchize you. Take your pick. I can't abide the sight of blood, so the tongs are better than the knife since they cauterize as they go along and still get the job done."

Lane looked around him wildly and yelled, "Somebody!" Getting no response, he shrieked, "Damn it. Somebody stop her!"

The hard faces of the punchers who saw this man as some kind of threat to the brand stared back at Lane, but nobody made a sound.

Then Dancer said, "Seen a white man gelded one time after he raped an Arapaho woman up in the Nations. But they done the cuttin' with a knife. I never seen it done with fire tongs. Should be a sight to see."

"Should be a thing to hear," Frank Cobb said.

"Mrs. Kerrigan, them tongs will get cold right quick," Dancer said.

"Marco, do your duty," Kate said.

The short, thickset blacksmith nodded and worked the handles of the tongs and their smoking jaws opened and shut with a metallic *chink-chink* sound. He advanced on the horrified Lane and said, "Señor, you are about to suffer a great loss, and for that I am sorry."

Dancer's hoarse whisper cut into the quiet that followed. "Well, I never seen the like."

Kate's breaths came in fast little gasps. She glanced

at Trace, whose face was ashen, and then at Frank, his jaw set as he stared not at Lane or Marco, but directly at Kate. She turned away and did not meet his eyes.

"For the love of God!" Lane roared, his face made terrible by fear.

The tongs were very close, their serrated jaws agape. Marco lifted the pincers closer to his mouth and spat. The hot iron sizzled. All the blacksmith's attention was fixed on Lane's naked loins as he shuffled closer still. "So sorry, señor. I hope you will forgive me . . . afterward."

Archie Lane felt the intense heat of the blue iron. Smelled the smoke. Smelled fear. "My name is Archie Lane and I work for Davis Salt!" It was a hoarse bellow of sheer terror. "Get them damn tongs away from me."

Kate waved Marco off. "Who is Davis Salt and why did he send you here?"

"I forget," Lane said.

"Marco," Kate said.

"To spy on the ranch buildings," Lane yelled. "Salty is an outlaw. Me, him, others, we're all outlaws."

"Why did Salt send you to spy on us?" Kate said, waving the blacksmith to a halt again.

"He plans an attack."

"Why?"

"He's working for someone."

"Who is he working for?"

"I don't know."

"Marco, give Mr. Lane a taste of the fire tongs," Kate said. "Perhaps they will jog his memory."

"No!" Lane yelled. "I remember! I remember! He's working for a feller by the name of Seth Koenig. His pa owns the biggest spread in the New Mexico Territory."

Kate felt a chill. "Seth Koenig hired him to attack my ranch?"

"Yeah, lady. He wants this spread for his ownself, at least that's what I heard."

"What does his father have to say about all this?" she said.

"Blade? He ain't in the picture, near as I can tell."

Kate hesitated a few moments and then said, "A couple of you men cut him down from there. Frank, question him, get him to tell you all he knows." Then, for Lane's benefit, "Marco, you can go now, but I may need you later."

"Anytime, Mrs. Kerrigan," the blacksmith said. He grinned and snapped the jaws of the tongs in Lane's face. "Bandito, I will keep these hot for you."

"Kate, Davis Salt plans to attack us, all right," Frank said. "Lane claims he's recruited around fifty riders, every one of them a named gun. I've heard of Salt. He's made a rep for himself as an outlaw, and he doesn't hire amateurs."

"When?" Surprised that her hand was steady, she poured Frank a whiskey, handed him the glass, and sat in her chair again.

"Soon. Lane says that's all he knows, and I believe him."

"Fifty gunmen, plus the Hellfire hands. We could be facing eighty or ninety riders."

"Seems about right to me, Kate."

"We can't fight that many."

"We can't fight half that many, at least not out in the open."

"What did Lane say about Blade Koenig?"

Frank shook his head. "About Blade, nothing. Lane says Seth is running the show. That's a mystery. I just don't see Blade stepping back and leaving the attack to his worthless son."

Kate adjusted the fall of her dress over her knees, more to gather her thoughts than anything else, but when she finally spoke all she could say was, "Yes, it's odd that, isn't it?"

"Yeah, it is, very strange," Frank said. "Blade is no spring chicken, but he isn't too old to run his ranch, not by a long stretch." The big segundo thought for a moment and then said, "Unless Blade has took sick and is feeling poorly."

"Has taken sick," Kate said. "I can't think of a man more unlikely to come down with a misery than Blade Koenig. When he was here he looked as big and strong as one of those Kodiak bears you read about in the dime novels."

Frank smiled. "Kate, you read dime novels?"

"From time to time I like to read about Bill's adventures."

"Buffalo or Wild?" Frank said, teasing.

"Buffalo Bill, of course. Unfortunately, I missed him in London before he left for Germany."

"We could use his riders. I wish he was here."

"So do I. Koenig and Salt have all those gunmen, Frank. How do we stand up to an army?"

"Well, there's me, Trace, the cook, and the blacksmith, that's four. We held on to eight hands, including one I recalled from the Rio Grande, all of them gun handy, and that makes twelve. If she doesn't leave, Aragon will throw in with us to protect Maria Ana, and we can probably count on Gabe Dancer and his rifle, now he's walking out with Biddy Kelly."

Kate said, "Add me and Mose and we can muster sixteen." She frowned. "The Kerrigan Fusiliers. Not much of a regiment, is it?"

"Well, I guess it all depends how we use it."

"If we use it well, do we have any chance, Frank?"

He drained his whiskey glass and was wishful for more. "Kate, I won't lie to you. Against fifty professional gunmen plus the Hellfire hands? We don't have a hope in hell."

"So it is hopeless. Like trying to argue a point with the grim reaper?"

"That's about the size of it," Frank said.

Kate sat in silence for a while as Frank got himself another drink. When he returned to his chair she'd come to a decision . . . she would swallow her pride, and it was a bitter pill to swallow.

"We can't spare a fighting man, but I'll put Nora on a good horse and have her ride to Hiram Clay and ask for his help. Nora is an excellent rider and a sensible girl."

Frank had to point out the obvious. "It's three days on the trail to the Clay spread, and even if Hiram leaves right away and rides night and day he may not get here in time." He looked into Kate's bleak eyes. "I guess it all depends on Davis Salt's next move."

"We can stand him off, Frank," Kate said. "Can we fortify the bunkhouse and fight from there?"

"Yes, we can. I'll get the hands started on it right away."

"We must make it a fortress."

"Yeah, Kerrigan Castle."

"You don't seem convinced."

"Men who are good with guns can wear us down and keep us penned up until we run out of ammunition and water. I'll do what I can to strengthen the bunkhouse, but it was built for sleeping, not fighting."

"Who is this Salt person?" Kate said. "Does he have a weakness we can exploit?"

Frank's smile was meager, grudging. "You read the Bible, Kate, so believe me when I tell you that Davis Salt is all Four Horsemen of the Apocalypse rolled into one. And if he has a weakness, no one has found it yet."

"Then tonight I'll say a rosary for our protection against such evil."

"Better say two, Kate. We're sure as hell gonna need them."

Nora Andrews was a tall, sunburned girl with brown eyes and dark hair that she habitually wore in a bun. She had returned from London with Kate, taking the place of Kate's lady's maid Flossie, who had gone back east to return to teaching. Aware of the imminent danger facing the Kerrigan ranch, Nora insisted on leaving right away while there was still three hours of daylight left.

"Be careful, Nora," Kate said. "I'll be so worried about you."

"I'll be just fine, Mrs. Kerrigan. I've camped out before, in England of course and in a tent," Nora said as she stepped into the saddle. She wore a man's shirt, hat, and boots and a tan-colored canvas skirt, split for riding, she'd borrowed from Kate. Under her knee a

Winchester was in the boot and tied to the saddle horn a burlap sack that, thanks to Jazmine, carried enough grub to last a strong man a week.

"Wait a moment, *s'il vous plait.*" Maria Ana hurried to Nora and handed her a silver medal on a chain. "Wear this around your neck, *mon enfant.* It's a medal of holy St. Christopher, the patron saint of travelers, and he'll protect you on your long journey."

Nora smiled her thanks and slipped the chain over her head. She looked at the small medal. "Who is he carrying on his shoulders?"

"The Christ child," Mara Ana said.

"Then I'm in good hands," Nora said.

"I'll say prayers for you until you're home safe and sound," Kate said.

The girl smiled. "A St. Christopher medal and prayers . . . what could possibly go wrong?"

"It's wild, empty country out there," Kate said. "Please be very careful."

"Shorty Hawkins taught me to shoot," Nora said. "It bored me at the time, but now I'm glad he took the time to do it."

Kate nodded. "Shorty is good with a rifle." She smiled. "I feel a little better now. Nora, tell Hiram Clay to come on at the gallop. Tell him that time is of the essence."

"Yes, Mrs. Kerrigan, I'll make sure he knows how urgently he's needed."

"I'm sorry I had to ask you to do this," Kate said.

"Don't be sorry. I'm part of the Kerrigan ranch now, and I know where my duty lies."

Kate smiled. "You ride for the brand."

"Yes, I do." Nora raised a hand in farewell, swung

her mare around, and galloped eastward under the fading sun. Behind her for a while she heard hammering as the hands boarded the bunkhouse windows and then there was only the drumbeat of her bay mare's hooves and the rush of the prairie wind past her ears.

Chapter Twenty-Five

This was perfect. Exquisite.

Seth Koenig felt a surge of elation, a moment of unadulterated joy. To kill without any danger to one's self was the dream of every self-respecting murderer. And here it was, right in front of him, the last mistake his pa would make, an error so grievous it would be Blade's passport to hell. Hanging from a peg to the right of the ranch house door was his holstered Colt, a well-worn .44-40, its black gutta-percha handles worn smooth from years of hard use.

Seth smiled to himself. *Dear Daddy, you killed more than your share with that revolver but your killing days are done.*

Concealing his mirth, Seth kept his back to his father as he unbuckled his gunbelt and hung it on another peg, a play for the big man's trust. He composed himself, checked that the tiny vial of poison was in his pocket, and stepped into the parlor. Blade sat in his easy chair, a pair of round reading glasses perched on his nose. He held a pigskin-bound volume of Sir Walter Scott's *Ivanhoe* and seemed to be engrossed in the tale.

He looked up when Seth entered and studied his son with a notable lack of enthusiasm. "You're back early."

Seth nodded. "Yeah, Pa, I left the hands to stack hay so we could talk without interruption."

Blade was surprised. "Then sit. Talk."

Seth pulled up a chair opposite his father and said, "I want to apologize."

"Apologize? Apologize for what?"

"For being a disloyal son and betraying your trust."

"You sound like a goddamned preacher," Blade said. *Ivanhoe* slid, unnoticed, off his knees. "Seth, is this more of your deviltry?"

"Pa, I know it sounds that way, and I realize I've said some pretty awful, hurtful, things to you in the past. My God, Pa, I've even threatened your life. But my conscience troubled me and I've thought things over. Hell, I've even prayed for divine guidance, if you can believe that. Maybe my prayers were answered, because from now on I plan to be, or at least try to be, the son you've always wanted."

"When did you get religion, Seth? Mighty sudden, isn't it?"

"Yeah, I know this is sudden, but I looked in the mirror a couple days ago and realized I didn't like the man staring back at me. Then I thought about you, Pa, and I asked myself if I'd take the bullet for you. Despite everything I may have said to you before, the answer was *yes!* Loud and clear." Seth tried to look sincere, and he succeeded. "Pa, let me love you as a son should." He felt a twinge in his belly. *Oh, God, I want to puke.* "I mean that, Pa. For the first time in my life, I really mean it."

A light gleamed in Blade's eyes that Seth tried and

failed to interpret. Hope? Suspicion? A mix of both? He didn't know.

Then his father solved the mystery.

"Seth, I want to believe you. I want to believe that you've changed, but it's too quick," Blade said. "You're coming on very strong."

"And that's a measure of how I feel, Pa. I'll use the years we have together to prove my love and admiration for you. I'll never stop trying to prove it."

"Seth, what about Caroline Briggs?" Blade said.

"What about her?"

"I want you to stop seeing her."

"I've no desire to spark her any longer, Pa. I want a respectable wife who can provide the grandson you deserve, another Koenig to inherit the Hellfire when we're both gone."

"A grandson? I've never seriously considered having grandchildren."

"I want to make it happen, Pa."

"You and your wife and me taking the kids to church in Deming on Sunday. Is that what you're talking about?"

"Yup, Pa, I sure am. My wife will dress the kids up nice so you'll be proud of them."

"Show them off, huh?"

Seth smiled. "That's what you'll do, for sure."

"I've never done that before."

"I know, but better times are coming. More loving times."

"A new beginning, you mean?"

"That's what I plan. We'll move on to better things, you and me."

Blade was silent, considering what his son had said. He picked up *Ivanhoe* and thumbed through its pages as though trying to find inspiration among all those noble Saxon knights and wicked Norman barons.

Which of them was Seth? Was he Wilfred of Ivanhoe or the cruel and treacherous Sir Reginald Front de Boeuf?

Because his heart dictated what his head would not, Blade chose Ivanhoe. "I want to believe you, son. I feel the need to make everything right between us."

"And you can, Pa. I know it's sudden, but I've changed. I looked in the mirror and saw what a worthless son I've been. From this day onward, I swear, I'll be a credit to you." *I'm lying to you again, Daddy, you disgusting, black-hearted piece of trash.* "Let's be father and son once more, and friends. Above all else, we must be good friends."

Blade Koenig smiled, but the smile fled quickly and left his lips stretched in a grimace. "There's been wrong on both sides, Seth. And, yes, I'm willing to spend my remaining years repairing the damage that's been done. But I have no guarantees."

"You'll try? Give it your all?"

"Yes, Seth, I'll try."

"That's all I wanted to hear. Maybe it's all I ever wanted to hear."

"It's going to take trust, Seth. And trust works both ways."

"And you have mine, Pa. All we need is time."

"Then so be it." Blade smiled. "This is the dawn of a new day."

Seth grinned. "Pa, you've made me very happy." Then the murderer slithered from the loathsome swamp of his being. "I'd say this calls for a drink."

"Sure, it does," Blade said. "I'll get them—son."

"No, sit where you are. I'll get the drinks," Seth said,

his viper eyes glowing. "From now on I take care of you, Pa, remember?"

Blade sat back in his chair and smiled. "Hell, I think I'm going to enjoy this."

"Oh, you will, Pa, you will. Depend on it."

"For many years to come, I hope"

"And I hope so too," Seth said.

Thc art of deccption lies in actions, not words, and he was tiring of all this meaningless prattle to a man he hated. Action demanded he poison Blade and then watch him die like a goggle-eyed trout flopping on a riverbank. And it was so easy, laughably easy, to empty the vial into the glass and pour whiskey on top. Colorless. Odorless. Such a bland agent of death.

"To us and a new beginning," Blade said, hoisting his glass.

"To us," Seth said.

Both men downed their drinks . . . and Blade Koenig began to die.

Oh, Blade knew he was dying all right, and he was aware of who had murdered him. What Seth found strange was that he didn't talk, not a word, not a single curse thrown at his treacherous offspring. He struggled, of course, foamed at the mouth and gritted his teeth against the poison's ravaging agony . . . and another pain that was beyond pain . . . the awful realization that his own son had killed him. He tried to rise from his chair, but could not, falling back with a terrible long, drawn-out sigh.

The whole time, and by Seth's watch it took Blade just under seventeen minutes to die, his grotesquely protruding eyes never left those of his son, staring, accusing, not angry . . . revealing something else . . . regret, perhaps.

Seth thought it all very amusing. He propped his elbows on his knees and leaned forward in his chair, moving closer to watch the fun. At one point, toward the end, around the twelve-minute mark—Seth was holding his watch in his hand, timing the course of the poison—Blade reached out a hand in a pathetic beseeching gesture and Seth slapped it violently aside.

Fourteen minutes . . . Blade groaned and clutched at his belly. His skin was the color of chalk dust scattered on dark blue paper.

Fifteen minutes . . . Seth poured himself a drink, his eyes never leaving his father.

Sixteen minutes . . . Blade had slipped into semiconsciousness. Lucky for him, Seth decided. He was vaguely disappointed that his dear daddy had died so quickly.

Seventeen minutes . . . Blade rattled deep in his throat and his staring eyes closed.

"That's it? It's over?" Seth said to a man who could no longer hear.

He was disappointed. Yeah, Pa's death had come too quickly. He hadn't suffered near enough.

Seth downed his whiskey and poured another. He sat opposite Blade's twisted body and smiled as a welcome thought came to him . . . it was time for a toast. He raised his glass and said aloud, "A toast to Seth Koenig, the new owner of the Hellfire."

He drained his whiskey and then something about his dead father's contorted face made him giggle, and he was still giggling when the hands rode in from the range.

Moving quickly, Seth smashed Blade's glass on the floor as though it had slipped from his hand. Then he staggered to the door and threw it wide. "Oh my God," he yelled to the startled punchers. "I think my pa is dead. I think his heart gave out. I think . . . I think . . ."

The hands rushed into the house and Seth, crocodile tears streaming down his cheeks, stepped aside to let them see the body.

Only Shield, the Pima scout, remained in the yard. He stared at the ranch house, and his face was as cold and stiff as stone.

CHAPTER TWENTY-SIX

"There's no reason for you to stay, Maria Ana," Kate Kerrigan said. "It's my fight, not yours."

The two women, made even more lovely by moonlight, stood outside the front door of the mansion, enjoying the Texas night air. The sky was full of stars, as though God had scattered handfuls of diamonds on black velvet to enhance the beauty of the evening.

Maria Ana smoked a slim cheroot, Toro lying at her feet as had become his habit. Out in the darkness Rodolfo Aragon stood in silence and watched . . . everything. The prairie wind fluttered the silken stuff of the women's nightdresses as though they were a pair of white doves that had just landed after a flight over the moonshined Pecos and back again.

Doña Maria Ana made no answer and Kate tried again. "I think you should go back to your husband. There's too much danger for you in Texas."

Maria Ana let blue cigar smoke trickle in tight spirals from between her parted lips. "You are my friend, Kate, perhaps my only friend. I will not desert you in your time of need."

"You could die. I mean, it's likely."

"Better to die with you than my mad dog of a husband."

"Maria Ana, you don't mean that."

"Mean what? That he's not a mad dog?"

"I don't think he is."

A moment's silence, then, "Kate, I really don't know what I mean."

"Then go to Don Pedro. Leave tomorrow."

"He hates me."

"I'm sure that's not true."

"He's a pig."

Kate smiled. "I'm sure that's not true either."

Maria Ana's face was tranquil. "Perhaps it is true, perhaps it is not. I don't know any longer. I've had many lovers, but none like Don Pedro."

"Leave then, Maria Ana," Kate said. "Your place is with your husband."

The woman shook her head, her raven hair rippling, shining, like an oncoming evening tide. "No, my place is here. I'm a selfish woman, Kate, and I know there are occasions when I say hurtful things that I shouldn't, but for the first time in my life allow me to do the right thing. Allow me to do something . . . noble."

Kate was touched, but found herself at a loss for words.

Maria Ana filled in the blanks for her. "I've arranged for my people to leave for Mexico tomorrow morning. I'm sending them home out of harm's way. They are peons, servants, and farmers, not soldiers, and I see no reason for them to die needlessly. Yolanda has agreed to stay with me. She says I cannot exist without the care of my lady's maid. And, of course, Rodolfo will remain at my side."

"But—"

"There is no but," Maria Ana said. She touched Kate's cheek. "*Ma chère*, how ignoble a thing it would be to desert you now to save my own skin."

"There is nothing I can say that would change your mind?"

"No, Kate. There is nothing."

"Then all I can say is thank you."

Mara Ana tossed away her cigarillo butt and smiled. "And now I must go to my bed." She sighed. "The mattress is lumpy and the room is small, but when visiting one must make do with what one is given, *n'est-ce pas*?"

Kate smiled. When it came to Maria Ana, some things would never change.

Before she went inside Kate felt a chill in the breeze. She stared into the darkness, imagining how dark and lonely it must be where Nora was, the vast grassland around her lit only by the fickle moon.

"My thoughts and prayers are with you, Nora," Kate whispered. "Take care . . . take care."

Nora Andrews' cold camp offered little by way of comfort, and the chilly darkness that closed around her was oppressive. She had unsaddled her horse, laid her Winchester by her side, and spread out her bedroll. The night was quiet, and even the yammering coyotes had fallen silent. Had Nora been more wilderness savvy she may have taken that silence as an omen, but London born and bred she gave it no thought. Wrapped in her blanket she was protected against the worst of the evening cold, helped by a nip now and then from the small flask of brandy Jazmine had included with her food.

While Nora stared at the rising moon and wished for morning, other, sharper eyes were on her, the green eyes of a predator driven by hunger, guided by instincts as old as time.

He was a big cougar, measuring more than nine feet from nose to tail, weighing around two hundred pounds. But he was old, thirteen, elderly for his species in the wild, and he was stiff and slow, slowed further by the bullet lodged in his hindquarters an inch from his spine. The winter before, the bullet had been fired from the rifle of a hunter and although the wound had healed, it still caused him gnawing pain. Younger, stronger males had forced him out of his hunting territory. Killing what he could to survive, he was an outcast, a wanderer . . .

Call him Ishmael.

Her horse warned Nora of danger and she caught her first glimpse of the lion as an amber flame in the darkness. She racked her Winchester, her lifetime—all that had gone before and all her hopes for the future—suddenly compressed into a few terrifying seconds as her existence hung in the balance. The scared mare reared, then turned, and stampeded to the west. Nora's hand dropped to the rifle at her side and she cried out in a sudden paroxysm of an ancient, primitive fear.

The cougar is an ambush killer, and Ishmael threw

aside his cloak of darkness and charged out of the shadows. He ignored the fleeing horse and concentrated on easier prey, the slow, weak human.

Despite his age and the wound that robbed him of fleetness, Ishmael hit Nora with appalling force. A mountain lion kill will often have puncture wounds to the back of the skull or neck, but the cougar attacked the girl head-on and slammed her into the ground as he overshot his target. The impact broke a couple of Nora's ribs on her left side and a slashing claw opened a three-inch gash on her forehead. Ishmael recovered quickly and spun around to renew his attack, snarling, his fanged jaws open wide. Nora screamed in rage and terror and triggered the Winchester. The cougar kept on coming and targeted the girl's neck and jugular. But he was slower as a fan-shaped eruption of blood rose above his head and splashed over Nora's face and shoulders like scarlet paint. The girl rolled to her right, the big cat on top of her, his rank breath hot on her neck. She expected to feel the bite that would tear out her throat, but it never came. Defeated by pain, his left shoulder smashed by Nora's bullet, Ishmael slunk back, growling, reassessing his dangerous prey. Nora got up on one knee, levered the Winchester and at point-blank range fired into the cougar's head. She fired, fired again and again, ran the rifle dry, pumping bullet after bullet into the lion, and above the roar of her bucking rifle her shrieks of rage and defiance shattered the night into a million shards of shattering sound.

Then it was over. The cougar was dead and the night quiet returned.

Nora tossed the Winchester aside, buried her

bloody face in her hands, and sobbed out all the fear and anger and outrage that was inside her. Sometime in the night, she collapsed onto her slide and slept, the dead cougar called Ishmael only a few feet away from her.

The mare was gone, probably back at the ranch by now.

Nora Andrews gave up the search and returned to where she'd killed the lion. In the dawn light, the dead cougar seemed much smaller, its coat ragged, flanks and hindquarters sunken and bony from starvation. It was fear and darkness that had made the animal look bigger. Nora stared at the beast. What was it she'd once heard Frank Cobb say? "Never trust a wolf until he's skun." Well, this wasn't a wolf. It was a mountain lion and as dead as she could make it.

Finding her horse was a lost cause and at a time of crisis when the KK needed all its fighting men close, Nora did not expect a search party to come looking for her. The way to the Clay ranch lay to the east across miles of open country and she had it to do. Kate Kerrigan was depending on her, though right then she'd rather be brushing her mistress's hair than standing in the middle of nowhere binding up her own aching ribs and gashed head with strips torn from her underwear.

Picking up her bedroll, rifle, and grub sack caused Nora considerable pain that didn't lessen as, in the wan light of the aborning sun, she began her trek eastward. On all sides the grasslands stretched away silent and empty, but after a while the birds came out and a jackrabbit bounded away from her and she felt less lonely.

At noon, she stopped to rest and drank sparingly from her canteen and ate a biscuit and a little bacon. She felt groggy from pain, and the cut on her head had begun to bleed again under the makeshift bandage, a thin, red trickle that seeped over her left cheekbone and down to her chin. Almost angrily, Nora dashed the blood aside with the back of her hand and then slowly struggled to her feet and resumed her travel. Riding boots are not made for walking, and every step became its own little ordeal, but she walked on . . . and on . . .

When darkness fell, Nora gratefully sought her blankets. Made wary by the lion attack, she nonetheless slept soundly with her Winchester by her side.

The moon was at its highest point in the sky when a young pronghorn stepped within a few feet of where the woman lay and raised a questioning nose. The little animal smelled blood on the wind and trotted silently away. Nora stirred and said something in her sleep. Her eyes fluttered open, but she saw only moonlit darkness and there was no sound but the soft whisper of the wind in the grass.

She closed her eyes and slept again.

Chapter Twenty-seven

Sleepless, Kate Kerrigan stood at her open bedroom window and stared into the night. Somewhere out there, alone and perhaps scared, Nora Andrews was dealing with a wild land she was not equipped to handle. A city girl from a good but impoverished family, it had been her ambition to enter service and become a lady's maid in Queen Victoria's household. But she was working as a hotel chambermaid when she had agreed to travel to Texas with Kate at the queen's request. Nora could be stiff as a whale-boned corset at times and somewhat prim, but Kate adored her, and now she waited and worried.

Then a tap at the door brought her the bad news she feared.

"Nora's hoss came in." Frank read Kate's concerned face and said, "Kate, just the hoss, no saddle."

Distraught, Kate couldn't find the words. "Frank . . ."

"Something happened and the mare ran," Frank said.

"But . . . but what?"

"I have no way of knowing. For what it's worth, the mare isn't hurt."

"We have to go after her."

Frank waited a few moments before he spoke again. "Kate, as it is I don't have enough men to defend the ranch. We'll make our stand from the bunkhouse and hope we kill enough of Seth Koenig's men to encourage them to leave. Our chances of pulling that off are slim to none and slim is already saddling up to leave town. I can't weaken us further by sending someone after Nora." Then, his face hard. "Like the rest of us, she'll have to take her chances."

"Then I'll go." As soon as she uttered those words, Kate knew she didn't mean them. "No, I won't. My place is here."

"Seems like," Frank said, just those words, spoken small and quiet.

Then, in a desperate bid to do something, Kate said, "I could send out another maid."

Frank shook his head. "I need all of them as rifle loaders and I'm sure one or two of them know how to shoot. Jasmine Salas knows how for sure."

"Yes, she does and so do I."

"Yes, you shoot good. You can take care of yourself in a fight."

"Frank, I'm so worried I don't know what I'm saying."

"We're all worried."

"Frank, suppose Nora is hurt, lying out there on the range with a broken leg or something?"

"Suppose she is? Suppose she isn't? Kate, suppose we can't hold the bunkhouse? Suppose Salt's boys torch the place and we're forced out into the open? Suppose we can't make a stand against his numbers? Suppose we're all dead and Seth Koenig is the new owner of the KK ranch?" Frank was slightly angry. "Right at this moment I can suppose a lot of things, but supposing a maid has a broken leg ain't one of them."

"Frank, you're yelling at me," Kate said, a frown gathering on her face.

"I am?" he looked startled. "I didn't mean to yell."

"Well, you're yelling."

His shoulders slumped. "Sorry. I have a lot on my mind right now."

"We all have," Kate said. "I'll say a prayer tonight and ask the Holy Trinity to help you control your temper."

He smiled. "And while you're at it, ask for fifty Texas Rangers. We could use them."

"Yes, that would be a worthy miracle indeed," Kate said.

"That's what we need, a miracle, but miracles don't happen with any regularity in West Texas, at least not on the open range."

"Then I'll pray for one. No, for two, one for us and one for Nora."

Frank's face softened. "Kate, I like Nora too. She's a fine girl, and she's got sand. If anyone can make it to Hiram Clay's spread she can."

"On foot and alone?"

Frank nodded. "Yeah, if that's what it takes."

"Then let's hope and pray she gets there on time. Frank, I'm going back to bed. Come for me after breakfast. I want to inspect our defenses and gauge the mood of the men."

"The men will stand. I told them that anyone who wanted to leave could, and no hard feelings. Nobody took me up on the offer, including Gabe Dancer."

"Doña Maria Ana says she'll stick."

"Good, I can use Aragon's gun." Frank gazed at Kate, his expression questioning. "How's the shoulder?"

"Fine. Much better, thank you."

"Kate, what do you see?"

"See? I don't understand."

"That gift of second sight you say all Irish women have, what does it tell you?"

"I can see nothing, Frank. Our future is a blank to me."

"Is that a good thing, or bad?"

Kate shook her head. "I don't know, Frank. I really don't know. What about you, Frank? What do you see?"

"We'll stand, Kate. Make a fight of it."

She knew that was no answer at all.

The dawn light washed away the dark shadows from the buildings and corrals around the Kerrigan mansion and the jays, quarreling already, fluttered in the trees. Over by the cookhouse Maria Ana's dog Toro crawled from under a parked wagon and yawned and stretched, making a concave arc of his back. The hands had eaten breakfast and were already saddling up for another day of hay stacking, but all wore belted guns and carried rifles. There was none of the early morning joshing that usually accompanied such occasions.

Frank waited until Trace rode out with the punchers before he crossed the yard in front of the house and knocked on the door. Kate opened the door herself. Instead of her usual morning dress she wore boots and a skirt, shirt, and vest. Around her hips she had buckled on a cartridge belt and holstered Colt. Her red hair was tied back with a green ribbon and as always Frank wondered at how lovely she was, even when her only beauty aids were soap and water.

He smiled. "Ready to inspect Fortress Kerrigan, General?"

Despite her worries, Kate laughed. "Right now I wish I was a general, like Ulysses S. Grant maybe."

"I'm sure you mean to say Robert E. Lee."

"Of course, I did," Kate said, putting on a show of penitence. Then, "The only problem is that Lee was the one who lost."

Frank grinned. "Lee didn't lose, Kate. It was the noble cause that was lost."

"Then I must be Grant. I don't want anything to do with lost causes."

Frank gave Kate his arm. "Then shall we proceed, General Grant?"

He and the hands had indeed turned the bunkhouse into a fortress. The windows were boarded and cut for rifle ports and the inside of the building's only door to the north was fitted with iron brackets to accommodate a hefty timber beam. The bunks had been dragged outside to clear the floor for the riflemen and boxes of ammunition were strategically placed at each firing station. Drops of water fell from the ceiling, the result of the efforts of a cowboy bucket brigade that had damped down the shingle roof as a precaution against fire. The place seemed impregnable and Kate complimented Frank on his efforts.

"I reckon we can hold off Salt and his gunmen until Hiram Clay and his riders get here," Frank said.

"So long as they come on at the gallop and don't stop for a picnic on the way."

"I'm sure that won't happen. Hiram will see himself as a knight in shining armor riding to my rescue. Now what about the cookhouse?"

A solid wall separated the cookhouse from the rest of the building, and Tom Ogilvy's only orders were to douse the stove at the first sign of trouble and then get the hell out of there . . . and take the cat.

"Mr. Ogilvy, the hands have done so well I'd like them to have a glass of wine with supper tonight," Kate said. "Jazmine will give you the key to the cellar."

For a moment, the cook seemed perplexed. "Beggin' your pardon, Mrs. Kerrigan, what kind of wine do I serve with sonofabitch stew?"

"Red, of course, you damned biscuit-roller." This from Gabe Dancer, who stood at the cookhouse door, his Henry rifle across his chest. "And what is your dessert tonight, to put it politely?"

"Vinegar pie, if'n it's any business of your'n," Ogilvy said.

"It is, if I got to eat the stuff. Then red will do just fine. The punchers won't care," Dancer said.

Ogilvy said to Kate, "I'll take care of it, ma'am."

"And I'll come with you," Dancer said. "I'll make sure you don't serve a fine Cabernet Sauvignon to a bunch of waddies who've drunk so much rotgut their taste buds were burned out by the time they reached adulthood."

"I know my wines," Ogilvy said.

"No, you don't," Dancer said. "But I'll teach you.'

The cook bristled. "I don't need—"

"I'm sure you will choose the right wine for tonight, Mr. Ogilvy," Kate said.

"And you can help, Mr. Dancer. Mr. Ogilvy, Mr. Dancer spent a lot of time in France, you know, and dined in some fine restaurants."

"And I spent a lot of time in Deadwood, Mrs. Kerrigan," the cook said. "There was more fine wine poured down throats in that town than ever was in Paris."

Dancer was delighted. "Mr. Ogilvy, that is crackerjack! Truer words was never spoke by mortal man. Why, I mind the time when Al Swearengen, the owner of the Gem Variety Theater, wait . . . you recollect him?"

"I'll say," Ogilvy said. "He was a rum one, was Al."

"Well, I mind when he paid five hundred dollars for a jeroboam of Don Pérignon that him and an actress drank in one night. Al was fine the next day, but it took the actress a week to sober up, or so they say."

Ogilvy beamed. "Sure, I remember that. The actress's name was Lucy Lacy and she was only as good as she needed to be."

Dancer put down his rifle, cackled, and slapped his thigh. "Yes, that was the lady! Hey, do you mind the time Wild Bill got drunk and him and Lucy . . ."

Kate and Frank made their escape and then Frank said, "I think those two will come to some agreement about the wine, don't you?"

"I'm sure of it, and if I'm not mistaken, they'll drink more than their share while they're at it."

When Trace and the hands came back to the ranch at dusk, Frank told them that no more hay would be cut and that starting tomorrow they would stand to arms.

Amid distant cheers as Ogilvy informed the punchers about the supper wine, Trace took Frank aside. "You think the attack will come soon?"

"It could come at any time. I'll let the boys have their fun tonight and at first light I'll send out scouts."

"How much warning will we get?" Trace said, his handsome young face troubled.

"Not much. We can't go out too far from the ranch or our scouts will ride in with Salt and his men right on their heels. I think a couple of the young hands with good eyes and field glasses could give us an hour."

"An hour? It's not much, is it?"

"No, it's not. But it's all we got."

"I've got far-seeing eyes. I'll play scout."

"No, Trace, you're too good with a gun. I need you in the bunkhouse when the ball opens."

"I'll make sure I'm back in time, Frank. Don't worry. When the shooting starts, I'll be here."

"You're right. I forgot that you've got eyes like a hawk. Just make sure you light a shuck back here the moment you spot Salt and his boys."

"You can depend on that."

"Take Chas Minor with you. He sees real good."

"Frank, how about we get Ma and the rest of the women away from the ranch? Maybe head them south to the river."

"Are you going to tell them to leave?"

Trace thought about that and shook his head. "They won't go, will they?"

"Not a chance. Kate won't leave and if she doesn't go, neither will the other women."

"Well let's hope that Hiram Clay gets here on time," Trace said. "That's all I can say."

Frank nodded, his eyes bleak. "Yeah, seems like we're all depending on Hiram Clay."

CHAPTER TWENTY-EIGHT

Seth Koenig buried his father at dusk . . . by lantern light . . . and in unseemly haste. It amused him to do so, reflecting as it did the dark hatred he'd harbored for the man.

Only one thing spoiled his fun, the constant chant of the damned Pima from somewhere out in the gloom.

The superstitious hands standing around the open grave were uneasy. Bathed in the orange glow of the lamps, they stood head-bowed and stone-faced and listened to the eerie rise and fall of the Indian's voice as he chanted Blade's death song. The punchers shared a single thought—no good could come of this.

Blade lay in a hastily hammered-together pine coffin and he was very still. As one of the hands whispered to the man standing beside him, only the dead lie without motion.

There was no preacher.

A puncher named Brown, whose father was a deacon, said the words, as much as he remembered them. "'Yea, though I walk through the valley of the shadow of death, I will fear no evil . . .'"

Lost in the shadows, the Pima's wild death song rose to a crescendo and echoed among the Hermanas foothills and chilled the punchers to the marrow of their bones.

"'. . . for thou art with me; thy rod and thy staff they comfort me.'" Brown's young voice faltered . . . weakened . . . choked to a halt.

And so too did the Pima's song . . . followed by a long, wailing scream—an animal cry of grief and loss that ripped apart the fabric of the evening and curdled the blood of every man at the graveside.

After a long silence, Seth Koenig said, "All right, boys. Let's get him in the ground."

"Damned wolves," a puncher said, his head cocked, listening into the gathering night. "Why the hell are they howling so close?"

"They know there's a burying," another puncher said.

"Maybe ol' Blade's ghost is among them," Brown said. "It's the kind of thing he'd do. Run with the wolves."

Then, a startled cry. "My God, look!" One of the hands, his face as pale as death, pointed to the coffin where the body of Blade Koenig . . . writhed . . .

The hair on the back of Seth's neck rose and his eyes threatened to jump right out of his head. Damn Ezora Chabert! The old bitch's poison hadn't worked. It didn't kill Blade . . . and it was wearing off!

The punchers raised lanterns above their heads and crowded around the coffin, light spilling over Blade's convulsing body like a yellow stain.

"Look at his face!" a puncher yelled. "My God, look at his face!"

The ranch hand had noticed what Seth had already seen, his father's ashen features contorted in agony. An owl glided over the grave on silent wings and startled the mourners. Yet another bad omen.

"He's dead!" Seth squealed. "Damn it. I watched him die."

"Well, he ain't dead now," Brown said.

"Get him out of there!" a puncher yelled.

"No!" Seth shrieked. "He's dead!"

Another puncher. "He ain't dead! He's alive."

And yet another, "Hell, the boss looks mighty sick, but he's still kicking."

Blade's huge body arched, twisted, and convulsed in the narrow confines of the coffin.

Seth felt his gorge rise. Oh, my God, his eyes are open! And somebody had called him the boss!

"Git the hell away from there!" Seth yelled. "He's dead, I tell you. Dead . . . dead . . . dead . . . I seen him die, damn it."

The hands, hard-bitten and tough though they were, harbored growing suspicions.

"No, Seth, your pa is alive," one said.

And then from Brown, "Hallelujah! Mr. Koenig has come back from the grave! The Lord be praised."

Several of the punchers got ready to lift Blade from the coffin. He was a big, heavy man and not easy to move.

Seth yelled his disgust. "He's come back from the gates of hell!" He pulled his Colt. "Get out of my way!"

A few quick steps took Seth to the coffin. He looked briefly at his father. Blade was fully conscious of what was happening, and he stared at his son, his terrified, pain-filled eyes accusing. Seth's bullet smashed neatly between those eyes and closed them forever.

"Get him into the ground! Now!" Seth yelled. "Bury the son of a bitch!"

The hands were stunned into immobility.

Then Brown stepped forward and yelled in Seth's face, "You murdered him!"

Frantic, an unreasonable anger spiking at him, Seth slammed his Colt into the side of the young puncher's head. The man groaned and fell beside the yawning grave.

Seth waved his gun. "Anybody else want to say I murdered him? I'll kill the next man who accuses me. He was dead, I tell you. The demons dragged him back from the pit, made his body move like he was a living person."

The punchers drew back, their faces drawn, unable to deal with what had just happened. But one, a big man braver than the rest with a reputation as a shootist, spoke for the other two dozen when he said, "Bury him yourself. We're done with you."

A couple men helped the groggy Brown to his feet and as one the Hellfire hands turned and walked to their horses.

Seth Koenig was incensed, his face black with anger, "Get back here, all of you! I'll tell you when you're through." When not a head turned in his direction he yelled, "All right. Damn you, you're all fired, every man jack of you. You're done at the Hellfire."

In silence the punchers mounted and in silence they rode away.

* * *

Blade Koenig was a big man, and he made a heavy corpse.

No matter how Seth tried to shove the coffin into the grave, he failed. Finally, he laid on his back and pushed with his booted feet. The pine coffin moved a couple inches. He tried again, breathing hard, sweat beading his forehead. A few more inches and then the momentum stopped.

Angry now, Seth yelled, "Move, damn you. Move."

The evening shaded into darkness, and the half-dozen lanterns at the graveside guttered in the rising breeze and became shifting orbs of amber light. A light rain pattered on the ground and fell on two up-turned human faces, one dead, contorted by its last agony, the other equally distorted, but by rage.

Seth removed his hat and wiped his sweaty brow with his sleeve, thinking. And then . . . yes, the feet would be lighter, much lighter than the head and shoulders. He'd push the damned coffin from there.

The rain cool on his face, Seth again put his boots against the rough timber of the coffin and shoved. It slid to the edge of the grave and teetered for several long seconds before sliding into the hole. But all was not well. The coffin lay at a right angle with Blade's feet at the bottom of the grave but his head and shoulders only six inches below ground level.

"Close enough, Daddy." Seth grinned, but his grin slipped when he saw Blade's terrible face. Even in death the eyes were still accusing. Seth's first few shovelfuls of dirt took care of that. He threw them directly into Blade's ugly mug and laughed, verging on hysteria while he was doing it.

* * *

Seth Koenig mounted his horse in a drizzling rain. Dirt covered Blade's body. Seth had thrown the lanterns in with the corpse. It was a waste of money, he knew, but he didn't feel like carrying them back to the Hellfire. So, the dead man's feet lay deep in the earth, but the other end of him was close to the surface. That didn't trouble Seth in the slightest. Situated as it was in the Hermanas foothills it was unlikely that a passing rider would come anywhere near the grave. The shallow burial was good enough, certainly good enough for Blade Koenig.

Despite the rain, the new owner of the Hellfire was as lighthearted as a pig in a peach orchard as he rode through darkness toward his ranch. He even sang a few versus of "Poor Sally Ann" at the top of his lungs just to hear the giddy happiness in his own voice.

Perhaps if he'd known what awaited him at the Hellfire, he would not have been so blithesome.

Chapter Twenty-nine

"We're riding out, Ma, me and Chas Minor," Trace said.

Kate was so surprised that she didn't correct her son's grammar. "But it's dark. Frank said he'd send out scouts at first light."

"I've seen a ranch house attacked at night, boss," Minor said. "When I was a younker I seen the Pinkertons do it when I rode for a spell with Jesse and Frank and them."

It was Kate's night to be surprised. "Chas, I never knew you were once an outlaw."

The kid smiled. "I wasn't much of one, ma'am. I was a horse holder and never rose any higher in the bank-robbing profession. Then one time Jesse told me, 'The Yankees denied me the right to live the life I believed in, so I'd no choice but to become an outlaw. Boy, you ain't got that reason, so get out of this business while you still can.'"

"And you took his advice?" Kate said.

"I sure did, ma'am. Jesse was an advising man and he never steered anybody wrong."

"Well, I'm glad you took his advice."

Minor smiled. "So am I."

Trace said, "Chas, with the hard times about to come down, maybe you'da been better off staying with Jesse."

Minor shook his head. "No sir. I ride for the brand and my place is right here."

Kate was touched. "I'm glad to hear you say that, Chas. Thank you."

"It weren't nothing, boss. I'm just saying things as I see them."

Kate rose from her chair and looked out the parlor window. "You have good horses?"

Trace seemed puzzled. "I'm riding the gray and Chas saddled Rat's Ass."

"The paint's name is Snip, Trace. I wish you would use it. You have field glasses? There are good ship's telescopes in the gun room, if you'd like to take one of those. And what about food. Did Jazmine—"

"Ma, you're trying to keep us here, aren't you?"

Without turning Kate nodded. "Yes, I am." She was silent for a while and then said, "I'm trying to keep my son with me just a little longer."

"Boss, Trace will be fine," Chas Minor said. "I'll keep an eye on him."

"Ma, I'm all grown up. I don't need Chas to keep an eye on me. I'm no longer a boy, so let me be a man."

Kate turned. "I know. I'm being foolish. But you could be riding into danger."

"Like Chas said, I ride for the brand." Trace said to Minor, "It's time to go."

"Wait, Trace," Kate said. "I have something to tell you."

Trace smiled, the reckless, confident smile of youth. "Will it take long?"

"No, not long," Kate said. "Trace, when Hiram Clay was visiting I could've asked him for help. His riders could be here now, and maybe the Rangers."

"Ma, the Kerrigans stand on their own two feet and ask help from no one. You've been telling me that since you tried to get me into velvet knee britches."

"And now my Kerrigan pride could get us all killed," Kate said.

"Begging your pardon for speaking out of turn, ma'am," Minor said. "But here in West Texas a man is expected to handle his own problems, and that goes for a woman as well. I mean, where does it end? The next time there's a drought or the KK has a problem with rustlers, do we run to Hiram Clay for help? No, ma'am, we don't. We handle them things ourselves."

Kate's smile was faint. "I've already sent to Hiram Clay for help."

"I know, ma'am, but meantime we're taking care of our own problem. If Mr. Clay gets here in time, we'll thank him kindly for his assistance. If he doesn't get here in time, well, we don't have to thank nobody because by then we'll have them outlaws licked anyhow." Minor blushed. "Boss, I ain't much for speechifying, and for me that was a long spell of talking, but I meant every word of it."

"I couldn't have said better myself, Chas," Trace said. "Now, Ma, will you give us the road?"

"Right now, at this very minute, we're standing on our own two feet, aren't we?" Kate said.

"Yup, on our own two feet, Ma. And standing mighty tall."

Kate smiled. "Then go, and take care of business."

"On our way, boss," Chas Minor said, grinning.

Only when her son and Chas Minor were gone, the hoofbeats of their horses fading into the distance, did Kate sit in her chair again and let the worry that nagged at her show in her face.

The big brindle longhorn that stared through the gloom at Nora Andrews showed a great deal of curiosity but no aggression. Exhausted, the girl didn't care much either way. All she wanted was sleep, hours of uninterrupted slumber until she woke with the dawn. Her head hurting, her ribs hurting worse, she spread her blanket roll and collapsed on top of it. The last thing she heard before she fell into deep slumber was the steady sound of the longhorn cropping grass.

When the first light of morning woke her, Nora sat up and looked around. The longhorn was gone. As far as her eyes could see, the rangeland was an immense panorama of emptiness without movement or sound, an achingly lonely land that ofttimes made prairie wives stand under the vast blue bowl of the unchanging sky and scream and scream until they could scream no longer.

Nora didn't have the strength nor the will to scream.

She struggled to her feet, ate a breakfast of a swig of wine and a few bites from a roast beef sandwich that was rapidly going stale, and then picked up her bedroll and rifle. She had slept reasonably well, though the night had been cold, but she felt terrible, weakened by loss of blood from the gash on her head and the constant pain in her ribs. But Kate was depending on her and the fate of the KK was in her hands so she had it to do.

Nora put one foot in front of the other and started walking again.

CHAPTER THIRTY

Seth Koenig saw the red glow in the night sky long before he noticed the acrid smell of burning in the night air. Despite the darkness, he hit Hellfire Pass at a dead run, raging at the treachery of the hands. Damn them! Damn them all! They'd burned him out! How else to explain the scarlet-bellied clouds above the very spot where the ranch house stood.

And it was as he'd feared.

Everything was aflame.

The house, the barn, even the outbuildings had been torched.

Silhouetted by fire, he stood in the open and watched his property burn. Everything he had worked for, killed for, was going up in smoke. Enraged, he vowed his revenge. He knew them all—their names, their faces—and he'd hunt them down one by one until he'd killed them all.

Wrapped in a cloak of self-love, what Seth didn't understand, that night or any other, was the depth of feeling the Hellfire hands had for Blade. They'd respected the man for his strength, feared him for his quick hands and fast gun, but loved him because no matter how rich and powerful he became, Blade Koenig remained one of them. He cared about the men who rode for him, paid them top wages, and looked after their welfare almost as a father to his many sons. Nor did Seth realize that to a man, the Hellfire hands considered him a bully and a braggart, a rapist who did not deserve to be the treacherous offspring of a much better man.

Burning the ranch had been a matter of spite, that and the fact that the punchers could not stand by and let Seth inherit what he'd gained by murder. They knew because of his ill-gotten gains he had the money to rebuild the place, but were content that they'd sent him a message written in fire that they held him in the deepest contempt.

Seth saw the burning as vandalism, nothing more, oblivious of the hatred that had spilled each can of coal oil and lit every match.

By dawn, the fire had burned itself out and all that remained of the house and the other buildings were ashes and a few blackened timbers. As he kicked through the rubble Seth told himself that there was no real need to rebuild a place that held so many bad memories for him. He had a house, a fine house, waiting for him. The Kerrigan place would suit him down to the ground and, if everything panned out the way he planned it, he would have the beautiful widow in his bed. Kate Kerrigan was a wildcat, but she was the kind to succumb to the strength and masculine charm of a man like himself. Oh, she might fight him at first, but a few encounters with the back of his hand would soon cure her of that.

Seth grinned, looking on the bright side. Today was the dawn of a new era. West Texas would be his permanent home, but he'd use the Hellfire to graze part of his herd. Very soon he'd be rich beyond his wildest dreams, live in a fancy mansion, and have an even fancier woman for mattress time. Nothing could stand in his way.

But first things first.

Davis Salt and his boys were still camped south of Deming. He'd ride there and tell the outlaw it was time to attack the Kerrigan ranch. So what if Salt didn't yet have the fifty men he needed? They could take the KK with half that number . . . if the rubes even put up a fight. He'd ridden right up to Kate Kerrigan's doorstep without a challenge before and he could do it again.

Such pleasant thoughts gave Seth an appetite. If he left right away, he reckoned he could be with Davis in time for lunch. He walked to his tired horse, and then froze, his entire body pinned in place.

Shield, the damned Pima, stood about fifty yards away, holding a Winchester across his chest, the stock decorated with brass studs. The Indian had stripped to a breechcloth, knee-high moccasins, and a red headband. The top half of his face was painted black, a sign of mourning, and his hair had been pulled back for war.

A spasm of fright spiked at Seth Koenig. The Pima didn't look human, more like an avenging spirit summoned from some terrifying Indian netherworld. Fear gave Seth a voice. "What the hell do you want?"

The Pima made no answer. Stared, unblinking, flaying Seth alive with his knife-edge eyes.

"Damn you!" Seth screamed. "Damn all of you!" He drew and fired. A miss. He fired again and then lowered his gun.

The Pima was gone . . . he'd been shooting at a phantom. Seth cursed. No, not a phantom. A damned Indian made of flesh, bone, and blood like himself. He holstered his gun and swung into the saddle. His Colt had failed him, but the Winchester would not. He slid the rifle from the boot, set spurs to his horse, and charged the spot where he'd last seen the Pima. It was open ground relieved from barrenness by a few wild oak and soapberry. Seth drew rein and dusted the entire area with shot after shot, levering the Winchester from his shoulder. He cursed wildly, damning the Indian and every breath he took, and when he lowered the rifle from his shoulder there was nothing to show for his efforts but a thick, greasy drift of gun smoke.

"Come out, damn you," Seth yelled. "Show yourself and fight like a man."

The silence mocked him, ridiculed his fear.

Seth grimaced and shoved the Winchester back into the boot. What was it an old-timer had once told him? *When an Indian don't want to be found, you won't find him.* Well, damn the Pima. Their paths would cross again. . . . "And I'll kill you," Seth roared. "You hear me, redskin? I'll kill you."

All right. He had to get away from there, be with white men again. Davis Salt would welcome him and they'd make a plan, maybe share a bottle and talk about cathouses and the whores they'd used and abused.

Seth swung his horse, took one last glance at the ruin of the Hellfire ranch house, and then pushed his mount into a canter. There were better days ahead, and that certain knowledge made him smile.

Seth Koenig was himself again.

Chapter Thirty-One

"I saw the parlor light was on and knew you were not in bed," Maria Ana said. She wore a dressing gown and slippers.

"I can't sleep," Kate said.

"Me neither."

"Were you thinking about Don Carlos?"

"No. He's a pig and I've forgotten he even exists." Maria Ana stepped to the drinks cart, moving like a goddess in a sheath of black silk. "Sherry?"

"Please," Kate said.

Maria Ana brought the drinks and sat in the chair opposite Kate. A log fire crackled between them. "Kate, are you afraid?"

"Yes, I think so. I'm afraid for Nora, for Trace, Frank . . . all of them."

Maria Ana smiled. "I thought you never got scared."

Kate's smile matched the doña's for beauty. "I've been afraid before."

"But not recently."

"Very recently. During my trip to London."

"I'd like to hear about that."

"All I'd do is bore you."

"Kate, nothing you do bores me," Maria Ana said. "Neither of us can sleep, so the night is young. Tell me about London. A pleasant enough city if it wasn't for the rain, fog, and Englishmen." She shivered. "I've always considered an Englishman too cold and aloof to take as a lover. Ah well, enough of that. I'm all ears, so now to your story, *ma chère.*"

A walnut box lay on top of a side table by Kate's chair. She opened the lid and took out the British Bulldog revolver. "Queen Victoria gave me this."

"How kind of her, though one of the royal diamond necklaces would have been kinder still," Maria Ana said.

"She said it was for my protection when I got back to Texas. But what the queen says she doesn't necessarily mean. At heart, Victoria is a politician, and when politicians talk, their real agenda is often hidden, the wheel within the wheel."

"Just so," Maria Ana. "Please continue."

"The evening of the day I met the queen I was visited in my hotel by a strange little man who introduced himself as Detective Chief Inspector Marmaduke Hawkes of Scotland Yard."

"Apart from his name, in what way was he strange?"

"Small, slender, wearing an enormous caped coat with sleeves that came over his knuckles. He had watery blue eyes, shaggy brows, and his face was the color of a fish's belly."

"La, la, a fish's belly no less," Maria Ana said. "I'm intrigued already."

"And a huge nose," Kate said. "When I told him that he might remove his coat, he wore a pale green ditto suit, quite new, and neat little brown boots with elastic sides. He looked more like a man who'd been a bank clerk for thirty years than a Scotland Yard detective."

"Did the queen send him to arrest you?"

"No, nothing like that. Believe me, the queen's plan was for something much worse."

"She wanted a favor from you?"

"You could call it that, I suppose. But it was a mighty big favor. She was asking me to lay my life on the line to catch a terrifying killer."

"The policemen told you this?"

"He did."

"And you said no, of course."

"I said I'd listen to what the detective had to say." As Kate told the story, she remembered every word the detective had said.

"Mrs. Kerrigan, or since we may be working together, may I call you Kate?

"I may? Thank you. And you can call me Marmaduke. May I smoke, Kate? I am much addicted to my pipe.

"Thank you again.

"Now perhaps you recall reading in today's newspaper that there has been a second bloody murder of a prostitute in the city's Whitechapel district.

"Whitechapel? It's in the city's East End, a vile morass of poverty, squalor, violence, and crime, where those lucky enough to find a bed sleep with rats and fleas and those not so lucky lie down in the foggy, filthy streets. Drunkenness and prostitution are everywhere and murder is a nightly occurrence. I know what you're thinking, Kate. With so much violence why should Her Royal Majesty concern herself with the deaths of two nameless prostitutes? The answer is a succinct

one—the Irish. Whitechapel has always been a hotbed of Irish unrest, rebels who would see an Ireland free of British rule. A dashed impertinence, if you ask me.

"Yes, I quite understand your feelings on the matter, Mrs. Kerrigan, and I will not press you on the subject. But therein lies the problem. Both murdered women were redheaded Irish girls, and if their murderers are not apprehended, the rebels will claim that Irish lives are of no consequence in Britain and use that as an excuse to riot and perhaps try to overthrow the government. Her Majesty will not allow such a thing to happen.

"Where do you fit in all this, dear lady? That is an excellent question, a wizard of a question, and I will get to the answer presently."

Maria Ana took a sip of sherry and made a sour face. "The detective was . . . how you say? Trying to push you into a corner. Irish girls with red hair indeed. Did he make that up for your benefit?'

"As it turned out, no. The girls were Irish and both were redheads. One was twenty-six and the other had just celebrated her eighteenth birthday."

"*Quelle horreur*! To die so young."

"And both were cut up horribly . . . mutilated almost beyond recognition, Detective Hawkes said."

"My dear Kate, what did he want you to do about it? I'm at a loss."

"He soon told me what he wanted me to do about it."

"So far, Scotland Yard's investigation into the murders has led to one dead end after another, but we do know that two killers were involved, this based on the testimony of one

Annie Spooner, age fifty-three, a known streetwalker. Spooner remembered that on the night Mary Collins was murdered—the younger victim—she saw her get into a carriage with two men and drive away. Spooner never saw Collins again after that night.

"The answer to your question is we don't know if the two men were the murderers or not, but right now it's the only lead we have. And please call me Marmaduke. Oh, and one thing more . . . Kate. Spooner's eyesight is not of the best, but she says she's sure that a cloak was thrown over the carriage door. To hide a nobleman's crest, perhaps?

"Yes, I know this grows tedious for you, dear lady, and that you're anxious to dress for dinner, so let me come straight to the point. Do you wish to save the lives of other Irish girls, especially those with red hair?

"Ah, that's the answer I expected, Kate. Why, of course you do. And how can you help? Well, let us go back a little. The queen gave you a parting gift, did she not? Yes, she informed me that it was the British Bulldog revolver. Did she tell you why?

"Oh dear, is that what she said? Of necessity, I fear Her Majesty told you a little fib. The revolver was never intended as a souvenir to take home to the wild Western lands. No, it was to protect you in Whitechapel."

"Pah, the man talked in riddles and was impertinent," Maria Ana said. "I hope at that point you showed him the door."

"No, I was fascinated and I wanted to hear what he said next."

"None of it good, I suspect."

"Well, he beat about the bush for a while and then finally confessed that he wanted me to be a decoy."

"Decoy! What is this word . . . *decoy*?"

"In my case it meant a person used to lure another person or persons into a trap."

Maria Ana was horrified. "I need more sherry!" She brought the decanter to Kate and filled her glass and then her own. "Please don't tell me that what I'm thinking is correct."

Kate smiled. "What are you thinking?"

"That the detective wanted to use you as a . . . decoy . . . to catch the murderer of those young Irish girls."

"He did, but he was obeying orders. The plan was not his."

"Then whose plan was it, for God's sake?"

"It was Queen Victoria's plan and hers alone."

"I don't understand."

"Neither did I at first, then Detective Hawkes explained it to me."

"Kate, the queen thinks very highly of you. She's aware that you own the biggest cattle ranch in Texas, and she admires your courage and derring-do. She asks a favor of you, yes, a favor to Her Majesty, but also to the nation and the empire.

"No, please. No need to be modest. You are a very remarkable woman and a beautiful one, if this old policeman may be so bold. Kate, you are ideally suited to carry out the monumental task the queen asks of you.

"Yes, you're right, I should get directly to the point, and the point is this. As I stated earlier, you can save lives, Kate, perhaps many lives.

"Yes, you just hit the nail on the head, dear lady. As our decoy, you will walk the foggy streets of Whitechapel in the

guise of a common prostitute, your head uncovered, the better to display your wonderful red hair. When the murderer accosts you, and we know he will, you will blow this whistle—as you can see it's regulation police issue—and a score of specially trained police constables hidden within earshot will run to your aid and capture the vile fiend.

"Kate, I can see your hesitancy and I don't blame you. There's no way around it, you will be placing yourself in great danger. Now, it's unlikely, but perhaps we could get someone else to take your place, but she won't have your courage and determination, and her chances of survival would be slim. If the woman was murdered like the others, people would talk, and the press would soon ferret out the story. Her Majesty would be accused of sacrificing the life of a prostitute in a futile attempt to solve a crime that Scotland Yard could not. The repercussions could be fatal for the crown.

"Yes, of course you can carry your revolver and you have the blessing of the Yard to use it to save your life. Since you are an American, I won't say that England needs you, Kate, but I will say that every prostitute in Whitechapel does . . . especially the young Irish girls."

"And that was when you showed him the door," Maria Ana said. "England needs you . . . the rogue."

Kate sipped her sherry and smiled behind the glass. "He had me at saving the lives of young Irish girls."

"Then let the police save them. That's what they're for, is it not?"

"Maria Ana, I was once an Irish girl living in a slum myself. I felt an affinity for those women. I could not turn my backs on those poor creatures and allow more of them to be slaughtered for some perverted maniac's pleasure."

"*Ma chère!* You didn't say yes? Please don't tell me you said yes."

"I did say yes. I told Detective Hawkes I would do it, but not for England, not for the queen, but for the poor Irish lass who could be the next to die."

The fire crackled and the wind sighed around the eaves of the house. Tom-Tom, the house cat, stretched out on the hearth, and red flames reflected in his eyes.

"Now I'm so afraid for you, Kate, *ma chère,*" Maria Ana said. "It's getting late, but I have to know what happened."

Kate smiled. "I led a double life, a tourist by day, a prostitute by night."

"But you didn't, I mean, you didn't really . . . do it?"

"No. Every time I was accosted by a drunken sailor or a sporting gent, there always seemed to be a policeman nearby to question him, search him, and then send him on his way."

"The detective's doing, I suppose?"

"Yes, Hawkes kept an eye on me, at least at first. During the day, I was shown the sights of London by a series of handsome young detectives who never let me out of their sight. It was fun, I will admit. I teased those young men mercilessly."

"And at night? What happened at night?"

"I dirtied my clothes a little, pulled down the neckline of my dress, and assumed my secret identity."

"Kate, do you know that you're clenching your hands so tightly your knuckles are white and you've sipped half a dozen times from an empty glass?" Maria

Ana poured Kate more sherry. "Drink it. It won't do you any harm and it will relax you." She sat again and said, "Well? What happened?"

Kate said, "So far it had been a lark, a little adventure, but on the fourth night all that changed and everything became deadly serious. It was foggy, a fog so dense that the pubs on Hanbury Street lit all the lamps inside to guide revelers to their door. As I'd been instructed, I took up my usual place under a gas lamp at the end of the street. It was cold and damp that night and the cobblestones had a wet sheen. I was close enough to the Eight Bells pub to faintly hear the voices inside, but far enough away that if I cried out for help no one would hear me."

"Oh, *mon enfant*, how horrible for you." Maria Ana leaned forward in her chair, her face eager. "And what happened?"

"After I was there for about thirty minutes I spoke briefly with a prostitute who said her name was Annie Chapman," Kate said. "She looked to be in her early forties, but was probably much younger. 'There will be no business for you tonight, dearie,' she said. 'This cold and fog will keep the gentlemen away.' Annie said she'd hoped to earn a shilling to pay for a bottle of gin and a place to flop. 'But there's not much chance of that, is there, dearie?' My purse was in my pocket, and I gave her two shillings. The poor creature was so grateful she blessed me and kissed my hand."

Maria Ana said, "Yes, the lower classes have novel ways of showing their gratitude. Now please get to the interesting stuff."

"More interesting than I care to remember," Kate said.

"Good. I'm all on edge."

"I'd just heard a steeple clock chime midnight . . . bad things always seem to happen at midnight, don't they?"

"I hadn't noticed, *mon ami.*"

"Well, they do."

"Please go on."

"I heard the horse first, the steady clang, clang, clang of shod hooves on the cobblestones and then a shiny hansom cab emerged from the fog and the coachmen reined it to a halt. For a long time the carriage just stood there, as though I was being studied."

"Hmm . . . you had much to offer," Maria Ana said. "That was the attraction."

"It would seem that way, because after a while the coachman climbed down from his perch. He wore a heavy greatcoat and a top hat, and his face was covered by a muffler. Only his eyes showed. He opened the carriage door and another gentleman stepped out onto the street. He also wore a top hat, but he was exquisitely dressed in evening wear, and his cloak was lined with scarlet silk. He smiled and stepped closer to me, and I saw his face for the first time."

"Was he handsome?"

"No, quite the opposite. His face was long and very pale as though he spent all his time indoors and his eyes were slightly protruding and watery with heavy lids. He had a small cruel mouth with a petulant bottom lip, and at the time I recall that I thought he bore more than a passing resemblance to Queen Victoria herself. He smelled of cologne, cigars, and whiskey, and I thought him a most unhealthy-looking man, though I soon discovered that he was not a man, but a demon in human guise."

"Oh, dear Kate, were you sore afraid?" Maria Ana said. "I know I would have been."

"No, I was not afraid, not at first, but when the coachman joined him and said, 'Stand against the wall and let the gentleman have his fun, Irish Eyes, and he'll give you a shilling.' It was then I saw the blade of a butcher's knife gleam in the gaslight in the hand of the man with the cruel mouth. He grinned at me like a wild animal and then he and the coachman stepped toward me."

"*Mère de Dieu!* Don't tell me anymore," Maria Ana said. "Not another word or I won't sleep tonight."

"Then I won't," Kate said. "I don't want to keep you awake."

"No, no, don't stop now. Tell me more," Maria Ana said. "If I get too afraid I'll put my hands over my ears."

"Very well then," Kate said. "It all happened very quickly. I found the police whistle in my pocket and blew . . ."

"Yes? And then?"

"Nothing. The whistle didn't whistle."

"I am distraught!" Maria Ana said, throwing up her hands. "I am devastated. A man in the fog with a butcher's knife, ready to plunge the blade into your heart! *Ma pauvre* Kate!"

"It seemed that he wasn't ready to use the knife, not quite yet. The coachman reached over and tore down the front of my dress, a cheap cotton thing that gave way easily . . . and then the bodice. My breasts were exposed and the man with the knife"—Kate touched the top of her chest—"drew the point from here, down between . . ."

"Your bubbies?"

"Yes, between my bubbies, and then all the way to

my stomach. He moved the knife slowly and didn't press hard, but he left a thin, red line of blood down my front. Then he got very close to me, bent his head, and began to lick the blood, making a strange smacking sound. At the same time, he pushed what was left of my dress and my underwear down over my hips, and I felt the point of the knife prick my abdomen. The coachman laughed and said, 'Gut her, my lord. Make the whore squeal.'"

Maria Ana jumped to her feet and placed her hands on Kate's shoulders. "Oh, thank God you're not a ghost. You're alive. But how did you—"

"I was wearing a short Zouave jacket that for some reason is very popular among women in London and this revolver"—Kate took the British Bulldog from its box—"was in the right-hand pocket."

"And what did you do?"

"I shoved the muzzle into My Lord the Knife Man's belly and pulled the trigger."

Maria Ana gasped in shock. "And then what? Oh, I won't sleep a wink tonight."

"He dropped at my feet, groaning. The coachman turned and ran, and I was good and mad, so I fired at him. I think I winged him, but I don't know for sure. I hauled up my dress and went after the piece of trash but lost him in the fog. And then about a dozen policemen arrived, including Detective Hawkes. I was hustled away from there in a police wagon and taken under escort to my hotel."

"What happened to the man you shot?" Maria Ana said.

"He died right there in the street," Kate said. "Or so I was told."

"And he was the man who'd murdered the Irish girls?"

"Detective Chief Inspector Marmaduke Hawkes said so, among other things."

"No, Kate, you are not a prisoner. For your services to the Crown, you are an honored guest of Her Majesty's government.

"Ah, yes, your luggage is already on board the steam frigate HMS Scylla, *currently docked at Portsmouth harbor, a fine warship eminently suited for the Atlantic crossing. You will leave tonight under cover of darkness, will be berthed in the captain's cabin, vacated by him of course, and Her Majesty has seen fit to supply you with a lady's maid, an obedient, intelligent girl named Nora Andrews, who will accompany you all the way to the wild Texas lands.*

"No, dear lady, the queen did not deceive you nor did she, as you say, use you. You were the right person at the right place and time, and she saw you as a savior.

"No, no, not as an assassin but as a brave woman who could rid this nation of a great evil.

"Very well then, since you ask. The man you killed in self-defense, let it be said, was William, Duke of Chelmsford, a nephew of the queen and a dangerous, degenerate sadist. This mentally unbalanced creature was already suspected of raping and murdering a sixteen-year-old kitchen maid, but Scotland Yard was ordered to cover up the crime.

"In answer to your question, Kate, that order came from the very highest level. But after the murder and mutilation of the two prostitutes, the queen realized that Chelmsford had to be disposed of like a dangerous animal. Anarchy is everywhere in this country, aided and abetted by the gutter press,

and a scandal of that proportion involving the queen's family could well topple the crown.

"You were chosen because, Kate, you would return to America and there would be no trail to follow. The story being supplied to the newspapers is that His Grace the Duke of Chelmsford was assassinated by anarchists and died bravely trying to thwart their evil plans. He is to be given a state funeral with full honors befitting a British hero.

"Yes, I know it's a falsehood, but look on the positive side . . . you are the real hero, and thanks to you, no more women will be murdered and mutilated in Whitechapel.

"Well, all we know yet is that the Duke's accomplice was not his regular coachman, but a hired thug who goes by the name of Jack. Rest assured, Kate, we'll arrest the bounder soon. Now before I go, this is from the queen in the hope that in a few years you can return to England and visit her again, wearing it."

"What was it?" Maria Ana said. "Diamonds?"

"No. It was a medal, the Order of the British Empire. I have it somewhere, and one day I'll show it to you."

"Kate, you were very brave. Much braver than I could have been. I think I would have fainted."

"No, you wouldn't, Maria Ana. You're made of sterner stuff. Despite what the detective told me, I was used by Queen Vic to assassinate a man who could have become a national embarrassment. I will never forgive her for her treachery." Kate smiled and stretched her slender arms. "Now it's time for bed, I think."

"Queens are bound by a different set of rules than the rest of us, Kate. That is the way of the world. But, *mon Dieu,* I won't sleep at all tonight, seeing that dreadful black carriage in the fog."

Maria Ana lay in bed and her mind conjured up an image of Don Pedro. She mentally stuck pins into his belly and then smiled and fell sound asleep. She'd forgotten all about the carriage.

BOOK THREE
Battleground

CHAPTER THIRTY-TWO

"When do we ride, Mr. Salt?" Having to say *Mr. Salt* rankled, but Seth Koenig needed the man, at least for now.

Salt's ravaged face was sour as he worked on his first cup of coffee. "We wait for Big John Waters and his riders."

"When will that be?"

"When will what be?"

"When will Waters arrive?" Koenig was irritable.

"Later today. Tomorrow. Who knows? Soon. Big John is his own man."

"Who is he?"

A thick morning mist hung over Salt's camp and the campfires of his assembled twenty-five gunmen created halos of dull red and yellow light. A man lost in the gloom coughed and then hawked and spat. It was not yet seven and the murmur of conversation among the men was desultory and subdued.

"Big John Waters? He's a Texarkana boy, an outlaw like the rest of us, him and his brother Dave and half a dozen assorted kin of one kind or another.

Mostly makes a living running rustled cattle into Mexico, but he'll rob a bank or hold up a stage if the opportunity presents itself."

"He a gun?" Koenig said.

Salt smiled behind the rim of his coffee cup. "Better than you'll ever be, Koenig, so don't even think about bracing him."

"No need to brace him. He's on our side." Seth returned Salt's smile, trying to look like everybody's friend. "I look forward to meeting him."

Salt made no comment to that and then said, "So ol' Blade is dead, huh?"

"Yeah. His heart gave out. He'd been feeling poorly for a spell."

"And you're the new boss of the Hellfire."

"Seems like."

"Where are your hands?"

"They quit on me."

"Why?"

Seth shrugged. "Didn't want me as a boss, I guess."

"I'm sorry to hear about Blade."

"Yeah, it was a tragedy. Very sad, especially since me and him became such great friends toward the end."

"How did Blade really die?"

"What do you mean?"

"Five words in my question. How-did-Blade-really-die? It was simple enough."

"Do you think I killed him?"

"Maybe."

"Do you care?"

"Not much. But if you killed one boss man you can kill another."

"He sat up in his coffin."

"Huh?"

"At the graveside, As we were about to bury him, Blade sat up in his coffin."

"He wasn't dead?"

"Maybe he was half-dead. I don't know."

Salt let a silence stretch.

Finally Seth said, "I shot him. Bedded him down for good."

"Shot him while he was sitting up in his coffin? Is that how it was?"

"Yeah. Dead men shouldn't come back from the edge of the grave. It ain't decent."

"And that's why the punchers quit? Because you killed Blade?"

'They would've quit anyway. Those boys didn't want a new boss."

"You mean they didn't want you?"

Seth said nothing and Salt shook his head. "You're a snake, Koenig."

"Hard thing to say to a man who's gonna make you rich, Salt."

"Could be, but you're still a snake." Then, "Archie Lane didn't come back."

"Who?"

"Archie Lane, one of my boys. I sent him to scout the Kerrigan ranch and he didn't come back."

Seth grinned. "Maybe he fell for the widow Kerrigan's charms, huh?"

"Or maybe they shot him. Could be that outfit is tougher than you think, Koenig."

"We can take them," Seth said. "Hell, I rode through them and opened the widow's front door the last time I was there."

"You're a tough hombre, huh?"

"I'm tough enough to warn you never to try me."

"I can't raise the number of men I wanted, so I'm in for a bigger risk," Salt said.

"You'll have enough."

"Maybe so, but I'm upping the ante." Salt poured coffee into his cup. His cratered face was grotesque in the harsh morning light.

"Upping the ante how?"

"I want the Hellfire."

"Salt, when you want, you want big."

"Time I settled down . . . hung up my guns and got me a wife . . . kids . . . stuff like that."

"They burned the Hellfire."

"Who did?"

"The punchers before they left. Burned everything to the ground."

"With the money you're paying me, I can rebuild the place," Salt said.

Seth Koenig thought about that. He wanted the Kerrigan ranch and the redheaded woman. Those were the real prizes. Salt could have the Hellfire and be damned to him.

"All right. It's yours, Salt. Right after we take the Kerrigan place and we all start living high on the hog."

"We? There's no *we*, Koenig. There's only you, remember? I'll take the KK, me and my boys, and then maybe I'll take it into my head to keep both places."

"I saw Blade's books," Seth said. "And his will. He has money stashed away in half a dozen banks, a lot of money. As his son and heir only I can access it. You'd be losing out on your share of a fortune."

"How much money?"

"The sort of money you can only dream about, Salt. I'm talking cash money, the kind that isn't tied up in land and cattle."

"All right. I was only joking about the Kerrigan place," Salt said. "I make little jokes now and then."

"Maybe you were, maybe you weren't. I don't give a damn, because you won't get the ranch or the woman."

"You can trust me."

Seth sniggered. "Trust among thieves? Is there such a thing?"

"Koenig, I told you, you can trust me. I'll hold up my end of the agreement like we planned."

"As will I."

"How much money can I expect?"

"You'll find out when the time comes. A lot, I can tell you that."

"So be it. I'll take your word for it, but you're still a snake."

Seth extended his hand. "A gentlemen's agreement, then, one snake to another. Let's shake on it."

Salt shook his head. "There's no call for me to shake your hand."

"Anything you say . . . partner." Seth Koenig forced a smile.

CHAPTER THIRTY-THREE

Big John Waters showed up at noon, an hour after the mist lifted. He was accompanied by just four riders.

"Cousin Billy Joe came down with a bloody flux and we had to leave him in Lordsburg," Waters said, talking to Davis Salt. "The Baxter twins never showed, and Boone Carter got hisself shot by a deputy sheriff up Las Cruces way and ain't expected to live." Waters shook his great nail keg of a head. "Hard times, Davis."

"The Baxter boys are a loss," Salt said, showing his disappointment.

"Yeah, especially Micah. Best with the iron I've ever seen."

Waters' gaze moved to Seth Koenig, who was sitting cross-legged, shoveling salt pork and beans into his mouth. "I don't think I've had the pleasure."

Without getting up, Seth extended his hand, chewing. "Seth Koenig. Pleased to meet you."

Waters, well over six feet tall with a great sagging belly that overhung his gunbelt, took Seth's hand. He immediately dropped it as though he'd just been stung. His florid face puzzled, the big man said, "You any kin to Blade Koenig, owns the Hellfire spread?" He rubbed his right palm on his pant leg.

"He's my pa, or was," Seth said, again talking around a mouthful of food. "He's dead."

"Sorry to hear that," Waters said. "How did it come about?"

"His ticker gave up on him."

Seth ignored Salt's bemused look as Waters said, "Hell, I thought men like Blade never died."

"Men like Blade die like any other men," Seth said.

"Then please accept my sympathy for your loss," Waters said.

Koenig shrugged and said nothing, all his concentration on his plate.

"Coffee's on the bile, John," Davis said. "You and your boys help yourself."

Waters waited until his four men, a tough-looking bunch with vague, inbred faces, poured coffee before he took his. He kept fussing with his right hand as though it was sticky. When he finally settled, he sat beside Davis, tried his smoking hot coffee, and then said, "What's the job, Davis?"

"It's big," Seth said. "A lot of money and land at stake."

Waters shot Seth an annoyed look, as though he'd talked out of turn.

"Yeah, John, it's big," Davis said. "We're going to get us a ranch."

With the back of his hand Waters wiped coffee from his mustache. "I need more than that, Davis. I ain't a man that's into ranching."

"The ranch belongs to a woman by the name of

Kate Kerrigan, and we're going to take it away from her," Salt said.

"I've heard the name. Biggest ranch in Texas, I heard."

"One of the biggest, for sure," Salt said.

"What are we up against?"

"Punchers, maybe a gun or two. I don't know."

"How many punchers?"

"Winter is cracking down and most of the hands will have been paid off," Salt said. "A big outfit like that might keep on ten, tops. We can take it."

Waters looked around him. "How many we got?"

Salt nodded in Seth's direction. "With him and me, twenty-seven. And you and your boys make thirty-two. We're all gun-handy and we'll be up against waddies who ain't."

"Yeah, that's enough, I guess," Waters said. "Davis, you said the money will be good. How good?"

Salt again nodded to Seth. "Ask him."

"Plenty," Seth said. "You won't be underpaid."

"Davis?" Waters said.

"I'll see you all right, John."

"Then it's settled," Waters said, knowing Salt was a man who stood behind his word. He said to Seth, "Where are the Hellfire hands?"

"There are none."

"How come?"

"They walked out on me."

Waters took a closer look at Seth Koenig. Tall, as big as his pa and just as handsome. Arrogant, probably as fast as Blade with a gun, but his face had a shuttered expression as though he harbored dark secrets. Waters recalled the young man's handshake—cold, stiff, like taking the mitt of a three-day-old corpse. He decided right there and then he didn't like Seth Koenig.

"How come the hands walked out on you, young feller?" Waters said. "I know they set store by your pa."

"But not me." Seth lifted cold eyes to the tall man's face. "By nature, are you a questioning man, Waters?"

"No, not as a rule."

"Then shut your trap. Do your job and you'll get paid. That's all you need to know."

"I'll do my job. I was killing men before you were born."

"Good. Then you'll know what to do when we hit the Kerrigan ranch. A word of warning, Waters. The redheaded woman is mine and I don't want her harmed."

"What redheaded woman?"

"The widow Kerrigan."

"I'll remember that."

"See you do."

Waters looked at Salt. "Davis, I don't like the company you keep."

Salt shrugged, staring at Seth. "I don't like him either, but he's the one with the money, John."

John Waters insisted that he and his men be given time to rest up that day and ride for the Kerrigan ranch at first light the following morning. Seth objected, but Davis Salt overruled him and that's where the matter stood as the day shaded into evening and the first stars appeared.

But trouble flares easily among a gathering of

rough and armed men when the whiskey bottle makes the rounds and voices grow loud and tempers short.

A man called Ray Ward, one of the Waters riders, lit the fuse. Small, with a pale, pinched face and vacant gray eyes, he sidled up to Seth Koenig and grinned. He asked about the redheaded woman, how big were her breasts and, once the battle was won, if she'd be willing to take on all comers.

Seth, already seething at the lack of respect shown him by Salt and Waters, was on the prod, and Ward's question was ill-timed.

Seth's answer was short and to the point. "Shut your filthy mouth. Go anywhere near my woman and I'll kill you." His words were shouted and attracted everyone's attention.

Ward was just drunk enough to be belligerent. He'd killed four men, but with a rifle at a distance. He'd never been in a spitting-distance revolver fight.

"Damn you, when I see a woman I want, I take her," Ward said. "And if I want your redheaded woman, I'll take her, too."

"You'll keep your dirty paws off her," Seth said.

From somewhere in the gloom, John Waters said, "Back off, Ray. It's a big ranch. There'll be women for everybody."

"The hell there will be." Ward stared at Seth, grinning, pushing it. "I want this boy's redheaded woman."

Waters stepped out of the shadows and said, "Ray, sit down. Have another drink."

"I don't want a drink," Ward said. Then to Seth, "You've been there, and you know I want some of what you had, huh?"

Seth, not angry but eager to kill and prove himself to Salt, made a rapid mental calculation. Thirty-two men in camp . . . well they could take the Kerrigan ranch with a couple less.

"You're a lying piece of trash." He smiled as his hand flashed to his Colt and he pulled the trigger.

Ray Ward staggered back. His face shocked and unbelieving, he stared at the bullet hole in his chest. He knew he was dead on his feet and he told Seth so. "Damn you. You've killed me."

Seth ignored the man. Big John Waters stood in place, frozen, stunned by what had happened, the sudden eruption of mindless violence. He showed no sign of making a play.

"You don't like my company, Waters?" Seth said. "Well here's a ticket that will take you the hell away from me." He triggered two fast shots into the big man.

Waters took a step back and had time to utter a roar of resentment and outrage before he hit the ground. A bullet tugged at Seth's sleeve. Waters' remaining men, all three close kin to him and each other, were firing. Out of the corner of his eyes Seth saw Salt on his feet, his Colt bucking in his hand. One of Waters' men went down, then a second. Seth slammed a shot into the third, and the man shrieked and fell.

"You damned idiot!" Salt yelled at Seth. His pocked face black with anger, he quickly crossed the distance between them and unloaded a tremendous right hook to Seth's chin.

Suddenly the sky cartwheeled around him, and Seth's legs buckled. He fought for balance but the shifting ground under his feet suddenly gave way and he crashed onto his back, his Colt thudding into the dirt beside him.

"You damned fool!" Salt yelled, thunder in his eyes.

"You're a mad dog killer, damn you. Why did you shoot Waters? He wasn't going to draw down on you on account of trash like Ray Ward."

Seth Koenig tried to grab hold of his reeling thoughts. "Wha . . . wha . . ."

"One of you men, take his revolver and Winchester," Salt said.

Finally, Seth found his tongue. "You hit me."

"Yeah, I did," Salt said, still dangerously angry. "You're lucky I didn't put a bullet in you. I saved your worthless life, Koenig, but we've got five men gone, good men we needed."

Seth sat up, put his hurting head in his hands and then looked up at Salt from between his palms. "We didn't need them. They were riffraff, spawned by sisters who couldn't outrun their brothers. Paying those white trash would've been a waste of good money."

"Money. Right now, money is all that's keeping you alive, Koenig," Salt said. "If there wasn't money in it for me, you'd be dead right now."

"Yeah, it's all about money and the power it brings, but you can't touch a penny of it unless I say so."

A gunman with a crafty face had been listening. His Texas spurs chimed as he stepped over a dead man and walked closer to Seth. "You keep talking about Blade's money, Koenig. How much money? We need dollars and cents."

This brought a chorus of agreement from some of the other gunmen.

"All right. Have you ever seen a hundred thousand dollars in one place at one time?" Seth said.

"Can't say as I have," the gunman said.

"You ever seen two hundred thousand dollars?"

"Nope." The gunman's cunning blue eyes had taken on a sheen of greed.

"How about three hundred thousand?"

The man shook his head.

Seth said, "Four hundred thousand? No, you ain't never seen that either." He got to his feet. "Mister, when this undertaking is done and I own the Kerrigan ranch, I'll put five hundred thousand dollars on a table and tell you boys to dig in and grab your share. And Salt, that also goes for you. Hell, it goes for you double."

His announcement was greeted with whoops of joy from most, skepticism from a few, among them Davis Salt.

Jaw muscles bunched, his ruined face a grotesque, angry mask, Salt said, "Koenig, if you're lying to me about the money, I swear, I'll kill you."

"You calling me a liar?"

"If the money isn't there and in the amount you claim, yeah, I'll call you a liar to your face and then I'll put a bullet in your belly."

Seth hesitated. He had no gun, but he wouldn't have braced Salt anyhow. The man was too fast on the draw and shoot, way too dangerous.

"Right after our business is done, the money will be there and you can count it," Seth said. *But you won't live to spend it, you scar-faced son of a bitch, because you'll be dead. A fast draw can't shade a bullet in the back.*

"Koenig, I hope for your sake you're right," Salt said.

"What about my guns?"

"You'll get them back before we attack," Salt said. "We ride for the Kerrigan ranch tomorrow at first light."

CHAPTER THIRTY-FOUR

Nora Andrews shivered in her blankets and longed for first light and the warming heat of the rising sun. She was sick, feverish, and in considerable pain. The trek across the grassland had tired her much more than she'd imagined it would, and her feet were so badly swollen that she hadn't removed her boots, worried that she'd never get them back on again.

The night sky was full of stars, and a gibbous moon cast a pale light that kept total darkness at bay and silvered the coats of the coyotes hunting among the wild oaks. A rising wind tugged at the girl, tossed strands of hair across her face, and whispered secrets to the buffalo grass.

Nora reached out and dragged her rifle closer, still shaken by the encounter with the cougar. She didn't know if coyotes that smelled blood in the wind attacked humans, but she was taking no chances.

She closed her eyes and willed sleep to come and relieve her of pain for a few hours.

The moon rose higher in the sky, and the coyotes kept their distance.

Nora dreamed that she was back in her native

London in the fog, listening to the hauntingly lonely horns of the great iron ships docked on the Thames.

The coming of morning woke Nora, and for a while she lay in her blankets, unwilling to move. More tired than she'd ever been in her life, she knew that the slightest movement would start the pain in her broken ribs again and set her head throbbing.

After a few minutes she struggled to her feet and put together her bedroll. On all sides of her the high prairie stretched into distance, silent, motionless. To the east where her destination lay, she saw only an endless, vast sea of grass until it met the lemon-colored sky of the dawn.

Nora did not feel like eating, but she forced herself to eat a crumbling piece of yellow cake and swallow a few sips of wine. Then she picked up her rifle and bedroll and began to walk, her feet dragging as though they were wrapped in sheets of lead.

As the sun rose, she struggled on . . . Happily there was no fog . . . and the iron ships had all gone to sea with their bold sailormen . . . Wait . . . what was the song about sailormen her mother used to sing to her when she was a child? Oh yes, she remembered. She turned her face to the sky and sang:

"What do you do with the drunken sailor,
What do you do with the drunken sailor,
What do you do with the drunken sailor,
Ear-lye in the morning?"

Nora's song stopped abruptly. Was that all she remembered? No, not all. There was more. Her voice rose, singing as she marched:

"Way hay and up she rises,
Way hay and up she rises,
Way hay and up she rises,
Ear-lye in the morning.

"Put him in the hold with the captain's daughter,
Put him in the hold with the captain's daughter,
Put him in the hold with the captain's daughter,
Ear-lye in the morning."

Nora stopped singing. It was a stupid song, and she didn't want to sing it any longer. Better save her breath for walking. Her feet hurt. Very swollen. And her ribs hurt. At least two broken, she guessed. Maybe three. She stopped and took a drink of water from her canteen. It was getting low. She'd need to find water soon. Ahead of her was an ocean of grass, but not a drop to drink. She thought that funny and she giggled, but it hurt her ribs and she stopped. Better to think sad thoughts. How far was Hiram Clay's ranch? A thousand miles probably. Now that was a sad thought, very, very melancholy indeed.

Nora walked on, first plodding, then dragging her feet. The sun was hot, fatiguing her, and the air was thick and hard to breathe. She staggered forward . . .

Then, three hours into her day's journey, she stumbled and fell . . . and would later have no recollection of hitting the ground.

At the same moment Nora Andrews began her walk eastward in the dawn light, Archie Lane finally freed himself of the ropes that bound him hand and foot.

He considered bloody, shredded wrists a small price to pay for his freedom.

Thrown into the Kerrigan barn with little regard for his comfort, he'd worked patiently for at least twelve hours, picking away at the hemp on the tine of a carelessly discarded pitchfork, its point fragmenting the rope, strand by agonizing strand. Lane untied his feet and stood, but only for a moment. His cramped legs gave out on him, and he collapsed heavily onto the wood floor. Cursing under his breath, he tried standing again, slowly, bit by bit, allowing circulation to come back to his legs. Finally, he could stand, then walk, and he stepped to the barn door and looked outside into the dawn. All was quiet, no lamps were lit, and nothing moved.

Quickly, he looked around for a weapon of some kind and took a ball-peen hammer from the wall and shoved its handle into his pants. It wasn't much of a weapon, but it sure beat a cross word. The only horse in the barn that morning was a bay mare, her saddle thrown over the timber partition between stalls.

Lane saddled the mare and put his boot into the stirrup . . . than stiffened in place as a voice came from the barn door.

"Going somewhere, señor?"

Lane slowly turned his head. A tall man with a patch over one eye, a vaquero by the cut of his jib, stood in the doorway, smiling. Something about the Mexican's presence was worth a second glance, and Lane gave him another look. The man was relaxed, hand near his holstered Colt, slim, confident, waiting for Lane to make a move. In a certain breed of men, the words *professional shootist* stand out like writing on a wall, and Lane read the words easily. Anyone who had the wits to understand knew the man was a gun.

The realization made Archie Lane wary. Even if he'd been wearing his revolver he'd have been wary. He took his foot from the stirrup and turned slowly. "We can talk about this."

"You and Señora Kerrigan can talk about this," Rodolfo Aragon said. "You and I have nothing to say to one another. We are strangers."

Lane smiled, trying to defuse the situation. "For a Mex you speak good English."

Aragon nodded. "And Spanish, French, and some Navajo."

"Let me ride out of here. I mean nothing to you."

"You are an enemy and therefore a threat to my patron, Doña Maria Ana de la Villa de Villar del Aguilla." Aragon shrugged. "In that regard, you mean much to me, hombre."

"I am unarmed."

"Armed or unarmed, I will shoot you if I have to. It will make little difference."

Lane took the ball-peen hammer from his waistband. "I have this."

"*Sí.* Perhaps you want to hammer a nail?"

"I don't want to surrender to a Mex. I have my pride."

"And it comes before a fall, does it not?"

"Yeah, so they say. Now go call a white man and I'll give myself up."

"No. You will come with me and you will speak with Señora Kerrigan."

"I told you, I have my pride."

"And it's foolish pride. Now come."

"The hell with you, greaser!"

As late as the 1950s, a historian claimed that as a boy growing up in Arkansas, Archie Lane was well known for his ability to chuck a rock and hit a glass canning jar at twenty paces. Perhaps Lane figured he had a chance of a successful hit and that's why he threw the ball-peen hammer at Rodolfo Aragon's head. But, more likely, he was motivated by a gunman's touchy pride and the anti-Mexican prejudice then rampant on the frontier.

As it happened, Aragon moved his head a little, the hammer flew past his left ear, and he fired. One shot, chest, dead center, and Archie Lane died standing. When his body hit the stable floor, he was already riding Aragon's bullet into hell.

The shot brought the alarmed Kerrigan ranch to its feet.

Frank Cobb was the first to run into the barn. Gun in hand, his eyes took in Rodolfo Aragon standing, Archie Lane sprawled on the floor, and a drift of gun smoke hanging in the air.

Behind Frank, Gabe Dancer asked the inevitable question. "What the hell happened?"

"Your prisoner tried to escape," Aragon said.

"And you plugged him?" Frank said.

"*Sí.* He threw a hammer at my head."

"A hammer? This hammer?" Dancer held up the ball-peen so Aragon could see it.

"That hammer," the Mexican said.

"How did he get untied?" Frank said.

"I didn't ask him," Aragon said.

Gabe Dancer tossed the hammer away, stepped to the door, and said over his shoulder, "I'm never coming into this goddamned barn again. The dead bodies keep piling up in here."

* * *

Nora Andrews woke to sunlight filtering through drawn lace curtains and the muffled sound of a gathering of excited men yelling. She lay in a soft bed with a patchwork quilt and above her was a high, plastered ceiling. From somewhere, she smelled bacon frying and coffee on the boil. Slowly it dawned on her that she wore a nightdress, some other woman's nightdress, and that her chest under her breasts was tightly bound. She touched her forehead where the cougar had wounded her, and that was also bandaged. Where was she?

Then a woman's voice. "Ah, you're awake at last, my dear." The concerned face of a middle-aged woman with beautiful gray eyes swam into Nora's line of vision.

"Where am I?" she said.

"At the ranch of the honorable Hiram Clay, Esquire. My name is Angie Docherty. My husband is Mr. Clay's foreman."

"How did I get here?"

"One of our hands found you this morning. He was hunting a cougar that's been playing hob around here for weeks."

"I think I met that cougar," Nora said. Then she remembered. "Oh my God. I must see Mr. Clay at once. The Kerrigan ranch is in danger."

Angie Docherty smiled. "We know, my dear. You were delirious but managed to tell us that Kate Kerrigan is in peril. Listen. Those horses you hear are Mr. Clay and his hands riding to the rescue."

A man's voice came from the bedside. "Hiram issued a call to arms and mounted everybody who can ride a horse, including the cook." Dr. Zebulon Farrell shrugged. "No great loss, that cook. How are you feeling, Miss Nora?"

The girl listened to the departing hoofbeats and then said. "I do hope Mr. Clay gets there in time. And I'm feeling a lot better than I was a while ago, Dr. Farrell."

"Hiram believes God is on the side of big ranchers in general and him in particular. If anyone can ride to the rescue in the nick of time, it's him." He scooted Mrs. Docherty over and sat on the bed. "You already look much better, Nora. Are you in pain?"

"It hurts to breathe," Nora said.

"I'm sure it does. You have three broken ribs, and I sutured the gash on your forehead. I'll give you something for the pain and then you'll need to rest in bed for at least a week."

Tears welled in Nora's eyes. "I should be with my mistress, not lying in bed."

"I'm sure Kate will manage just fine without you for a while." He smiled, a rare event. "Let Hiram have his chance to be her knight in shining armor."

Then, because she was young and concerned about such things, Nora said, "Doctor, will I have a scar—"

"On your forehead? Yes, a small one, but it will fade with time. Don't worry. You'll be just as pretty." Dr. Farrell was not a demonstrative man, but he took Nora's hand and said, "You did well. You were very brave. When the puncher brought you in, you were delirious, still battling the cougar. Kate will be very proud of you."

"After it was over, I felt sorry for the cougar. He was very thin."

"Even a thin cougar is a handful in a fight, I imagine."

"He was. For a while I thought I was dead."

"Are you hungry? I'm sure Mrs. Docherty can fix you something."

"No, I'm not hungry."

Dr. Farrell squeezed the girl's hand. "We're all proud of you. Well done."

"Thank you," Nora said. Suddenly she was very tired. She closed her eyes and slept.

Chapter Thirty-five

"Yes, two of them," Davis Salt said, lowering his field glasses.

"Do you think they see us?" Seth Koenig said.

"Damn right they do." He put the binoculars to his eyes again. "Yup, there they go, hightailing it back to the ranch."

Behind Salt, his twenty-five mounted gunmen had spread out in a ragged skirmish line, half expecting an order to charge after the fleeing Kerrigan riders. But none came.

Salt glanced at the sky and then said to Seth, "Maybe two hours of daylight left. The men are tired, and I don't want to fight in the dark."

"Then how do you want to play it?"

"We'll camp here tonight and hit them at sunup."

"Catch them napping, huh?"

"No chance of that. Those two will raise the alarm and they'll be waiting for us."

Seth glared at the older man. "Hell, if that's the case I say we go now. We can kill them all by sundown, and I'll sleep in Kate Kerrigan's bed tonight."

Salt shook his head. "A night battle is too risky. One time I recollect a feller telling me he tried to pull a train robbery in the dark. Turned out somebody had informed on him and there were eight Pinkertons hidden in the baggage car. He said people were running back and forth all over the damned place and he and his boys ended up shooting two of their own men, and not a penny of profit to show for it. No, we'll wait until dawn. I want to see what the hell I'm shooting at."

Seth Koenig was irritated. "Salt, I can tell you're scared, so give me half of the men now and I'll get the job done."

Davis Salt turned his head slowly. "Koenig, I'm only going to say this once, so listen up—shut your damned trap and follow orders."

Anger spiked in Seth's belly. "Salt, you're a big talker, but you've never had to deal with this . . ." His hand dropped to his gun. The move was meant to intimidate Salt, but it was a mistake. Behind Seth rifles rattled and he turned and saw a dozen Winchesters aimed at his head, some mighty unfriendly eyes looking through the sights.

"Koenig, get this into your thick skull," Salt said, smiling. "You just ain't popular around here."

"Davis Salt is nobody's fool. I don't think he'll attack us until tomorrow at sunup," Frank Cobb said. "But we can't take chances. We'll stand to all night in the bunkhouse."

"Does that include me and Mose and the maids?" Kate Kerrigan said.

Frank nodded. "Everybody, including Doña Maria

Ana. Starting now. It's going to be crowded in there, Kate, but there's no other way."

"Then let's get started. Trace, help me get everyone into the bunkhouse." She looked at Frank. "Salt and Koenig have around thirty men. That's not so bad, is it?"

"It depends how good they are, Kate."

"How good are they? You must have some idea."

"My guess is they'll be the best Salt could find and they'll be a handful. Counting the Hellfire hands, I expected fifty, so the odds have been reduced some."

"Unless there's more of them on the way," Trace Kerrigan said.

"That has occurred to me," Frank said. "And it's worrisome. Kate, I'm riding out to make sure Salt is staying put for the night. He's a crafty one and he might be trying to fool us."

"Frank, I'll go with you," Trace said.

"No. Best you stay here and make sure everyone gets into the bunkhouse. And have a couple hands help Tom Ogilvy bring plenty of grub and water. We may be in for a long siege."

"Frank, he's already done that," Trace said.

"I know, but my guess is we'll need twice that amount."

Doña Maria Ana understood the gravity of the situation and arrived in the bunkhouse dressed for war in a riding skirt, shirt, and boots. She'd tied her hair back and carried a pile of petticoats and other garments. "For bandages," she said, answering the question on Kate's face.

"Let's hope to God we don't need them," Kate said.

Rodolfo Aragon listened to that exchange in silence and then took station by a partly boarded window. The man looked calm and competent, and Kate was glad he was there.

The hands, intimidated by the presence of two beautiful women, one of them their boss, took up their places by the windows and stared out into the waning day. They were quiet, unusual for young punchers. When Kate looked at their faces one by one she saw tension but no fear, and she felt proud of them.

She saw no fear in Maria Ana's face either.

"Kate, perhaps your beau, um . . . what's his name?"

"Hiram Clay." It occurred to Kate to say, "He's not my beau," but considering the danger they were facing, it seemed petty.

"Yes, dear Hiram," Maria Ana said. "Perhaps at this very moment he's charging across the prairie to our rescue."

"Perhaps. It all depends on Nora Andrews."

"Yes, a sulky girl, but I like her. I'm sure she made it to Hiram's ranch without mishap."

"Walking," Kate said.

"*Excusez-moi*? I don't understand."

"Her horse came back, remember?

"Ah yes, she's on foot. But those big-boned English girls love to walk, always striding up and down hills and the like in their sensible shoes. I'm sure she made it just fine."

"I'm sure she did." Kate said, more in hope than in certainty.

"Kate, I've never been shot at before," Maria Ana said. "Have you?"

"Yes, several times."

"I imagine it's unpleasant."

"It is. Very unpleasant."

"I plan to be brave, Kate."

"I'm sure you will."

"Suppose I'm not? Suppose I'm not brave?"

Kate smiled. "Maria Ana, don't build houses on a bridge you haven't crossed yet. Once the shooting starts you'll find your courage."

"Do you really think so?"

"Yes, I do. You'll be as brave as any of us, and perhaps braver."

"Then, thank you. I feel much better now," Maria Ana said. "Kate, sometimes just talking with you gives me courage."

Davis Salt was staying put for the night. And it looked to Frank Cobb that Salt's numbers had not been increased by late arrivals. Through his field glasses Frank saw smoke rise from cow-chip fires that would burn hot enough to boil coffee. A horse line was at the rear of the camp.

Frank nodded to himself, his smile grim. It seemed that hell was postponed until daybreak.

Chapter Thirty-six

Maria Ana slept, her head resting on Kate Kerrigan's shoulder as the long night wore on and bathed the silent ranch in moonlight. The hands dozed on their feet at their positions by the bunkhouse windows, and every now and then one of them jerked his head upright and then peered outside with renewed interest, as though to convince the wakeful Kate that he hadn't been sleeping at all.

Gabe Dancer, rifle in hand, tiptoed his way through the slumbering maids and crossed the floor to where a pale Biddy Kelly sat with her back against a wall. The girl's eyes were wide, unblinking, as she stared into the middle distance, seeing nothing but the cold gray ashes of what had been her own searing fear. She seemed numb, resigned to her fate whatever it might be.

Kate's gaze followed Dancer as, his knees cracking, he groaned and took a seat beside Biddy.

He put his arm around her shoulders and said, "How are you feeling, pretty Irish girl?"

The girl yielded to his comforting arm but remained stiff, distant as though she hadn't heard him.

After a few moments she said, "When will they come and will they kill us all, Gabe?"

Dancer smiled and hugged her closer. "Not much chance of that happening, girl. They'll have to get past me first, and that ain't an easy thing to do. I've been in a fix like this afore."

Biddy looked into his grizzled face and whispered, "I'm scared, Gabe."

"We're all scared," Dancer said. "Look over there at the tall gent by the window."

"It's Mr. Cobb."

"Right, it is. In his day, outlaw, shootist, all-round hell-raiser and as near as I can figure, a brave man. Know something?"

"What, Gabe?"

"Frank is just as scared as you are, and that's a natural fact. But like the rest of us, he shoves his fear to the back of the stove and lets it simmer there while he does what has to be done."

"Gabe, you won't let them hurt me?" Biddy said.

"Nobody's gonna hurt you, little girl. Believe me. I won't let them."

"Gabe, have you ever been scared? I mean really scared, as scared as me?"

"Sure, plenty of times. Apaches spooked me a time or three, and once a war party of Utes, kind of like the Comanche only nastier, kept me and three other tinpans holed up in a rock cabin for the best part of a week . . . around Christmastime as I recollect."

Biddy showed unexpected interest. "And what happened?"

"Oh, they finally gave up and rode away, but only after they ate my mule and wounded ol' Lanky Lawson with an arrow. Funny thing was, Lanky had been hit by arrows two times afore, but he always said the Ute arrow hurt the most." He leaned closer to Biddy and whispered. "Maybe because it was stuck in his ass."

The girl giggled, and Dancer said, "There, that's better. Now you're smiling again like I remember."

"Gabe, tell me another story," Biddy said. "I don't feel as afraid when you talk to me."

"Well, all right then, Biddy, here's a story that's as true as the day is long. One time me, Jesse James, and Billy the Kid was up on the Platte, panning for gold nuggets as big as your fist and . . ."

Kate smiled, her own fear abating as a straight-faced Dancer told his big windy. Maria Ana stirred restlessly in her sleep and whispered words of endearment to a long-forgotten lover, and over by a window Frank Cobb turned and smiled. The oil lamps smoked and created shifting shadows in the corners and over at Kate's mansion the grandfather clock in the hallway chimed two . . . but there was no one there to hear it.

Rodolfo Aragon, who had stood alone, talking to no one, left the bunkhouse about two hours before sunup and stepped out into the darkness. Frank Cobb watched him leave and after a discreet couple minutes followed, aware that Kate's eyes were on him, her expression puzzled.

Frank didn't doubt the Mexican's loyalty, not when Maria Ana's life was in danger, but the man's actions were strange. The door's barricades were not yet in place, but it wasn't the time to go wandering outside unless Aragon was answering an urgent call of nature. Frank smiled at his own distrust. He could be following a man who only wanted to take a piss. Yet something niggled at him, a strange feeling that all was not well with Aragon. Was the famous shootist showing yellow? A fast draw would not be of any help in the coming battle and Aragon knew it.

Frank stood in the shadows and his eyes reached into the darkness. Nothing moved. There was no sign of Aragon. And then, from the direction of the wild oak that grew near the cookhouse, a whisper, a string of words spoken in Spanish, soft, but with a tone of urgency. Aware that there was no future in surprising a draw fighter by walking silently up behind him unannounced, Frank moved to his left on cat feet, drawing a little closer to the oak but still hidden in shadow.

A lilac cloud edged in silver glided past the face of the moon and in the waxing light Frank saw Aragon outlined under the oak. The man was on his knees, head bowed, whispering what sounded like a prayer. Frank listened for a while, decided he was intruding on Aragon's devotions, and retreated toward the bunkhouse. He was at a loss. Why was the Mexican praying? For the success of the upcoming battle? For the safety of Maria Ana? Or for something else? Frank had no answers for those questions. But whatever the reason, he hoped Aragon's God was listening.

Chapter Thirty-seven

Seth Koenig and Davis Salt led a probing attack at dawn. It was a brief, hit-and-run affair that occasioned a lot of shooting from both sides but resulted in no casualties. Salt's men were content to ride past the bunkhouse, firing at the gallop and then quickly retreating, their mission accomplished.

Salt learned a couple lesson from the encounter, One, that there were at least a dozen riflemen in the fortified bunkhouse, and two, his attack would not be made by mounted riders. His gunmen would go in on foot, using every scrap of cover they could find.

It would be a battle of attrition.

Seth was angry. "Hell, Salt, you're talking about a siege that could go on for a long time. I planned to sleep in the Kerrigan mansion tonight."

"Tonight, tomorrow night, next week, the Kerrigan woman will still be there," Salt said. "And playing it my way, so will most of my men."

"I say we ride right up to the bunkhouse in force and cut loose through the windows," Seth said. "With all of us firing at the same time we can kill them real fast."

"Did you note the return fire?" Salt said. "Front and back there are a total of six partly boarded-up windows and twice as many gun ports cut in the walls. If I do what you suggest, the shooting will make the horses unruly and the mounted men will cram together, trying to get their work in. They'd be cut down like ducks in a shooting gallery. I learned this morning what generals took so long to learn in the war . . . you don't send cavalry against entrenched infantry."

"Salt, this ain't the war and you're not Robert E. Lee. There's a bunch of scared cowhands and women in the bunkhouse and a volley or two from our mounted men will kill some and the others will keep their heads down. The rest will be easy." Seth stood in the stirrups and yelled to the men around him. "I need volunteers for another mounted attack. Who's with me?"

He got no takers.

A few of the assembled gunmen had fought in the war, and they knew what infantry in a strong position could do to cavalry. The younger men read the doubt in the veterans' faces and ignored Seth's plea.

"Like I said, we do it my way," Salt said.

Seth gave the man a look of pure hatred. "Damn you, Salt. A few shots fired and you're scared out of your britches. You could cost us the fight."

Before Salt could answer, one of the older gunmen called out, "Koenig, if you're so damned sure them cowboys will give up, why don't you gallop over there and cut loose through those windows your ownself?"

"Yeah," another man yelled. "And we'll all wait and see what happens."

Salt had heard enough. "All right. Men, we'll go in on foot. Boggs, McCoy, you two stay with the horses."

Then to a gunman with a tough, bearded face, "Bill Graham, take half the men and hit the bunkhouse from the north. I'll attack from the south. Koenig, you come with me."

"Salt, you're doing this all wrong," Seth said. "This is going to be a disaster."

"That remains to be seen. Men, conserve your ammunition and pick your targets. Now move out." Salt looked at Koenig and smiled. "The die is cast."

"Is anyone hurt?" Kate Kerrigan said, rifle in hand, looking through a veil of gun smoke.

"No." Frank stepped beside her. "Shorty Hawkins got hit by a splinter, but it's only a scratch."

"Our men cheered, Frank. Does that mean we scared them off?" Kate said, her voice hopeful.

He shook his head. "No, Kate. Salt was testing our defenses was all. He'll be back to try again."

"I thought I saw Seth Koenig."

"I saw him, too. Took a shot at him through dust but missed."

Maria Ana had just taken around a platter of bacon and sourdough sandwiches for the hands. She offered the last one on the plate to Frank and said, "Mr. Cobb, have you seen Rodolfo?"

"Not since last night," Frank said, chewing. He didn't go into detail.

The doña looked concerned. "I wonder where he is?"

Frank bit his tongue. He suspected Aragon had fled to save his own skin, but to Maria Ana he said,

"He'll show up, I'm sure." Then forcing the words, he said, "He wouldn't leave you."

"No, he wouldn't," Maria Ana said. "But it's very strange."

"They're back!" A hand at one of the windows shouldered his rifle and fired.

What would go down in Kerrigan family history as the Battle of the Bunkhouse began in earnest.

Salt's men fired on the bunkhouse from two sides and after an hour the thin timber boards that fortified the windows were shredded by outlaw lead.

One of the Kerrigan hands was dead, another wounded, and Tom Ogilvy had tripped, fallen hard, and may have broken a leg. The inside of the bunkhouse was thick with gun smoke and became stifling hot as the sun rose. Empty shells littered the floor and the noise was incredible. A steady roar of rifle and revolver fire made the ears of the besieged ring, forcing men to yell hoarsely to one another to make themselves heard above the din.

As the morning dragged slowly toward noon, bullets constantly rattled through the building. Just as Maria Ana handed a puncher a Winchester she'd loaded, the man took a rifle slug to the head. A scarlet eruption of blood and brains splashed across the doña's face, and she screamed in sudden terror. Gabe Dancer, thinking faster than anyone else, grabbed the woman, pulled her to the floor, and yelled to Kate, "Take care of her!"

Kate laid her rifle against the wall, shoved a piece

of petticoat into Biddy Kelly's hand, and shouted into her ear, "Wipe her face!"

For a moment, Biddy just sat on the floor, stunned, staring at the glistening, crimson and gray nightmare of Maria Ana's face, her eyes filled with fear and panic.

Kate slapped the girl hard, and shoved Biddy's hand downward. "Wipe!"

Tears welled in the girl's eyes but, sobbing, she began to rub away the mess, smearing Maria Ana's cheeks and forehead, making a red mask of her face.

Kate returned to her place by the window and snapped off a shot as one of the gunmen ran to change position. The man fell, flopped around for a moment, and then crawled behind cover. She didn't know if she'd killed him or not.

The firing continued unabated. Making the rounds of the defenders, Frank counted eleven claims of downed enemy gunmen. He congratulated the shooters, but secretly put the real figure at two or three. Salt's men moved constantly as they inched their way closer to the bunkhouse, and it was easy to mistake a man diving for cover as a gunman with a bullet in him.

What Frank did know for sure was that the bunkhouse was turning into a sieve and that with two dead and another badly wounded the KK was surely and steadily losing the battle.

It was Trace Kerrigan who first caught sight of Rodolfo Aragon sacrificing his life to save Maria Ana, the woman he adored. His head bleeding from a flesh wound, Trace made his voice heard over the rolling thunder of gunfire. "Frank! Look!"

Frank ran to a window facing the outlaw contingent

led by Davis Salt and Seth Koenig. He saw Aragon come on at a gallop, reins trailing, a bucking Colt in each hand, blazing away at Salt's gunmen. The Mexican leaped from the saddle, backed against the bunkhouse wall, and kept up a steady fire. One of Salt's men cried out and went down, then another. Aragon was hit. Blood splashed his embroidered shirt and he dropped to one knee. Salt and Seth Koenig, ignoring the fire from the bunkhouse, yelled their men forward, every round from every gun directed at Aragon. The shootist suffered hit after hit and in a dying act of defiance he emptied his Colts into the oncoming gunmen and then fell forward onto the dirt and lay still.

Salt's men had been stung. Badly. Five men down, three wounded, all in the space of a few hell-firing seconds. A bullet had burned across Seth Koenig's left shoulder and as he took cover beside Salt, he cursed Aragon.

Salt shook his head, his eyes bright. "He was a *macho* hombre. I would've been proud to ride with him."

Seth was outraged. "Damn him. He shot me."

"He missed you, Koenig, but, God bless him, he tried," Salt said.

For the moment, the gunmen around Salt and Seth were demoralized, still shaken by Aragon's shattering attack. Their firing was desultory and sullen. On the other side of the bunkhouse, the gunmen under the command of Bill Graham kept up a steady fire that was proving accurate and deadly.

As volley after smashing volley ripped through the bunkhouse, another puncher was hit. He dragged himself to a corner, where he groaned and coughed up blood. A sixteen-year-old orphan, the young man called himself the Sabine Kid, probably because he had no other name. Maria Ana crossed the floor and cradled the youngster's head in her lap, her lips moving in prayer . . . for the dead. A kitchen maid yelped in pain as a bullet slammed across her shoulder, tearing muscle. Jazmine Salas hurried to the sobbing girl's aid.

After another hour of taking punishing fire, Kate looked around her at a bunkhouse rapidly becoming a charnel house. It was time to end it. The ranch, her honor, the avoidance of the harsh fate that awaited her, none of those things was worth the life of another young person . . . or, as she looked through the gun smoke at Gabe Dancer, firing steadily from his window, an old one.

There was only one option open to Kate, and she must take it.

Surrender.

"Frank!" she called out.

As he turned to look at her through the thick, gray mist of smoke, Kate said, "It's over." She tied a piece of torn petticoat to the barrel of her rifle.

The white flag of shame.

Chapter Thirty-Eight

Within the chest of the short, rotund Don Pedro de la Villa de Villar del Aguilla beat a contrite heart. It was his opinion that no peasant, priest, or potentate could understand the anguish he suffered, his desire to throw himself at the feet of his beloved Maria Ana, kiss the hem of her very expensive French gown, and humbly beg her forgiveness.

As he'd told his confessor before he left the hacienda, "I thought she'd have come back to me by now after what was just a foolish lovers' quarrel, but lo, I fear she's left forever, and I am heartbroken."

The new padre had been stern, just as stern as the old one. "Don Pedro, you told Doña Maria Ana that she must don the dress of a peasant woman, reduce the number of her servants—"

"She had a great multitude of servants," Don Pedro had humbly pointed out.

"No matter. And you said she may no longer visit her beloved Paris more than once a year."

"Twice. I think I said twice a year."

"My son, no wonder she left you. You've been very cruel."

Don Pedro had wailed in great torment. "Yes, you are right, Padre, I've been an unfeeling pig. Oh, wicked Don Pedro, oh, selfish Don Pedro, oh—"

"Sinful Don Pedro."

"Yes, that too, Padre. I much regret the squeezing of the tit."

"As does the Blessed Virgin, I'm sure."

"I will never do it again." Don Pedro had held up his right hand and stared at it. "This is the hand that squeezed. Oh, that I'd cut it off rather than commit such a sin."

"What's done is done and has been forgiven."

"Then I'm in good standing with God?"

"Fair standing with God. Now go in peace, my son, and bring your wife home and love and cherish her so long as you both shall live."

And so it was that Don Pedro, dressed like an ardent groom in all his embroidered finery, had set out for the wild Texas lands with a hundred merry vaqueros at his back and a love song in his heart.

The younger vaqueros heard distant gunfire before the slightly deaf Don Pedro did.

"Ahead of us, you say?"

"*Sí, patron,*" a vaquero said.

"The ranch of the Señora Kate Kerrigan lies in that direction. Could the firing be coming from there?"

"Maybe so," the vaquero said. "Yes, from the hacienda of Señora Kerrigan, I think."

Don Pedro felt a spike of alarm. He was certain that Maria Ana had fled to the Kerrigan ranch since Kate was her only friend that side of the Rio Grande. And if guns were firing, then his beloved could be in danger.

A man always looks his best when he's on a horse, but alas that did not apply to Don Pedro. When he stood in the stirrups he presented a potbellied little figure, balding under his huge sombrero. But he was a man of proven courage and determination and, like Kate, he'd carved a vast cattle empire out of a wilderness. Heedless of the risks, he was ready for any battle. He raised his revolver and ordered his men forward. "*Adelante, mi compañeros!*"

A dust cloud rose like a thunderhead above a hundred riders as they charged northward at the gallop,

The sudden cessation of gunfire from the bunkhouse surprised Davis Salt . . . until he saw the white flag. "They've quit," he said to Seth Koenig. "They're surrendering."

Seth licked his thick lips. "So be it. Kill all the men, but save the women for yourself and the others. Remember, I don't want Kate Kerrigan harmed."

"Hell, she may be harmed already," Salt said. Wary of a trap, he ordered his men to cease firing and then rose slowly to his feet. For a while the gunmen on the other side of the bunkhouse continued, but then faltered and stopped as Kate waved the white flag.

Salt stepped closer and then yelled, "Come out, the damned lot of you. I see anyone carrying a weapon and you all die."

Seth Koenig was flushed with excitement, exhilarated beyond reason. Everything he'd hoped to achieve was coming to pass . . . the Kerrigan ranch and the redheaded woman were within his grasp. He stood beside Salt and said, "Kate Kerrigan, you come out first." And then, grinning at his moment of brilliant inspiration, "Naked."

He felt Salt's eyes on him and he said, "Davis"—now speaking to the outlaw on equal terms—"to the victors belong the spoils."

As Kate, her face like stone, began to unbutton her bloodstained shirt, Maria Ana ran to her and said, "Kate, I'll go outside. Let them take me instead. I've got no one who cares, but you have sons, a family . . ."

Kate shook her head. "No, it's me Seth Koenig wants. I won't let you go in my place."

"No, Ma! The only one going outside is me," Trace Kerrigan said. "I can drop Koenig and Salt and—"

"And I'll be with you, Trace," Frank Cobb said.

"And me," Chas Minor said. He had a fat bandage around his head, but his young face was determined.

Kate shed her blouse and then untied the pink ribbon at the neck of her bodice. "I won't have anyone else die on my account."

"I won't let you go out there, Ma. Biddy, Doña Maria Ana, hold her. Tie her up if you have to." Trace drew his Colt. "Frank, Chas, let's get it done."

Kate struggled like a wildcat with the other women as Frank and Gabe Dancer pulled the timber boards away from the inside of the bunkhouse door.

"Count me in, Frank," Dancer said.

"Glad to have you, Gabe." Frank tossed the last board aside and opened the door.

And at that moment, a roaring tidal wave of horsemen crashed onto the Kerrigan ranch.

CHAPTER THIRTY-NINE

Don Pedro was a smart man and he saw at once that the Kerrigans were holed up inside the bunkhouse. His vaqueros, crazed with battle lust, were less analytical. If a man was running or shooting and he was a gringo, he was the foe and must be dealt with. They had little grasp of the concept of extending mercy to a surrendering enemy.

Aware of the thinking of his men, Don Pedro rode directly for the bunkhouse, threw himself out of the saddle, and ran for the door. Being a prudent man, before he dared enter he yelled above the rattle of gunfire, "It is I, Don Pedro!"

The little nobleman was rewarded by a shriek from inside and Maria Ana's call of, "Don Pedro! You have come for me!"

"*Mi querido amor*!" the don yelled. He rushed inside, ignored the guns pointed at him, tossed his sombrero aside, and then he and Maria Ana rushed into each other's arms.

"Maria Ana!" Don Pedro said.

"Pedro!" his wife said.

They clung to each other, both sobbing. Maria Ana's joyful tears fell on the top of her husband's bald head.

Outnumbered ten to one, Davis Salt and his men were gunned down in the first wave of horsemen. Seth Koenig dived to the ground and feigned death as the berserk vaqueros shot at anything that moved. After a few moments of frenzied, gun-blazing havoc, the Mexicans rode on in search of other prey.

Koenig saw his chance and took it.

He jumped to his feet and then hesitated as he heard Salt's pleading voice behind him.

"Koenig, my knee is all busted up. Help me."

"Hell, no," Seth said. "You ain't going nowhere with that leg."

"Please . . ."

"I got to go." Seth raised his Colt, ignored Salt's terrified face, and shot the outlaw in the head. "I've had all from you I'm gonna take."

The vaqueros were busily shooting down the gunmen around the bunkhouse and Koenig sprinted unseen for the door of the Kerrigan mansion and ran inside. His path to the back was immediately blocked by Moses Rice, who had stalwartly refused to desert his butler's post.

"You can't come in here," Moses said.

"Get the hell out of my way!" Koenig yelled. He threw the old man aside and bolted out the back door. It was a sprint to the horses while trying to remain out of sight, keeping the mansion between himself and the rampaging vaqueros.

The two gunmen Salt had left with the horses were already mounted. For several minutes, they watched

Seth stumble toward them but made no effort to bring him a horse.

When he reached them, breathless, it took a while before he could answer the questions thrown at him. Finally, he said, "Get the hell out of here. Salt is dead and you'll be next."

"What happened?" one of the men said.

"Mexicans, hundreds of them. They've killed everybody."

The two gunmen stared at the pall of dust and gun smoke that obscured the ranch buildings.

"*Rurales*, bandits?" one of them said.

"How the hell should I know?" Seth said.

"Ol' Salty is dead? Are you sure?"

"He's got a .45 slug in his brainpan. Is that sure enough?"

The gunmen exchanged glances and swung their horses around and cantered away, heading in the direction of the New Mexico border.

Seth Koenig watched them go and then swung into the saddle. He took a last, bitter look at the Kerrigan ranch, his face set and hard. To be sure, it had been a setback, but he still had his pa's money and he could hire guns, plenty of guns, the best there was. He'd be back. Back in force, and he'd play it smarter. The redheaded woman had given him a taste of what she had to offer and whetted his appetite. She might feel safe in her bed tonight, but she wasn't, not that night or any other. He'd bet the farm that Kate Kerrigan would have disturbing dreams, terrified that Seth Koenig was in bed beside her, his panting breath on the back of her neck. One night she'd wake . . . and he'd really be there.

Seth kicked his horse into motion, and like the two

riders ahead of him, he headed for the New Mexico Territory. He would return to the Hellfire to rest up for a few days at the only home he'd ever known, and then visit the Deming bankers to claim his inheritance.

Seth Koenig smiled to himself. He'd lost the battle, but he'd win the war.

Chapter Forty

There were no wounded among Davis Salt's men. Frank Cobb counted twenty-nine dead, all the corpses shot full of holes. Salt was identified by his pockmarked face, but there was no sign of Seth Koenig.

"So, he got away clean," Kate said.

"Seems like," Frank said. "But we'll get him, Kate. You have my word on that."

Her own wounded had been carried into the house and her three dead had been laid out in the parlor, awaiting coffins. She was exhausted, her ashen face streaked with gunpowder, spotted with blood. She found it difficult to speak. "I want Seth Koenig brought back here and I want him to hang." And then, after a few moments, she asked Frank, "Do you still correspond with Jacob O'Brien?"

He nodded. "Maybe two or three times a year when he's back in the New Mexico Territory. Jake's a bounty hunter, as you know, Kate, and he moves around a lot. He's so strange and his letters so interesting I read them over and over and pretty much memorize every word. Last I heard he was studying Buddhism, traveling around the country as a bodyguard to a Japanese Zen master by the name of Soyen Shaku."

"What is a Zen master?" Kate said.

"I have no idea," Frank said, "but that's what Jake called the Japanese man."

"Can we hire him to track down Seth Koenig?"

Frank shook his head. "No, Kate, we can't. Jacob O'Brien is the best there is, but he's a hard man to pin down. He's one of a restless breed and attempting to corral him is kind of like trying to dab a loop on the wind." Frank's face tightened and the lines showed on his face. "I'll go after Koenig."

"I need you here," Kate said.

"I have some experience as a manhunter."

"You're also the segundo of this ranch, and your place is here with the KK."

"Winter is cracking down, Kate. I could bring Koenig in before the start of the spring roundup."

"No, Frank," Kate said. "We have a ranch to run, and Koenig has already done enough damage. I'll find some other way. I have friends among the Pinkertons and I'll seek their advice."

"You're the boss, Kate, and you have to play it the way you see it." Frank's face softened. "Why don't you get some rest? Me and the others can do what has to be done."

"I'll take a bath and change my clothes. Then I want a report on range conditions, the state of the wells, and how much hay we have stacked. And then . . ."

Frank waited.

"I'll bury my dead."

* * *

Late afternoon sunlight angled through the windows of Maria Ana's room in the Kerrigan mansion. Outside, the vaqueros shared mescal with the surviving KK hands, and Gabe Dancer seemed merry enough to sing "Put Thy Little Hand in Mine" at the top of his lungs.

Don Pedro ignored the din and pulled a chair close to Maria Ana's bathtub. "Can you forgive your Pedro, my love? For all the wrongs I've done you in the past."

The doña laid her neck on the copper rim of the tub and closed her eyes. "Pedro, there is nothing to forgive."

"I reduced the number of your servants, forced you to wear the dress of a peasant woman. There is much to forgive, my love." He shoved his face into his hands. "Wicked, wicked Pedro. Why has the devil entered you so?"

Maria Ana opened her beautiful black eyes. "Earlier today a boy died with his head on my lap. Before he passed away he looked up at me and said, 'I'll be fine, Ma. Don't worry. I'll be just fine.' Then I felt his head grow heavy and a moment later his soul fled to his Creator."

"*Mi amor*, it is good that you brought the boy such comfort," Don Pedro said. "Surely the good Lord will light another star in your honor."

As though she hadn't heard, Maria Ana said, "Though wounded, my faithful Yolanda stayed by my side, and Rodolfo Aragon . . . the gallant and faithful servant I treated with such disdain . . . laid down his life for me. Amid the inferno of blood and death, I came to realize that French gowns, trips to Paris, are so unimportant. They are the empty desires of a spoiled, selfish woman."

Don Pedro was wise enough to say nothing

Maria Ana shifted a little, and soapy water slopped over the rim of the tub. "I have never been faithful to you, Pedro. Over the years, I've taken many lovers. Until now, I've never regretted them. Now I regret them terribly, all those empty, meaningless affairs I used to flatter my own vanity."

The little don's expression remained the same. "Yes, this I know. I was aware that there were other men, but I turned a blind eye. Through it all, my love for you never waned. Maria Ana, you were always my moon and stars, my whole life, and that did not change and will never change."

"Then who should seek forgiveness? Not you, Pedro. It is I who should ask for pardon. I should fall at your feet and beg you to take me back and never stop loving me."

"I will love you always, Maria Ana. Until the end of my days."

For the first time that day Maria Ana smiled. "Then take me home, Pedro. I vow that never again will anything stand between us." She stood in the tub, water rippling from her magnificent body, then stepped out and, unheeding of her husband's finery, sat on his lap.

"I love you, Pedro," Maria Ana said, staring into her husband's eyes, her slender arms around his neck. "Will you take me back as your wife?"

"And I love you," Don Pedro said. "And you will always be my wife . . . forever and a day."

Chapter Forty-one

The vaqueros buried Davis Salt and his gunmen on the prairie. The Kerrigan hands buried their own dead in the cemetery on the rise above the ranch.

The wake is the Irish way to celebrate the life of the deceased and give them a fine send-off, and Kate Kerrigan ordered it was how the dead punchers should be mourned. The stories were told, the old songs were sung, and the whiskey flowed like water.

When Maria Ana and Don Pedro prepared to leave the next morning, it seemed that everybody at the Kerrigan ranch nursed an aching head, and Kate was no exception.

She and Maria Ana said their farewells in the parlor, two women who had shared the same dangers and had grown closer as a result.

Kate released Maria Ana from her hug and smiled. "Have you quite recovered?"

"The dying boy will stay with me for the rest of my life, Kate."

"With all of us. And the memory of the dead boys who gave their lives for this ranch."

"We will never forget, ever."

"In the end, Don Pedro came for you."

"Yes. Yes, he did,"

"He saved us."

"He's a fine man."

"I agree with that assessment," Kate said.

"I don't deserve him. On our wedding day, I should have realized that I didn't deserve him. I think we'd have been happier had I known that and lived my life accordingly."

"Well, you can be happy now, both of you."

"Yes. I will make Don Pedro happy . . . but as for me, I just don't know."

"You wondered if you were going to be brave, remember? Well, you were brave, very brave, and now you must be braver still. A successful marriage takes courage from both sides. It's not for weaklings."

Maria Ana nodded. "I understand that now. I had lovers, Kate. The whole time we've been married I cheated with other men. They were handsome, charming, and shallow. Just like I was."

"Don Pedro knows this?"

"He knows. He knew all along. He says he's forgiven me and I believe he has."

"And now you must forgive yourself."

"That will be the work of a lifetime, Kate, but I willingly accept it."

Kate glanced out the parlor window, where an impatient Don Pedro and his men were already mounted, except for four wounded vaqueros who rode in a wagon. A peon held the reins of Rodolfo Aragon's horse that Maria Ana had decided to ride back to Mexico.

"I think it's time to leave, Maria Ana." Kate took the woman's hand. "You will come back and see me?"

"Of course, I will." Maria Ana smiled. "Don Pedro told me he wants us to have a child. The next time I visit I'll have a fine son or a pretty daughter"—she made a big belly with her hand—"or I'll be out to here."

"Either way, you'll always be welcome at the Kerrigan ranch," Kate said.

The women hugged as Maria Ana said, "*Vaya con Dios*, Kate Kerrigan."

"And you too, Maria Ana . . . *Vaya con Dios.*"

Her hand shading her eyes, Kate watched Maria Ana and the others leave. She watched until they faded behind a dust cloud and felt a great sense of loss, but through it all she smiled.

Texas had a way of turning girls into women.

Another departure that day caused great consternation among Kate's maids, but brought grins to the faces of the menfolk. Gabe Dancer had decided to pull out . . . and he was taking a blushing Biddy Kelly with him.

"Kate, there's just too much excitement around the Kerrigan ranch for a man of my advancing years," Gabe said. "Hell . . . begging your pardon . . . that there bunkhouse battle gave me the croup and I ain't recovered from it yet."

Biddy was tentative, almost fearful. "Mrs. Kerrigan, ma'am, I'm sorry I couldn't give you more notice, but Gabe asked me to come with him and I accepted."

"We plan to get hitched, just as soon as we can find a preacher," Dancer said. "Make it all legal, like."

Biddy blushed. "Gabe wants us to have a child."

"Boy or girl, I don't care," Dancer said. "He or she will be a great comfort to me in my old age."

This brought a cheer from the hands who'd gathered to bid Dancer farewell, and even the normally serious Frank Cobb grinned ear to ear.

Trace, who slapped the old man on the back, grinned too. "Go at it, Gabe."

That remark would normally have brought a rebuke from Kate and a possible mention of Our Lady's tears, but surprised as she was at Biddy's leaving, she acted as though she didn't hear. "You'd no need to give me notice, Biddy, but I'm sorry to lose you. Have you thought about this?"

"I surely did, ma'am. Gabe asked me to leave with him and I told him that I had to pack a bag. The whole time I was packing, I thought about what I was doing and I knew it was the right thing." She leaned closer to Kate and whispered, "Gabe is such a gentleman and so handsome."

There is no accounting for taste, and Kate made no comment at that.

"Well, I hope you will both be very happy," she said. "Biddy, if you ever want to come back, there will always be a place for you at the Kerrigan ranch. That goes for you too, Mr. Dancer."

Gabe Dancer swept off his cap. "Thank you, dear lady, and let me say that I feel honored to have made your acquaintance. You are a fine woman."

Kate accepted the old man's compliment with a smile. "Wait, just a moment." She walked back to the house.

When she returned she handed Dancer a small canvas poke containing two hundred dollars in gold double eagles. "Every Irish bride should have a dowry, and since Biddy's father died a martyr's death and can't be here, this is her dowry from me, standing in his place. Health and life to both of you."

Biddy sobbed at that, and Gabe Dancer was touched. "God bless you, Kate." He shook his head. "I'm too overcome to say more."

Kate and the others watched as Dancer helped Biddy onto his mustang and propped her carpetbag on the saddle in front of him. He waved a hand in farewell, and Trace, Frank Cobb, the hands, and the damp-eyed maids cheered as the happy couple left, riding east into the grasslands and their uncertain future.

But the excitement of the long day was not yet over for Kate Kerrigan.

Just as the afternoon light gave way to a gray dusk, Hiram I. Clay and his riders charged into the ranch at a gallop, whooping and hollering as though they were relieving the Alamo. To Clay's disappointment it was obvious that the battle was over and the victory already won.

"Dear Kate, your Hiram is wrecked, desolated . . . in a word, *crushed* . . . that he was too late to save you." Clay squeezed Kate's hand and pressed it to his lips that were quite damp from his copious tears.

Kate rescued her hand and said, "You're here now, Hiram, and that's what matters. I am so glad to see you and your gallant band."

"I care for you deeply, dear Kate. More deeply than I have the words to express. I am at a loss. Oh, that I was a poet that I could express my feelings in romantic verse."

"And I care deeply for you, Hiram. You have the soul of a poet, and that's quite enough." Then, to deflect the little man's ardor, "Obviously, Nora reached you. How is she?"

"A brave girl, very. She will be on her feet soon and I will see that she gets an escort back to the bosom of the Kerrigan family."

Kate would have asked more questions about her maid, but Clay was still stuck in warrior mode. "Now I am here, point out an enemy, dearest lady. Let your Hiram smite him, hip and thigh."

"The enemy is gone, Hiram, and won't return now that you are here," Kate said.

Clay grabbed Kate's hand again, pressing it to his chest. "This conflict has taught us a timely lesson, Kate. It tells your Hiram that now is the time to wed you, so that he can protect you forever from, as the Bard of Avon said, 'the slings and arrows of outrageous fortune.'" Tears again started in the little man's eyes and he said, "Be mine, my beloved. Do me the honor of becoming my blushing bride."

It was fortunate for Kate that Frank Cobb happened to be passing and read the pained expression on her face. "Mr. Clay, Jazmine Salas just made a batch of bear sign if you and your boys are interested."

"No, sir! I say again, *no sir!* Until Kate says 'I do,' I won't eat a crumb, not a morsel, not as much as an iota." Then, as Clay watched hungry punchers drift toward the kitchen, "Ah . . . how much bear sign did Jazmine make?"

Frank kept a straight face. "Judging by how sharp set those boys look, not enough."

Hiram Clay knew a predicament when he met one, and since the partaking of one of his favorite indulgences was at stake, he wanted a way out of the situation fast. Edging his way toward the house and the wonderful aroma wafting from its kitchen, he said, "Kate, true love makes a man weak at the knees, and I will take your advice and eat a little something to sustain me before I continue to press my suit."

As far as she was aware, Kate had not mentioned food, but she jumped at the chance. "Yes, that's a splendid idea, Hiram. After your long and tiring journey, you need to eat a little something. I always say that a man . . ." She was talking to empty spacc.

Hiram Clay was already hustling to the kitchen as fast as his stubby legs could carry him.

Chapter Forty-two

Seth Koenig rode through Hellfire Pass as the sun dropped lower in the sky. After the disastrous attack on the Kerrigan ranch he was in a foul mood and as dangerous as a cornered rattler. His plan was to spend the night in his blankets at the ruin of the old house and then head for Deming at first light. As he rode his mind raced, busy with schemes centering around the redheaded woman and her cattle empire. Kate Kerrigan and all she owned would soon be his and despite his seething anger the realization made him smile.

He drew rein and studied the ruins of what had been the Koenig ranch headquarters. Everything—the blackened foundations of the house and outbuildings—was as he'd left it. Probably Blade's vengeful spirit, too. That thought didn't trouble Seth in the least. He feared no man, living or dead.

He kneed his horse forward, scanning the empty land around him. His red-rimmed blue eyes missed nothing, the cold stare of a man holding no hint of mercy or kindness. Seth had for too long looked at life over a gun barrel, a man who lived a wild, lawless life, his attitudes framed by the all-consuming hatred he held for the father he'd murdered.

Hungry and tired, Seth unsaddled his horse then poked around the ashes and scorched timbers of the cookhouse. A pile of fire-scorched cans and several sides of bacon, burned to a blackened crisp, littered the floor. The labels had burned away, and he had no idea what the cans contained. He figured they'd be spoiled or even poisonous and let them be. With a bright future in sight, it was not the time to take chances with his health.

He spread his blanket roll and lay on his back, smoking a cigar. He watched the sky change from blue to gray and a chill wind picked up. Over the Tres Hermanas Mountains thunder rumbled high among the peaks where bighorn sheep were said to be, though none had been seen for many years.

Seth stubbed out his cigar, pulled his blankets to his chin, and shivered. *Damn.* It was getting downright cold. He thought about starting a fire, but decided it was too much trouble. By that time tomorrow he figured he'd be in Deming, sleeping between sheets under a quilt.

He dozed as darkness fell and night birds called out among the wild oaks behind the ruined house. In the distance, eternally optimistic coyotes hunted and yipped, searching for something to kill. Thunder still grumbled among the mountains but seemed no closer, though lightning flashed and splashed the sky with dazzling blue light.

He sat upright in his blankets. "What the hell was that?"

There, he heard it again, a rustling in the brush

between the trees. His eyes probed the gloom. A glimpse of white. Fleeting. One moment there and then gone.

Seth slid his Colt out of the leather. It had been a bird or maybe a steer that had strayed off the range. Or Blade's gibbering ghost? As he got to his feet, Seth grinned. He'd killed the son of a bitch twice . . . he could kill him a third time.

Moving warily, every muscle in his body tense, he stepped toward the oaks, his revolver up and ready. He stopped, peered ahead of him, and said, "Who's there? Show yourself and state your intentions."

The slow drumbeat of thunder was his only answer.

Seth walked on again. He reached the stand of wild oak and looked around him, rubbing the residue of sleep from his face. Nothing was there. A big daddy raccoon had probably passed through and rustled the dead leaves.

From behind him came a man's hoarse whisper, not hostile, almost friendly. "Seth . . . Seth . . ."

He turned and fired, shot again, gun flares momentarily blinding him. The thunderheads finally came down off the mountains, roaring, and lightning scrawled across the sky.

"You son of a bitch!" Seth yelled. "I'll kill you!"

From somewhere in the lightning-scarred murk came a derisive laugh, then words. "I've come for you, Seth."

He almost shrieked. Was it his father's voice? Had he come back from the fires of hell to torment the living? No! Seth refused to accept that. Out there, a man was pretending to be Blade, a mortal man who could be killed like any other.

The voice had come from a few yards to his right

and maybe ten paces away. Seth pinned the man in place against the inky backdrop of the night and cut loose. Three shots hammered fast in the impersonator's direction.

He blinked from the gun flare. After some fumbling, he managed to reload his Colt and ready himself for further action. Seth's heart thumped in his chest and his mouth was dry as though he'd inhaled mummy dust. "Come out and let me see them hands."

Seth listened, waiting for a reply, but heard only the sound of the lamenting wind and the boom of thunder as it brawled with the clouds. And then . . . laughter.

Behind him!

Seth spun around, his revolver coming up fast. Rain ticked around him. His eyes searched the darkness for a target, but he saw nothing. "Damn you, show yourself!" he yelled. Then, with a crafty look on his face, he said, "I got money. Big money. We can share. I can make you rich."

"Seth . . ."

The whisper came from his left, no, his right. Damn! It was all around him.

"Pa! Is that you, Pa? I'm sorry. It was all a mistake!"

"Seth . . . I'm coming for you . . . Seth . . ."

For the first time that night, fear lanced at Seth's belly and the hand that held his Colt was slick with sweat. He had to get to his horse, ride away from this haunted place. Yeah, that was it. He'd ride through the storm and wouldn't draw rein until he reached Deming.

Seth stepped through the rain-lashed gloom to where he'd left his mount.

Above him the thunderstorm was in full voice. Bellowing. Lightning shimmered around him, illuminating the landscape a split second at a time and starkly revealing the charred skeleton of the ranch house.

His horse was gone!

Seth Koenig cursed, venting his spleen at God, his dead father, and the world and everybody in it. Using the spiking lightning flashes to light his way, he searched for the horse, but it was gone, nowhere to be found. Rain pounded on him and made a waterfall off his hat brim.

Something big and black hurtled through the air at him.

Seth snapped off a shot . . . and drilled a hole in his saddle.

From somewhere close the man's voice said, "Soon now, Seth . . . very soon."

Seth bit back his panic and charged directly at the spot where he judged his tormentor was hiding, firing as he ran. The area had recently been cleared of brush to make way for the construction of a windmill, and stacks of lumber were still in place. He ran into the open space but stumbled on something metallic that rolled under his feet, causing him to fall heavily onto his right side. Stunned for a moment, he climbed to his feet and scanned the darkness. A lightning flash revealed no sign of a man, dead or alive, but he did see the round object at his feet . . . the fire and smoke-blackened cooking pot that once hung in Ezora Chabert's cabin.

It took a tremendous effort, but Seth forced himself to remain calm. Someone was playing dirty tricks on him—but who would know that he'd been at the old witch's cabin? He had a few suspects in mind and—Wait! Before the last peal of thunder, he thought he'd heard something . . . and there it was again. The whinny of a horse.

Seth angrily kicked the pot away from him and turned, his eyes searching the gloom. Lightning flashed and he saw his salvation. A saddled sorrel pony stood head down in the rain, now and then visible in the flickering glare.

It was a trap, of course. Seth knew it, but one he could use to turn the tables on his taunting tormentor. With a lot of open space around the horse, he reckoned he'd see any attacker coming at him, giving him plenty of time to make a fast play with the iron. He reloaded his revolver.

The rain had let up as the thunderstorm moved to the east and the thunder died to an ill-tempered growl, leaving the night as dark as the inside of a coffin. Seth stepped carefully, leading the way with his outstretched Colt. He was being watched. Hidden eyes were on him. Hostile eyes. Maybe not mortal eyes.

He yelled into murk that smelled of damp earth and seemed as black and thick as molasses. "Yeah, I'm leaving, you son of a bitch. Why don't you step out into the open and stop me?"

No answer. The ravaged night was suddenly silent as a tomb.

Seth threw back his head and howled the victory cry of the lobo wolf. He shoved his boot into the stirrup and then stopped. Footsteps, soft as thistledown falling on grass, came from behind him. Alarmed, he turned his head, his hand dropping to his gun. Too late. Something hard crashed into the back of his skull, and he hit the ground in an unconscious heap.

* * *

Seth Koenig opened his eyes to a pale blue, washed-out morning sky and the smell of burning wood. Slowly, as his mind began to focus, he recalled the events of the night and the blow to his head. What happened after that was a blank. He lay on his back, and when he tried to get up he was unable to move. Then, frantically jerking his head back and forth, the awful realization hit him that he'd been stripped naked, spread-eagled, and his wrists and ankles were staked to the ground. A fire, enclosed by a circle of rocks, burned nearby and what was thrust into the glowing coals made Seth's eyes nearly bulge out of his head. Red-hot irons. Pincers, pliers, rods, dehorners, awls, a wooden-handled knife with a sharp point . . . tools that had once hung on the walls of the Koenig stable.

He felt a surge of panic mixed with dread, seasoned by terror. "Where are you?" he yelled. "Untie me or by God, I'll kill you."

No answer, but footsteps, soft as thistledown, drew nearer.

"You!" It was a croak of fear.

Shield, the Pima scout, kneeled beside Seth. His face was painted black, his hair hung over his shoulders, and his eyes glittered. He picked up a red-hot iron . . .

Seth Koenig was a big man and strong, nourished since childhood on the best grass-fed beef in the world, toughened by years of hard work. And all that was most unfortunate . . .

It took him four days and three nights to die.

CHAPTER FORTY-THREE

Kate Kerrigan welcomed her daughters Ivy and Shannon back to the ranch, and the girls were disappointed that they'd missed all the excitement. To Kate's considerable chagrin, the fact that their mother could have been killed was news that took second place to the visit of the glamorous and deliciously wicked Doña Maria Ana.

"What was she wearing, Ma?"

"Is she still married to old Don Pedro?"

"Did she bring a new lover?"

"Is she still as complaining?"

"Did she tell you about her romantic adventures in Paris? Huh? Huh? Huh?"

"That's young'uns for you in these modern times," Frank said. "They love to hear about anything that has a touch of scandal."

"Well, they each got a penance of a rosary to be said every night for a month," Kate said. "Touch of scandal, indeed." She drew rein, her eyes reaching out to the horizon. "The range looks good, Frank. I worry about overgrazing."

He nodded. "There's plenty of grass to sustain the cattle we have. We've enough stacked hay to see us through the winter and the wells are working fine. The cows are in good shape. I expect a record number of calves come spring."

For a moment, the eyes Kate turned to Frank seemed troubled. "The land was worth it, wasn't it, Frank? All that fighting and dying."

"It was worth it and still is. The fight was brought to you by violent, vengeful men, Kate. It wasn't of your choosing. You didn't seek it out."

She had a stubborn set to her chin. "I won't be run off my range by anyone, but I pray to God we never have to fight for it again."

"Amen to that. But there will always be a breed of men who use the power of envy to destroy or take what is not their own. They can never be underestimated, Kate, and if need be, must be fought to the death."

"If such a time comes again, I want you here at my side, Frank. I need your strength and courage."

"You don't lack in those yourself, Kate, but I won't leave you. This ranch is my home. It's where I lay my head at night and where I wake up in the morning."

Kate smiled. "You've come a long way, Frank. We've both come a long way. Me from the slums of New York and you—"

"From the owlhoot trail, though I never did see a bright future in the outlaw profession."

"Your future is here, Frank." She pointed at the ground. "Right here."

"I know, but it's good to hear you say it."

Kate touched the back of Frank's gloved hand with the tips of her fingers. "And I've got an exciting surprise for you."

Frank smiled. "Well, that sounds interesting."

"What's your favorite food in the whole world?"

"Jeez, I'd have to think about that. Maybe—"

"You don't have to tell me. I already know. It's my sponge cake, and I'm baking one for tonight's dessert just for you!"

Frank forced himself to look pleased, visions of Tom Ogilvy's promised dried apple, raisin, and cinnamon pie popping like soap bubbles in his head. Despite hobbling around on a splinted leg, Ogilvy swore that the pie would be something special, a masterpiece. *Poof!* It was gone, replaced by . . . sponge cake.

"This will be the first time I'll use Queen Victoria's secret ingredient," Kate said. "I know how well you love my sponge cake, Frank, but the big secret is to add rosewater to the mix. I promise it will be even better. Aren't you excited?"

"Very," Frank said, the polite Southern gentleman lying through his teeth.

Kate laughed. "I just knew you would be. And I'm giving you an extra-large portion since you love it so much."

"Now I have something to look forward to." Figuring that one lie was not enough, he added, "I can hardly wait."

Night lay over the Kerrigan ranch like a purple fog. Here and there glowed orbs of orange light from oil lamps as a hazy moon had begun its climb into the sky. There was no sound, only the hallowed silence of the plains and the drowsy hush of sleeping people. A barn cat crossed in front of the mansion on whispering feet, then stopped as its amber eyes searched the darkness before it melted into the shadows.

The midnight hour chimed.

Did you ever hear the screech of a bobcat? If you have, then you've heard the closest sound there is to the ancient Pima war cry. Accompanied by the hammer of a running horse, the primitive shriek shattered the quiet and brought the Kerrigan punchers tumbling out of the newly repaired bunkhouse.

The Pima had already disappeared into the night, but he'd left behind a memento, a heavy object in a burlap sack that had thudded into the mansion door.

Frank Cobb and Trace Kerrigan, both in hat, boots, and combinations, were the first to reach the door.

"What the hell is it?" Trace said.

The door opened and Kate, maids in various stages of undress crowding behind her, stood on the step. "What happened, Frank?"

"Somebody, an Indian by the sound of his whoop, left this." He picked up the sack. "It's heavy."

"Do we want to see what's in it?" Kate said.

"The Indian, whoever he was, wants us to. I reckon he made that pretty obvious." Trace took the sack from Frank, untied it, and dumped its contents on the ground.

The grimacing head of Seth Koenig rolled to Kate's feet, and she stepped back in alarm. "Jesus, Mary and Joseph, and all the saints in heaven preserve us. It has no eyes."

"No nose either," Frank said. "But I recognize him. It's Seth Koenig, or part of him."

"Frank, are you sure?" Kate said. "It could be anybody."

"When I shoot at a man and he shoots at me, I tend to remember his face. It's Koenig all right."

It took Kate a while, and then she said, "Yes, now I look closer I see that its him. The hair . . . yes, I remember . . ."

Frank's gaze went to Kate's pale face. "Well, I reckon it's over now, Kate. Somebody evened the score for us."

"Who?" Kate said. "Wait. I remember. There was an Indian with the Koenigs. He saved the Tillett baby's life, laid the child by my side."

Frank shook his head. "I guess we may never know if he was the one that did for Seth. Blade maybe? He's capable of something like this, but I doubt he'd do it to his own son. Look at the burn marks on the cheeks and forehead, and right there, on his lips. Seth Koenig was tortured before he died, maybe for a long time."

"Well, whoever it was did us a favor," Trace said. "Now we've no need to go after him."

Old Moses Rice surprised everybody. "Yes, it's Seth Koenig, and the Indian who was here did this to him. One time I saw a man after Apache women worked on him for a few days and his face looked like that." He looked at Frank. "It was the Indian, Mr. Cobb, not the boy's father. If Blade Koenig couldn't stop this, then he too is dead."

That last was greeted by silence.

Then Kate said, "Mose, what you say is true. They're both dead, father and son, and the Indian who saved the baby was the one who killed Seth Koenig. I know it."

Moses smiled. "You have the gift, Miz Kerrigan."

"Yes, I do. We both have, Mose."

A week later Nora Andrews returned to the Kerrigan ranch. Apart from a scar on her forehead, she looked well and ready to resume her duties. When she told Kate of her adventures and her battle with the cougar, Kate pinned Queen Victoria's medal to the bib of the girl's pinafore and told her she could wear it for a week.

"Nora, you are the real heroine of this household."

Keep reading for a special preview of the next book in the bestselling Jensen Boys series!

THOSE JENSEN BOYS!
RIDE THE SAVAGE LAND

William W. Johnstone. Keeping the West Wild.

Those Jensen boys, Ace and Chance, know how to ride the savage land. But when they agree to lead a wagon full of women across Texas, they're just asking for trouble—times five . . .

FIVE MAIL-ORDER BRIDES
A prostitute. A virgin. A tomboy. A woman on the run. And a bank robber's girlfriend. These five brides-to-be are ready to get hitched in San Angelo, Texas—and it's Ace and Chance's job to get them to the church on time. But this is no easy walk down the aisle. It's one hard journey that could get them all killed . . .

ONE WILD RIDE
One of the brides has a crazy ex-husband gunning for her. Another has a secret stash of $50,000, stolen by her outlaw boyfriend. He's not letting go—of her or the money. Then there's a creepy, woman-hungry clan of backwoodsmen who want the brides for themselves, not to mention a fierce, deadly band of Comanche kidnappers. But Ace and Chance swear they'll protect these ladies—till death do they part . . .

ON SALE NOW!

The Jensen Family
First Family of the American Frontier

Smoke Jensen—*The Mountain Man*

The youngest of three children and orphaned as a young boy, Smoke Jensen is considered one of the fastest draws in the West. His quest to tame the lawless West has become the stuff of legend. Smoke owns the Sugarloaf Ranch in Colorado. Married to Sally Jensen, father to Denise ("Denny") and Louis.

Preacher—*The First Mountain Man*

Though not a blood relative, grizzled frontiersman Preacher became a father figure to the young Smoke Jensen, teaching him how to survive in the brutal, often deadly Rocky Mountains. Fought the battles that forged his destiny. Armed with a long gun, Preacher is as fierce as the land itself.

Matt Jensen—*The Last Mountain Man*

Orphaned but taken in by Smoke Jensen, Matt Jensen has become like a younger brother to Smoke and even took the Jensen name. And like Smoke, Matt has carved out his destiny on the American frontier. He lives by the gun and surrenders to no man.

Luke Jensen—*Bounty Hunter*
Mountain Man Smoke Jensen's long-lost brother Luke Jensen is scarred by war and a dead shot—the right qualities to be a bounty hunter. And he's cunning, and fierce enough, to bring down the deadliest outlaws of his day.

Ace Jensen and Chance Jensen—*Those Jensen Boys!*
Smoke Jensen's long-lost nephews, Ace and Chance, are a pair of young-gun twins as reckless and wild as the frontier itself . . . Their father is Luke Jensen, thought killed in the Civil War. Their uncle Smoke Jensen is one of the fiercest gunfighters the West has ever known. It's no surprise that the inseparable Ace and Chance Jensen have a knack for taking risks—even if they have to blast their way out of them.

Chapter One

It began with a rattlesnake in a glass jar and Chance Jensen's inability to pass up a bet he believed he could win.

A balding, beefy-faced bartender with curlicue mustaches reached under the bar, came up with the big glass jar, and set it on the hardwood with a solid thump. The top of the jar had a board sitting across it. Somebody had drilled airholes in the board so the fat diamondback rattler coiled inside the jar wouldn't suffocate.

"Five bucks says no man can tap on the glass and hold his finger there when Chauncey here strikes at it," the bartender announced.

A cowboy standing a few feet down the bar with a beer in front of him looked at the jar and its deadly occupant and said, "Step aside, boys! This here is gonna be the easiest five dollars I ever earned!"

The men along the bar shifted so the cowboy could stand in front of the jar. Chance and his brother Ace had to move a little to their left, but they could still see the show.

The cowboy leaned closer and peered through the glass at the snake, which hadn't moved when the bartender set him down. "He's alive, ain't he?"

"Tap on the glass and find out," the bartender said.

The cowboy lifted a hand covered with rope calluses. He held up his index finger and thumped it three times against the glass, lightly.

Inside the jar, the snake's head raised slightly. Its tail began to vibrate, moving so fast that it was just a blur.

The saloon was quiet as everyone looked on, and even through the glass, the men closest to the bar could hear the distinctive buzzing. That sound could strike fear into the stoutest-hearted man in Texas.

"Yeah, uh, he's alive, all right," the cowboy said. "What do I do now?"

"Show me that you actually have five bucks," the bartender said.

The cowboy reached into his pocket, pulled out a five-dollar gold piece, and slapped it down on the hardwood. Grinning, the bartender took an identical coin from the till and set it next to the cowboy's stake.

"All right. Tap on the glass a few more times to get Chauncey stirred up good and proper, and then hold your finger there. Then we wait. Shouldn't be too long."

Another man said, "Chauncey's a boy's name, ain't it?"

"Yeah, I suppose so," the bartender said with a frown. "What's your point?"

"I was just wonderin' how you know for sure that there snake is a male. Did you check?"

That brought a few hoots of laughter from the crowd.

The bartender glared. "Never you mind about that. If I say he's a boy, then he's a boy. If you want to prove different, you reach in there and show me the evidence."

"No, no," the bystander said, holding his hands up in surrender. "I'm fine with whatever you say, Dugan."

The bartender looked at the cowboy. "Well? You gonna give it a try or not? You were mighty quick to brag about how you could do it. You decide you don't want to back that up with cold, hard cash after all?"

"I'm gonna, I'm gonna," the cowboy said. "Just hang on a minute." He swallowed, then tapped three more times on the glass, harder this time.

"Hold your finger there," Dugan said.

From a few feet away, Chance watched with all his attention focused on the jar and the cowboy who was daring the snake to strike at him. Ace watched Chance and felt a stirring of concern at the expression he saw on his brother's face.

The cowboy rested his fingertip against the glass. Inside the jar, the snake's head was still up, its tiny forked tongue flickering as it darted in and out of his mouth. The buzzing from the rattles on the tip of its tail steadily grew louder.

Then, faster than the eye could follow, the snake uncoiled and struck at the glass where the cowboy's finger was pressed.

"*Yeeeowww!*" the cowboy yelled as he jumped back. The rattler's sudden movement startled half a dozen other people in the Lucky Panther Saloon into shouting, too.

For a couple seconds, the cowboy stared wide-eyed at the jar, where the snake had coiled up again, and then looked down at his hand. The index finger still stuck straight out, but it was nowhere near the glass anymore. Obviously disgusted, he said, "Well, hell."

Grinning, Dugan scooped up both five-dollar gold pieces and dropped them into the till. "Told you. Nobody can do it. It just ain't natural for a man to be able to hold still when a rattler's fangs are comin' at him, whether there's glass in between or not."

Ace tried to catch Chance's eye and shake his head, but it was too late. Chance stepped closer to the spot on the bar where the jar rested and said, "I can do it."

People looked around to see who had made that bold declaration. If not for what happened next, they would have seen a handsome, sandy-haired man in his early twenties, well dressed in a brown tweed suit, white shirt, and a dark brown cravat and hat.

But all their attention turned to the man who shouldered Chance aside, said, "Outta my way, kid," and stepped up to the bar. "I've never been afraid of a rattler in my life, and sure as hell not one penned up in a jar." He was tall and lean, dressed in black from head to foot, and probably ten years older than Chance and Ace, who were fraternal twins. His smile had a cocky arrogance to it.

Ace was more interested in the gun holstered on the man's hip. In keeping with the rest of his outfit, that holster was black. The revolver was the only thing flashy about him. It was nickel plated and had ivory grips.

However, the gun wasn't just for show. Those grips showed the marks of a great deal of use. Maybe the man just practiced with it a lot—or maybe he actually *was* the gunslinger he obviously fancied himself to be.

The man in black held the edge of a coin against the bar and gave it a spin. It whirled there for a long moment, so fast it was just a blur, but finally ran out of momentum and clattered on the hardwood. "I reckon my money's good, Dugan?"

"Sure, Shelby," the bartender said. "You're welcome to give it a try."

A spade-bearded man in a frock coat stepped up. He hooked his thumbs in the gold-brocaded vest he wore and said, "I have fifty dollars that says Lew can do it."

That wager was too rich for the blood of most of the patrons in that particular saloon in Fort Worth's notorious Hell's Half Acre, but the tinhorn gambler got a couple takers. Coins and greenbacks were put on the bar for Dugan to hold while Shelby made his try.

Ace nudged a bearded old-timer who stood next to him and asked, "Who are those two?"

"The gun-hung feller in black is Lew Shelby," the codger replied. "The one in the fancy vest is Henry Baylor."

"He looks like a card sharp."

"Good reason for that. He is. Or at least the rumor has it so. Nobody's ever caught him cheatin', though, as far as I know. If they have, they've had sense enough not to call him on it." The old-timer licked his lips, his tongue emerging from the shaggy white whiskers for a second. "Baylor might be even slicker at handlin' shootin' irons than he is at cards. Him and Shelby is two of a kind, and they run with a bunch just about as bad."

Ace nodded. Chance didn't look happy about Shelby pushing in ahead of him, but for the moment at least, he was keeping his annoyance under control. Ace would say something to him if necessary, to keep him calmed down. They didn't need a gunfight in the middle of the saloon—or anywhere else, for that matter. The Jensen brothers were peaceable sorts.

That was what Ace aspired to, anyway. Oftentimes fate seemed to be plotting against them, however.

Lew Shelby stood in front of the bar, feet planted solidly, hands held out in front of him and slightly spread. He rubbed his thumbs over his fingertips and took deep breaths, as if he were working himself up to slap leather against the snake, not hold his finger against a glass jar.

The crowd began to stir restlessly.

Shelby sensed that impatience, glanced over his shoulder, and sneered. "Hold your damn horses." Then he reached out and tapped the glass several times, fast and hard. He pressed his finger against the jar as the snake reacted, coiling tighter in preparation to strike.

Everybody in the place knew it was coming. Nobody should have been surprised, least of all Shelby. But when the rattler struck with the same sort of blinding speed as before, Shelby jumped back a step and yelped, "Son of a bitch!"

Several men in the crowd cursed, too. Others laughed, which made Shelby's face flush.

Dugan picked up the gold piece that was all he'd had riding on the bet, but the other men who'd placed wagers moved quickly up to the bar to claim their winnings. Shelby and Baylor looked startled and angry.

That anger deepened as Dugan smirked. "Told you so, boys. No man alive has got icy enough nerves to manage that little trick."

Ace tried to get hold of Chance's coat sleeve and pull him away, but Chance was a little too quick for him. He stepped forward and said, "I told you, I can do it."

Lew Shelby looked at him and scowled. "Run along, sonny. This business is for men, not boys."

Chance's voice held an edge as he said, "I'm full-grown, in case you hadn't noticed." He moved his coat aside a little, revealing a .38 caliber Smith & Wesson Second Model revolver with ivory grips resting in a cross-draw rig on his left hip.

Shelby's dark eyes slitted, giving him a certain resemblance to the snake. "You better walk soft, boy. I don't cotton to being challenged."

Ace stepped up next to his brother. He had been born a few minutes earlier than Chance, and he was slightly taller and heavier, too. Dark hair curled out from under a thumbed-back Stetson. He wore range clothes, denim trousers and a bib-front shirt, and his boots showed plenty of wear. He didn't take the time or trouble to polish them up, the way Chance did his. The walnut-butted Colt .45 Peacemaker leathered on Ace's right hip was strictly functional, too.

"Nobody's challenging anybody." Ace had plenty of experience trying to head off trouble when Chance was in the middle of it.

"That's not true," Chance said. "I'm challenging that rattlesnake, as well as Mr. Dugan here. I can hold my finger on the glass without budging when the snake strikes at it."

"If I can't do it, kid, you sure as hell can't," Shelby snapped.

"The two hundred dollars in my pocket says I can."

Ace bit back a groan. Actually, the two hundred

bucks was in his pocket, not Chance's, but they had that much, all right. They had worked for several months on a ranch north of Fort Worth to earn it, and they were ready to take it easy and drift for a while, which was their usual pattern.

They couldn't do that if Chance's reckless stubbornness caused them to lose their stake.

Things had gone too far to stop. Chance had thrown the bet out there.

Henry Baylor stroked his beard. "I'm down a hundred dollars tonight. Winning two hundred from you would allow me to show a profit for the evening, son."

"I'm not your son," Chance said.

In truth, he and Ace didn't know whose sons they were. They had been raised by a drifting gambler named Ennis "Doc" Monday, after their mother died giving birth to them.

Once they were old enough to think about such things, they had speculated about whether Doc Monday was really their father, but there was no proof one way or the other and they had never worked up the nerve to ask him about it, since his health had grown bad over the years and he was living in a sanitarium. A big emotional upset wouldn't be good for him.

"If you actually have the money," Baylor said, "you have a wager."

"I've got it." Chance glanced around at his brother. "Ace?"

With a sigh, Ace dug out the roll of greenbacks and set it on the bar. He said to Dugan, "That's our whole poke. We don't have an extra five dollars to cover the bet with you."

The bartender laughed and waved a hand. "Hell,

kid, I'll waive that for the occasion. In fact, I'm so sure your . . . brother, is it? . . . can't do it that if he does, I'll add a nice new double eagle to your payoff. How's that sound?"

Chance said, "We're obliged to you, Mr. Dugan. But get ready to pay up as soon as this fella"—he nodded toward Baylor—"proves that *he* can cover the bet."

Lew Shelby bristled at that. He tensed and started, "Why, you impudent little bas—"

"That's all right, Lew." Baylor stopped him with an easy but insincere smile. "It's fair enough for the lad to ask for proof, since I did." He took a sheaf of bills from a pocket inside the frock coat, counted out two hundred dollars, and placed the money next to the Jensen brothers' roll. "Satisfied?"

"Yes, sir, I am." Chance turned to the bar and studied the snake in the glass jar. He asked Dugan, "His name's Chauncey, you said?"

"That's what I call him," the bartender replied. "Caught him in the alley out back earlier today. I started to kill him, then realized that maybe I could use him to make some money."

"All right, Chauncey." Chance leaned closer, putting his face almost on the glass as he peered at the rattler. "Get good and mad now, you scaly little varmint."

The snake stared back, as inscrutable as ever. The buzzing from its rattles sounded angry.

Three times, Chance thumped his fingertip against the glass. With the last thump, he left his finger there, pressed hard against the jar. The snake didn't waste any time. It uncoiled and struck furiously, jaws gaping wide to display wicked fangs dripping with venom.

Chapter Two

Just like the other two times, several men in the Lucky Panther let out involuntary shouts when the snake's head darted at the glass. One gaudily dressed saloon girl pressed her hands to rouged cheeks and trilled a little scream.

A few seconds of stunned silence ticked past before the place erupted in cheers.

Chance Jensen was still standing in front of the bar with his finger pressed against the glass. He hadn't budged.

He remained where he was in the middle of the excited commotion, other than turning his head and smiling at Henry Baylor. "I believe you owe me two hundred dollars, my friend."

Baylor smiled in return, but his lips were tight and his eyes hooded. "It appears that I do."

A few feet away, the bearded old-timer Ace had been talking to tugged on his sleeve. Ace had to lean down to make out what the old man was saying.

"Better collect your winnin's and get outta here in a hurry, kid! And keep your eyes open! Baylor won't like losin' that money, and Lew Shelby sure as hell will be mad about your brother showin' him up."

Based on the expressions on the faces of Baylor and Shelby, Ace agreed with the old man. He reached out, scooped up their roll from the bar, and shoved the stack of greenbacks from Baylor into his pocket, as well. Dugan grinned ruefully and handed him the double eagle he had promised as an extra payoff.

"Come on, Chance," Ace said. "Time for us to drift."

Chance still hadn't taken his finger away from the glass. He did it leisurely, mockingly, then lifted the finger to his lips and blew across the top of it as if he were blowing away a curl of smoke from a gun muzzle.

"Wait just a damn minute," Shelby rasped.

"Why? You're not going to claim that I cheated, are you? That would have been hard to do with this many people watching me the whole time."

"But *were* they watching you the whole time?" Shelby turned to the bar. "Dugan! Did you have your eye on this kid? You didn't look away any?"

"I don't think so," the bartender said.

"You didn't even blink when the snake struck?"

"Well . . . I was trying to watch pretty close . . ."

Shelby glared as he jerked his gaze around the room. "I'll bet everybody in here blinked just then! Nobody was watching the kid the whole time. He could've taken his finger off the glass for a split second, and nobody would have noticed." When nobody spoke up to agree with him, he scowled even more and demanded, "Isn't that right?"

Shelby had a reputation in Fort Worth as a gunman. Nobody wanted to disagree with him. Some men shuffled their feet and looked down at the floor in obvious discomfort. Others edged toward the door, figuring it was better to leave than to wait and see how things played out.

Then one grizzled hombre spoke up. He looked like a successful cattleman, the sort who didn't take any guff from anybody. "I was watching the whole time, and I didn't blink. The kid's finger didn't move."

Emboldened by that blunt declaration, several other men muttered agreement.

"You know I didn't move my finger," Chance said to Shelby. "You're just mad because I was able to do it and you couldn't."

A feral hatred came into Shelby's eyes as he said, "I can do it! By God, double or nothing! I'll show you."

"Lew, I'm not sure that's wise," Baylor cautioned. "We've already lost enough tonight."

"I'm not gonna let this damn kid think he can get the best of me!" Shelby's jaw jutted out as he said to Chance, "How about it? You willing to bet the four hundred that I can't do it?"

"Chance . . ." Ace said.

"Relax, Ace," Chance said with a smile. "If we lose, we're no worse off than we were before."

"Yeah, we are. Two hundred bucks worse!"

"Life would be mighty dull without a little risk now and then to spice it up." Chance nodded to Shelby. "We'll take that bet, mister. Go ahead." He glanced at Baylor. "I won't even ask if you can cover it."

The gambler was grim-faced. His friend had put him in a bad position, but he jerked his head in a nod and made a little gesture with his slender, long-fingered hand. "Go ahead,"

As Shelby faced the jar, Dugan said, "I don't know

about this. Chauncey's been banging his head against the glass every time he strikes. He's liable to be gettin' a little addled by now. I don't want him to hurt himself."

"You gettin' soft on a rattlesnake, Dugan?" one of the customers asked with a jeering grin.

"No, but if he bashes his brains out, he can't win me any more bets, can he?"

"Does a snake even have a brain?" another man asked.

"Got to," his companion said. "Ever'thing that's alive has got a brain. Don't it?"

"Don't know. I never studied up on snakes. Just shot 'em or chopped their heads off with a bowie knife."

Shelby snapped, "Shut your damn yammering! A man can't hear himself think." Once again he went through the routine he had performed earlier.

Silence descended on the saloon, broken only by the sound of men breathing. Even that seemed to die away as Shelby hunched his shoulders a little. He was ready. His hand stabbed forward. His finger shoved hard against the jar. He didn't even have to tap on the glass this time. The snake was so keyed up it struck immediately.

Shelby's finger jerked back as the fangs hit the inside of the jar. He didn't flinch much, maybe half an inch, but his fingertip definitely left the glass, and everybody who was watching saw that. Shelby tried to press his finger against the jar again, but it was too late.

"That'll be another four hundred dollars," Chance said into the awed hush that followed.

Shelby took a quick step back, away from the bar. A stream of obscenity poured from his mouth as his hand dropped to the fancy gun on his hip. Ace grabbed the back of his brother's coat collar and yanked Chance out of the way as he used his other hand to grab his Colt.

The gunman wasn't aiming to shoot either of the Jensen brothers, however. He was still facing the bar when his gun leaped up and spouted noise and flame.

The first bullet shattered the jar and sent glass shards flying through the air. The second swiftly triggered round whipped past Chauncey's weaving head and blew a bottle of busthead on the back bar to smithereens. The snake shot out of the wreckage, slithered across the bar, and dropped writhing to the sawdust-littered floor, the thick body landing with what must have been a thump.

Nobody could hear it, though, because the saloon still echoed from the reports of Shelby's gun. At least half the people in the Lucky Panther started yelling and screaming when they realized the big rattler was loose.

"Chauncey!" Dugan bellowed to Shelby, "You bastard. You tried to kill my snake!"

Shelby snarled and shouted, "Get outta the way! I'm gonna blast the damn thing!"

Dugan reached under the bar, came up with a bungstarter, and raised it as he leaned across the hardwood. Another second and he would have brought the bungstarter down across the wrist of Shelby's gun hand, probably breaking the bone.

Before the blow could fall another pistol cracked, this one a small weapon that Henry Baylor had grabbed from concealment under his frock coat. The slug tore through Dugan's forearm and made him drop the bungstarter and howl in pain.

The Lucky Panther had two entrances—the bat-winged main one facing Throckmorton Street and a regular door on the side that faced Second Street. The customers stampeded for both. The furious gunman and the equally agitated rattlesnake had everybody scrambling to get out of there before they caught a bullet or got bit.

Everybody except Ace and Chance Jensen. They knew Shelby was liable to hurt an innocent person if he kept flinging lead around.

Ace scooped up the beer mug he had emptied a few minutes earlier and heaved it at Shelby's head. The heavy glass mug struck the gunman a good enough lick to stagger him. At the same time, Baylor swung his gun toward Ace. Acting instinctively to defend his brother, Chance tackled the gambler before he could fire.

The collision drove Baylor's back against the bar. He grunted and swiped at Chance's head with the pistol. The blow knocked off Chance's flat-crowned brown hat but missed otherwise.

Charging into the fray were two of the three men Shelby and Baylor had been sitting at a table with earlier. The third man, an Indian by the looks of him, drew a knife from his belt and stalked across the room, ignoring the rapidly developing brawl. Probably all three were the bad bunch the old-timer had warned Ace about.

Getting walloped by the beer mug had stunned Lew Shelby enough to leave him stumbling around in aimless circles. One of his friends took up the battle for him and went after Ace. The other man looped an arm around Chance's neck from behind and dragged him away from Baylor.

Ace ducked a roundhouse right that his attacker threw at him. He brushed his hat back off his head so it hung from its chin strap behind him. He crouched even lower and waded in, hooking punches to the man's soft-looking belly. That paunch was deceptive. Hitting it was like hammering his fists against the wall of a log cabin, Ace discovered.

The man hit Ace a backhanded blow with his forearm. The impact knocked Ace halfway across the bar. He caught himself and managed not to slide all the way over. As his opponent charged in, he raised both legs and straightened them in a double kick to the chest.

That sent the man flying. He landed on a table that collapsed under him and dumped him among its shattered debris. He sat up and shook his head groggily.

Halfway along the bar, Baylor was slugging Chance in the belly while the other man hung on to him from behind. Chance was red in the face from the choking grip around his neck.

Ace swerved wide, picked up a chair, and crashed it down on the back of the man who had hold of Chance. That knocked him loose.

Chance twisted free, grabbed Baylor's arm as the gambler tried to hit him in the stomach again, and pivoted, throwing Baylor over his hip in a wrestling move he had learned during a rough-and-tumble childhood spent traveling with Doc Monday. Chance might look like a bit of a dandy, but he could handle himself just fine in a fight.

Baylor rolled across the floor, dirtying his nice frock coat. In the scuffle, he had lost the little pistol with which he had shot Dugan, but that wasn't the only weapon he carried. As Chance closed in on him, ready to continue the fight, Baylor came up slashing with a folding straight razor that he flicked open with a practiced twist of his wrist.

Chance had to jump back to avoid being cut. Baylor came after him, backing him against the bar.

Ace was being hemmed in by Shelby and the man he had kicked in the chest, both of whom had recovered their wits and appeared to be ready to beat him to death.

The Jensen brothers found themselves standing side by side, backs against the bar, with no place to run as trouble closed in on them. Sadly, it wasn't the first time they had found themselves in such a perilous position. Judging by the anger and hatred twisting the cruel faces of the men stalking toward them, they might not get out of it.

With no warning, the deafening roar of another shot slammed through the room and made everybody freeze.

Chapter Three

All eyes turned toward the saloon's main entrance. A dapper man in a dark suit and vest, silk tie, and narrow-brimmed hat stood there with a smoking gun in his hand. He was rather handsome, with a full mustache and tawny hair long enough to sweep back in waves behind his ears.

What really drew the eyes, though—besides the gun—was the badge pinned to his vest.

"All right," he said quietly, "what's the trouble?"

"Baylor shot me!" Dugan said. Using his left hand to hold up his ventilated right arm, he displayed the blood staining his sleeve.

"I had to," Baylor said. "He was about to kill Lew. I've got a right to protect my friend, don't I?"

Dugan stared. "What? Kill him? I was gonna knock the gun out of his hand, that's all."

Baylor said, "It looked to me like you were about to stave his head in with that bungstarter. I couldn't take the chance."

Shelby spat disgustedly on the floor. "Hell, he just wounded you. I would've shot to kill."

The lawman came farther into the room. He didn't holster his gun but used it to gesture. "That explains one of the shots. How about all the others? And what's all that broken glass doing on the bar?"

"He tried to kill Chauncey, too, Marshal Courtright," Dugan said. "You need to arrest him!"

"Who the devil is Chauncey?"

Dugan suddenly looked a little sheepish. "My, uh, snake. He's a rattlesnake."

Courtright raised an eyebrow. "I didn't know you were keeping a pet rattlesnake in here, Dugan, or I might have locked you up for being a public menace and a damned fool."

"The snake wasn't a pet," Chance said. "He was using it to win bets and make money. He bet that a man couldn't hold his finger against the glass and keep it there while the snake struck at it." A grin spread across Chance's face. "I did, though."

"And Shelby here couldn't," Ace put in. "That's why he got so upset he shot the jar and busted it."

Coolly, the marshal asked, "And who might you boys be?"

"I'm Ace Jensen. This is my brother Chance."

That perked up the lawman's interest. "Jensen, eh?"

"Yeah, but we're not related to Smoke or Luke," Ace said, mentioning the two Jensens whose names were most likely to be known to a star packer.

Smoke Jensen was widely regarded as the West's fastest, deadliest gunfighter, despite the fact that these days he lived a mostly peaceful life as a rancher in Colorado. Anybody who had ever read a newspaper or a dime novel had heard about him.

Luke Jensen was Smoke's older brother, a bounty

hunter whose name might well be familiar to a lawman. Ace and Chance had met both men and shared adventures with them in the past.

"Not related that we know of," Chance added. "Personally, I lean toward the idea that we're actually the long-lost black sheep of the family."

Ace just rolled his eyes at that.

"Well, even if you're not blood kin to that hell-raising bunch, you seem to take after them," the marshal observed. "You two were at the center of this ruckus. Maybe I should arrest you as well while I'm locking up Shelby and Baylor and their friends." Courtright cast a baleful eye on the four men. "I've had run-ins with you before, and I'm tired of it."

"Marshal, these boys didn't do anything wrong," Dugan said. "That one there won his bet fair and square." He pointed at Chance.

"We all claim that he didn't," Baylor put in hastily. "The five of us will swear that the boy pulled away when the snake struck, so it's our word against Dugan's." A satisfied smirk appeared on the gambler's face. "I'd say that makes the count five to one in our favor."

"Five to three," Ace said. "Chance and I both know he didn't flinch."

Baylor shook his head. "Still not a winning hand."

Courtright appeared to consider that for a moment, then nodded. "Much as I hate to agree with you, Baylor, it seems that you're right." He looked at Ace and Chance. "Whatever money you won from this tinhorn, give it back. I'm declaring all bets null and void."

"You can't do that!" Chance protested. "I won!"

"We try to discourage gambling around here,"

Courtright said with a look of bland righteousness on his face. That statement was a blatant falsehood since Hell's Half Acre was full of gambling dens. "You're fortunate I don't lock you up for that."

Ace sighed and pulled out the bills he had picked up from the bar. He started to hand them to Baylor, but Courtright intercepted them.

He peeled off a bill and dropped it on the bar. "For the damages and for the pain of Dugan's wounded arm."

Shelby pointed at Ace and Chance. "These two little bastards ought to pay for part of the damages. They were fighting just like we were."

"Legally speaking, you may be right. But I don't like you, Shelby, and I'm still reserving judgment on these youngsters." Courtright handed the rest of the money to Baylor. "You can keep that with you while you spend the night in my lockup. Let's go." He glanced around. "Where's the Kiowa?"

"He had nothing to do with this," Baylor said. "He stayed out of the fight completely."

"That's true," Ace said. "We were just scuffling with these four."

"All right." Courtright frowned. "Something else I just thought of. What happened to the snake?"

"Over here, Marshal," said a man with a deep, calm voice.

Everyone looked around and saw the Indian who had been sitting with Shelby, Baylor, and the others before the battle erupted. He held up his knife. Skewered on the end of it was the limp, lifeless body of the big rattlesnake. "Good eatin'."

"Chauncey!" Dugan wailed.

* * *

Shelby, Baylor, and the other two men were disarmed and ushered out by Marshal Courtright. A doctor carrying a medical bag bustled in to tend to Dugan's wounded arm. Obviously someone had sent for the medico. Since Ace and Chance hadn't been arrested, they remained in the Lucky Panther and sat down at one of the tables.

Chance sighed, and Ace said. "I don't know what you're looking so glum about. We're not behind bars."

"Yeah, but I won that bet fair and square." He held up a hand to stall Ace's protest. "I know, I know. We're not any worse off than we were before, but that lawman didn't have any right to make us give our winnings back. It's the principle of the thing."

A new voice spoke up. "When Longhair Jim lays down the law, it *stays* laid down."

Ace and Chance looked up to see the whiskery old-timer Ace had been talking to earlier. Most of the saloon's customers were filtering back into the place now that the fight was over and word had spread about the rattlesnake's demise.

"That's the marshal?" Ace said.

"Yep. Longhair Jim Courtright. Fast on the draw and a dead shot. Lew Shelby may have thought about takin' him on, but with Jim's gun already drawed, Shelby knew he'd be stretched out on the floor gettin' cold iffen he tried." The old-timer looked hopeful. "You boys fixin' to have a drink?"

"I'm sure you'll want to join us if the answer is yes," Chance said.

"Weeellll . . . if you're askin' . . . reckon I don't mind if I do."

"Sit down." Ace caught the attention of the aproned man who had taken over as bartender while Dugan was getting patched up and held up three fingers.

The old-timer sat down. "I heard you boys say your name's Jensen. Mine's Greendale. Harley Greendale. Fancy moniker for an old pelican like me, ain't it?"

"Glad to meet you, Mr. Greendale."

"Call me Harley. Mr. Greendale was my pa, damn his black heart to hell."

Ace didn't ask what that comment was about. There was a good chance Harley would tell them sooner or later anyway. The old man was the garrulous sort.

"You boys always carry this much excitement around in your back pockets?"

"That ruckus wasn't our fault," Chance said. "Nothing would have happened if Shelby and Baylor had just admitted I won that bet fair and square."

"Them two ain't the sort to take kindly to losin', like I was tellin' your brother earlier."

One of the serving girls delivered three overflowing mugs of beer on a wooden tray. Harley leaned forward eagerly, picked up one of them, and sucked the foam off the top. He sighed in satisfaction. "That bunch drifted into town a couple months ago."

The Jensen brothers hadn't asked him to fill them in on Shelby and the others, but Ace thought it might not be a bad idea to learn more about the men with whom they had clashed. Shelby especially struck him as the sort of hombre who would hold a grudge and try to act on it.

Harley took a healthy swallow of beer and wiped the back of his hand across his mouth. "Inside a week, Shelby was mixed up in a killin'. Plenty of witnesses saw the other feller reach first, so Shelby didn't go to jail for it. Nor for the other two shootin's he's been part of since then. Both of them were over card games. Fellas didn't like losin' to Baylor. Didn't come right out and accuse him of cheatin'—there wasn't no proof of that—but they pushed it hard enough that guns was drawed anyways."

"It sounds like they have a partnership," Chance said. "Baylor fleeces the lambs, and Shelby shoots the ones who object too strenuously to being shorn."

"Reckon that's about the size of it."

Ace asked, "What about the other three?"

"They just sort of hang around with Shelby and Baylor. Jack Loomis is the bald-headed one with the big belly. Feller who always looks like he just bit into somethin' sour is called Prewitt. Don't know that I've ever heard his first name." Harley paused. "Then there's the Kiowa. Nobody ever calls him anything else."

The Indian had left the saloon after Marshal Courtright herded his friends off to jail. As far as Ace and Chance knew, he had taken the dead snake with him and might be cooking it over an open fire at this very moment.

"He never says much," Harley went on. "I don't like the look in his eyes. Just as likely to scalp you as to say howdy. Probably more likely." He swallowed more suds. "All I know is that they're a bad bunch. Iffen I was you boys, I reckon I'd be ridin' out of Fort Worth tonight. First thing in the mornin' at the latest, 'fore Longhair Jim lets those varmints outta jail. Shelby is liable to come lookin' for you."

"Let him come," Chance said. "I'm not going to run away from anybody."

"That's a good attitude to have, son. But in this case, you might ought to give it some extry thought."

Chance was going to argue with the old-timer, but Ace lifted a hand from the table to forestall the wrangling. When he had Chance's attention, he tipped his head toward the saloon's main entrance.

Marshal Jim Courtright had just come in and was looking around the place. When his gaze landed on the table where the Jensen boys sat with Harley, he started across the room toward them with a stern look on his face.